The Silent Count

a thriller by E. A. Smiroldo

Publisher's Note:

This is a work of fiction. All names, characters, places, and
events are the work of the author's imagination.

Any resemblance to real persons, places, or events is
coincidental.

Solstice Publishing - http://www.solsticeempire.com/

To my mother, Santa, and my cousin, Annette.
I miss them both every day.

T-minus Ten

"Some said the world would end in fire. Others said it would end in ice. We know better now."

Brigadier General Alexander Fallsworth acknowledged his audience in the windowless room lit with PowerPoint slides and the words 'Top Secret-SCI' (for 'Sensitive Compartmented Information') in red LED letters on each wall. His presentation to the Intergovernmental Committee on Climate Affairs beamed from a laptop that normally resided in a padlocked Class 6 file cabinet. Both the cabinet and the computer were nearing capacity.

The meeting participants had come to CIA headquarters in Langley, Virginia, from several other agencies — the Joint Chiefs of Staff, the Department of Defense, the Environmental Protection Agency, the Department of Energy. They gathered around a large conference table, all furrowed brows, crossed arms and pointed features.

Alexander, silver-blue irises shifting, felt adrenaline course through him as words shot past his tongue. "Colleagues, the world hasn't ended at all. It's left us the task of dealing with the consequences. That's why I've gathered you here today. I'd like to talk about Project Plowshares."

A few in the audience fidgeted, coughed. *Afghanistan was a walk in the park compared to an afternoon with this crowd.* He pressed on, quoting from the Bible's Book of Isaiah: "'...they shall... beat their swords into plowshares, and their spears into pruning hooks; nation shall not lift up their sword against nation, neither shall they learn war anymore.'"

The PowerPoint transmitted a video of a nuclear explosion, ending in a mushroom cloud of fission products. Pacing himself with a few sips of water, Alexander delved into the history of the program.

Most of the audience members had been students of nuclear history at one time or other, so they were familiar with Project Plowshares, at least the version of the program envisioned during the Cold War era. Alexander explained that Plowshares resulted after President Eisenhower's 'Atoms for Peace' speech before the United Nations in 1953, when the president said of the atomic bomb, "It is not enough to take this weapon out of the hands of the soldiers. It must be put into the hands of those who will know how to strip its military casing and adapt it to the arts of peace."

He took a breath, hoping his listeners couldn't see the perspiration beading where his blond crew cut ended and his forehead began. "The brass at the U.S. Atomic Energy Agency took the Atoms for Peace ball and ran with it, funding programs to find peaceful uses for atomic bombs. Beyond the obvious nuclear energy applications, Plowshares included large-scale civil engineering projects that harnessed the power of nuclear explosives." He advanced to the next slide, willing himself to keep talking.

"The Soviets ran a similar 'peaceful uses' program during the Cold War era. Some would argue that India was able to develop atomic weapons due to this program by exploiting gaps in the Treaty on Nuclear Non-Proliferation, since it originally referenced 'nuclear weapons' rather than 'nuclear explosives,' as it does today. We're aware that India consulted with the Russians on using nuclear explosives to create artificial lakes. Unlike us, the Soviets actually tested and implemented infrastructure projects under their version of Plowshares, including a dam in Kazakhstan.

"Now here's a blast from the past for many of you," Alexander said, stifling a chuckle as he drew circles on the next slide with his laser pointer. "Nearly every undergraduate nuclear engineering student in the United States uses the classic textbook *Introduction to Nuclear Engineering*, by the late John Lamarsh. Perhaps you remember this book from your college days. Early editions of the book contained the following excerpt:

'...there are a number of ways in which nuclear explosives may be used for peaceful purposes...natural gas trapped in underground formations can be released by the detonation of a nuclear explosive...New harbors, canals, and mountain passes can be excavated with nuclear explosives at a fraction of the cost of conventional methods.'"

He paused, looked around the table, and clicked to the next slide that contained the rest of the Lamarsh quote: "'It should even be possible to alter unfavorable weather patterns in many parts of the world by removing mountain ranges which obstruct the flow of air.'"

Alexander swallowed, his mouth dry. "Do we have any questions so far?"

One of the meeting participants, a man in a U.S. Air Force uniform, spoke up. "General Fallsworth, what are you suggesting?"

Alexander attempted to modulate his breathing, which grew at a clip to keep up with his heart rate. "I'm proposing what Lamarsh said was possible, the one thing no one has tried. I propose that we use nuclear explosives to eliminate targeted mountain ranges in order to reposition the Jet Stream, create more favorable weather patterns and heat sinks, and reverse the impacts of climate change."

Silence and stillness now. Every eye in the room bored through him. "Ladies and gentlemen, I'm going to speak plainly. Fire, drought, floods, and extreme weather have rendered swaths of our country uninhabitable and burdened other areas due to countless citizens who've been displaced. Agriculture is in ruins, insurance premiums have skyrocketed, and the chasm between rich and poor continues to grow. Besides the obvious financial impacts, these problems threaten our national security. Our enemies are well aware of our weaknesses, and, domestically, civil unrest is on the rise. Worst of all, people have died." Alexander's voice caught in his throat. "Thousands of people have died," he continued, "and all we have done is react."

He paused, pressing his lips together, then added, "This has gone on far too long. We carry on as if everything is fine, letting the years slip through our fingers. Well, time has run out for conventional methods, and now we must explore the desperate measures I've discussed. These measures could save us, not to mention future generations."

Moments later, a woman in the corner, eyes focused on the birch table's grain, broke the silence. "Is this even legal?" she asked.

"The U.S. never ratified the Comprehensive Test Ban Treaty, and we're not planning to do anything outside our own territory. The general counsel reviewed my proposal and, technically, it's completely legal."

She nodded, her tight expression easing. "I lost several family members when Cheniak flooded. My niece was only three months old when she..." The woman hesitated, adjusted her glasses. "...when she drowned. The water rose so fast, there was nothing anyone could do."

The representative from the Joint Chiefs of Staff piped up. "What do you recommend as a path forward?"

Alexander felt his shoulders lighten. *Steady, Fallsworth,* he said to himself. "I plan to reach out to the Chair of the Nuclear Engineering Department at Chambers

University. One of her Ph.D. students, the 'Bouldin, D.' on the journal articles I've handed out, developed software that simulates nuclear detonations and removal of geological obstructions for geo-engineering purposes. The dissertation examines how technical parameters related to nuclear explosions can impact weather patterns and long-term climate outcomes. As far as I can tell, a model already exists and would only need to be adapted and beta-tested, then implemented."

The committee members exchanged looks across the table. "What about radioactive fallout?" asked the woman from the Department of Energy.

"We can conduct the detonations underground," replied Alexander, his voice firm.

Then the man in the Air Force uniform spoke for the group. "I think we owe it to ourselves and our nation to at least consider geo-engineering as a way out of our difficulties. Let's think about it. If we agree, authorizing a black fund shouldn't be hard."

Alexander studied the participants, mentally beseeching each one to please, please accept the proposal. *Thank them for their time, Fallsworth. You've got this.*

It was all he could do to keep from calling out, "So who's with me?"

***

President Donahue's voice betrayed a practiced cadence through the car radio speaker. Dara Bouldin, fingers clutching the steering wheel, recalled Donahue's appearances on TV, his American flag lapel pin and brilliantine hair gleaming in high definition.

"Watch out!" Avery Bouldin, Dara's father, back-seat drove from the shotgun position, yelling over the downpour pummeling the car's roof. Another obliterated power line, another patch of black road leading into black horizon.

"Don't worry, I've got cat's eyes." Dara's ashen knuckles told another story.

The president droned on. "Acres of forest, critical infrastructure, and entire cities have burned off the map. Wildfires, floods, mass relocations — biblical proportions have nothing on what's happening now. Nature has dealt us a cruel hand."

"You shouldn't listen to his speeches, Dara. They upset —"

Before Avery could finish his thought, a splintered branch, dangling from a half-fallen tree, hurtled through the darkness toward the windshield.

"Hold on!" Dara cried out.

She swerved to avoid the wayward limb, but before she could exhale the vehicle began hydroplaning.

"Turn in the direction of the skid!" said Avery through clenched teeth, grabbing for the armrest.

Understanding the physics behind defensive driving didn't stop every muscle in Dara's body from twitching to turn the other way. Her old Hyundai weighed over a ton, yet it would meet its match in six inches of floodwater. How many inches were there tonight?

No time to calculate. Dara breathed a silent prayer, steered against her instincts, and righted the vehicle. *So this is what they mean by 'Jesus take the wheel,'* she thought. Her dark curls puffed into frizz in the humidity.

A few feet away, an orange detour sign mocked Dara's progress. Emerging from the shadows, a police officer in a neon poncho flashed a light in her window, motioning for her to pull over.

"What the hell are you doing on the road?" he demanded, dispensing with formalities. "Don't you know what could happen to you in a storm like this?"

Dara knew all too well about natural disasters and repercussions, but the last thing she needed was trouble with law enforcement. She had a government job, a security clearance, and zero intention of jeopardizing either one.

"I'm sorry, officer," she said. "I'm taking my father to work."

Dara caught Avery in her peripheral vision nodding from the passenger seat.

"Does he work at the hospital?"

She noticed Avery hadn't stopped nodding, so she blurted the verbal equivalent of a kick under the table. "No, sir. He works at the Slot Lot Casino."

Avery spent much of his free time there as well, which is why his own vehicle got repossessed. Dara knew better than to lend him her good-for-a-few-bucks beater, so she took it upon herself to transport him to work whenever his carpool bailed.

"License and registration," said the police officer, rolling his eyes.

She rummaged through her purse, producing her driver's permit, while Avery dug up the vehicle registration from the glove compartment. The cop returned to his cruiser to scan the documents, leaving Dara and her father waiting, water pouring over her faded silver Hyundai as if from an enormous bucket. They were quiet for a moment.

President Donahue rambled in the background, his words now infused with radio static. "My fellow Americans, my thoughts and prayers are with you. We, must all join together and move forward toward a stronger, brighter tomorrow."

Dara swatted at the on/off switch. "Shut up!"

Avery sighed. "It's okay, sweetheart."

"No, it isn't." She glared at the radio. Climate change was all around them, yet all Donahue ever did was deny, deny, deny, blather, rinse, repeat.

"They'll listen to you someday. Have faith."

Avery said this to his daughter so often that it had lost all meaning, especially now that the only job she could get since finishing her Ph.D. had nothing to do with her dissertation on climate change.

The officer returned, scowling. "Miss Bouldin, I advise you and your father to return home. Driving in this weather isn't safe."

"Thank you, officer." She refrained from adding the second part of her sentence, at least out loud – *but we need the money, so I'm going to drive my dad to his job anyway.*

She stared at the detour sign, calculating how long it would take to get to the casino using the alternate route.

The cop must have read her mind, given his sharpened tone. "If you don't turn back, you're taking an unnecessary risk. Blackjack is not a life or death situation."

"I know," said Dara, not making eye contact.

He sent them on their way, shaking his head as they rolled past.

Dara figured her dad could hitch a ride back to their apartment from a coworker once his shift was over. The forecasts all promised an end to the storm by daybreak, the new normal of cataclysm today, business-as-usual tomorrow. She could wait out the worst of the downpour in the Slot Lot's parking garage, then make her way home and rest up before commuting to her own job.

Her own job – *oh joy*. Another day spent testing nuclear safety codes, when all she wanted to do was sell the climate simulation software she'd designed in school.

Driving mostly uphill at earthworm-speed, dodging piles of debris and God knows how many abandoned vehicles, Dara spotted the Slot Lot sign, its generator-fueled glow stabbing her retinas. She was nothing like a cat and she knew it, except maybe for having nine lives.

"Thanks for the ride, sweetheart," said Avery, reaching over for a quick hug. "Be careful going home."

"I will." Dara watched her father, lanky in his yellow slicker, enter the casino, the workplace that never closed. A blessing and a curse.

For now, she'd shake off the stress of the drive, forget that it was the second hundred-year flood in two years. In the morning, she'd get back on the merry-go-round, one of thousands of civil servant drones in the nation's capital, waiting on the Metro platform, wandering the halls of her agency, the ghost image you see after looking at bright light.

***

The song of the summer, "Break the Skin," rasped through Dara's earbuds. Her fellow commuters would have glared at her were they not similarly lost in whatever pulsed through their own gear, although, given its popularity, it was probably the same song. The breakthrough hit for the DC-based music style called Dark Reverb was everywhere. Its characteristic bluesy guitars against punk rock beats struck a chord with doomed youth in search of a new anthem.

Reverberator-in-chief was Jericho Wells, descendant of Cab Calloway on his dad's side of the family, Irish immigrants on his mom's. His voice – strong yet world-weary, melodic yet forceful – drifted in and out of Dara's consciousness thanks to constant radio airplay and TV appearances. His green-eyed visage was omnipresent as tabloids and social media caught up with the public's fascination.

Jericho Wells was also Dara's ex.

Months before he'd written the lyrics, Jericho played the chords to "Break the Skin" for Dara on his battered Martin acoustic. The words came later:

It's been five years
Light years long and dark but now I find
I found my way
Away from you
But not from me
And I thought I'd arrived
Sign said you are here
But I am lost

And if you break the skin
You'll see the state I'm in
Don't break the skin
You'll see the state I'm in, state I'm in

Seven years ago, Dara was an immediate outcast when she and her father moved to the Washington, D.C.-area from Colorado. She'd tested out of a couple of grades, rendering her a 14-year-old among 16-year-old classmates.

When Jericho wasn't getting beat up, he likewise was ignored. It didn't help that he had "straightedge" proclivities ("I don't drink, don't smoke, don't do drugs," he'd say, in line with the straightedge movement) when the other kids all drank, smoked, and did drugs. Or that he was into Dark Reverb when the other kids had never even heard of it.

Dara and Jericho lived on the same street, a few houses apart. She'd hear music pumping from his basement like an insistent heartbeat, certain he didn't know she existed. But Jericho knew exactly who Dara was because she'd break the curve on science exams and hole up in the computer lab most nights after school. Everyone else hated her for it, but Jericho was no fool. One day he asked her if she knew how to use Pro Tools, the audio recording software. No, but she could learn.

Thought I could
Handle all but sticks and stones
And I should know
A stick figure, I
And your heart made of stone
I'm alone with this
A word to the wise fool
Tell me and I swear
I'll change, I'll change

And if you break the skin
You'll see the state I'm in
Don't break the skin
You'll see the state I'm in, state I'm in

She did a credible job recording his first demo, and later his EP. Jericho decided to start a record label with delusions of attracting other bands and taking over the world. He called it Tyrannosaurus Regina. The name originated one night in junior year when Dara and Jericho were debating some topic or other. Jericho found himself shaking his head: "You have to be right all the time," he said to Dara. "You're like a pit pull, or a T-Rex."

She looked him in the eye. "That's Tyrannosaurus Regina to you, Jericho Wells." After that, they'd call each other Regina and Rex, depending on who felt feistier.

They were outcasts together. "I'm going to take over the world, too," said Dara, eventually mustering the courage to tell her friend about her computer project. "I got the idea from a book all the nuclear engineering majors in college use." She went on to describe the geo-engineering climate simulation program she was coding, based on the ideas in the textbook. "You can reposition the Jet Stream — take a look at the results when I input these parameters." She flashed a rare smile, one that made Jericho wonder where he ever got the idea that she was plain.

Jericho dreamed of being like Bob Marley, Bob Geldof, or John Lennon — someone who used music to make the world a better place. Dara dreamed of being like Marie Curie, Louis Pasteur, or Jonas Salk – someone who used science to make the world a better place. These were lofty ambitions, downright laughable to all but each other. But like blood brother and sister, they'd plot and plan next steps and guide each other out of self-doubt.

Of course, the brother and sister act didn't last. The friendship blossomed and grew wings. Pandora's kiss. They were too young to understand what was happening, or the inevitable burn-and-crash of romance. It didn't help when Dara's dream began to eclipse Jericho's.

Broken
That's what I am
Scarred
And scared of who I am
Born or made?
But stuck with what I've become
The strength that I feign
The power of one
The power of none

Forever wasn't nearly long enough until they found themselves there, five years after their first kiss. They talked about getting married; they argued about getting married (and everything else). They got engaged, they got estranged, they got back together. Then the reversal of fortune came: Jericho soared, Dara spiraled. He went on tour with his band and decided it was better if they remained apart. "We can still be friends," he said.

Since finishing grad school, Dara had only spoken to Jericho a couple of times, going through the motions of remaining friends without having to deal with him in person due to the distance. She moved back in with her father and got a job, forcing herself up every morning and onto her train.

Emerging from the Metro station, the fecund scent from last night's storm filling her nostrils, Jericho's gaze greeted her in 2-D from the side of a bus. *Well, Rex,* she thought, *you're doing what you said you'd do. Hope you're feeling powerful now.*

***

Dmitri Andreevich Ivanov studied the biographies and photographs of his new coworkers at the Agency for Advanced Energy Research well in advance of the first day of his Washington assignment. Nonetheless, he went through the formality of introductions, trailing the Division Director Jason Houseman around the office to meet the team. The Americanisms always amused him — the sports metaphors, the 'welcome aboards,' the easy smiles. He knew not to mistake any of those for sincerity.

"We look forward to having you here," said Jason, administering what is known in government parlance as 'the grip and grin.' "We haven't had a visiting scientist from Russia in several years."

"It is my pleasure to be here," Dmitri said in barely-accented English, returning Jason's handshake. This was not his first assignment in an English-speaking country and his accent reflected it. Dmitri took in the surroundings: the newish office furniture, the fresh faces of young Ph.D.s, the open doors. It was evident that the Agency for Advanced Energy Research, also known as the AAER, was one of the more well-funded U.S. government entities.

"I'm just glad our governments have agreed that nuclear safety has no border so you can participate in our scientific exchange program. We look forward to learning what we can from you while you're here."

"I hope to do the same," Dmitri replied, maintaining eye contact.

Fortunately for Dmitri, U.S.-Russia scientific and technical cooperation wasn't entirely dead, with several programs having survived the political tensions of the past decade. The Department of Energy's international nuclear fusion research program, agreed to by the governments of the United States and the Soviet Union in 1958, remained in continuous operation. The International Space Station projects between NASA and Russia's Roscosmos weren't ending anytime soon. Likewise, the technology-neutral Reactor Safety Simulation Program (RSSP) at AAER lived to see another fiscal year.

Dmitri's Ph.D. in nuclear engineering from the prestigious Moscow Engineering Physics Institute (a.k.a., MEPhi) along with his advanced programming skills made him an ideal candidate for the RSSP. More importantly, he cut his teeth on fast reactors. Fast neutron reactor technology was already in commercial operation in Russia, yet it barely existed, even experimentally, in the United States, despite the fact that Americans invented it. Now the U.S. government was playing catch up.

Jason Houseman and company hoped the esteemed Dr. Ivanov could help AAER get ahead, and Dmitri knew it. Not that this urgency sped up the vetting process. Dmitri spent a full year in Yekaterinburg waiting for AAER's security office to complete his background check. The so-called "Gateway to Siberia," Yekaterinburg was the Russian city where Tsar Nicholas II and his entire family were executed. Whiling away the endless winter writing safety code for the breeder reactor at Beloyarsk, he concluded that the Romanovs got off easy.

At AAER, Dmitri's work plan allowed him to focus on unclassified safety research and code development as long as he stayed away from nuclear fuel production technologies and anything related to atomic weapons design. He wouldn't be allowed on the agency's local area network (LAN), so most of what he'd learn would be from talking to his new coworkers. Establishing rapport was crucial to his mission.

Making his way with his new supervisor down a narrow corridor, one of the office doors was closed. Jason smirked, knocked, and opened the door a crack. "Dara, I'd like to introduce you to our new visiting scientist."

She got up. Her desk was strewn with crumpled papers and empty soda cans. There were several computers in the office and a touch-screen monitor on the opposite wall. A screen saver displayed gifs of a rock band in action. Other screens showed various charts, which Dmitri recognized as depicting nuclear accident modeling in progress.

Dmitri noticed that a poster of Albert Einstein behind Dara's chair made more eye contact with him than she did. Her own eyes, brown and almond-shaped, seemed fixed on his lapel pin that depicted a two-headed eagle, the symbol of the Russian Federation. He wondered if it was because she was so small that the pin was at eye level for her. Or maybe she was just shy.

She wore a black-fringed shawl over a black wool skirt, an incongruous outfit for summer. Dark hair curled around her ears. Dmitri noticed scarring along her right hand and forearm.

"I see that you are modeling severe accidents, Dr. Bouldin," Dmitri offered, shaking her hand, trying to ignore the scaly texture.

"I developed the code that we use. It's not very exciting." Dmitri already knew about the code. Dara was right about the lack of excitement.

According to her bio she was twenty-one, but in person she looked even younger. Her lack of makeup, high heels, or jewelry — accoutrements the other women in the office wore in abundance – didn't help. Dmitri thought about the other young staffers he'd met. Even the ones with only Master's degrees seemed happy to play grip and grin, yammering about recent projects and promotions. They were not nearly as accomplished as Dara, from what he'd read of her educational background and publications.

"I'm sure you'll enjoy your time here," Dara added.

Dmitri, late twenties, tall and lean with dark blue eyes and wavy brown hair, nodded. Unlike Dara, her female colleagues made eye contact easily, even flirtatiously. Perhaps he would enjoy his time here, in more ways than one.

Jason shut the door as they left. "She always wants her door closed," he said. "She's like that."

***

Dara emerged after lunch holding a blank copy of her performance appraisal in anticipation of her appointment with Jason. Not that she ate much. Today was quarterly review day at AAER, her first professional appraisal. The form listed five metrics: Competence on Assigned Projects, Technical Initiatives, Communication — Written, Communication — Interpersonal, and Teamwork. The ratings for each rubric went from one to five: 5) Superior; 4) Excellent; 3) Average; 2) Below Average; 1) Poor.

"Have a seat, Dara," Jason said, giving the once over to her outfit, which suggested a brunette Stevie Nicks circa 1978. Other days her look called to mind what Wednesday Addams or Pippi Longstocking might have worn to an office job. Mostly she just draped herself in head-to-toe black.

"Dara, I'll start by saying that you've demonstrated superior competence on your assigned projects. The reactor safety code you developed resolved a vulnerability the old software couldn't. We've already licensed the code to several foreign nuclear regulators for substantial fees. Thanks to that, we've been able to increase our travel budget for international conferences. We're also funding employee training requests and taking on more black projects later this year. We won't need to ask Congress for additional appropriations, which is great. I'll rate your performance on this rubric a five."

Dara watched Jason tap the number five on his keyboard. She thought about the licensing fees for the code but knew the drill — when you develop software for the U.S. government, it becomes property of the U.S. government. Uncle Sam keeps any royalties.

She also knew that her coworkers enjoyed the fruits of her labors. She'd overhear them discussing upcoming travel to exotic locations for conferences, approvals for expensive training classes (usually the latest management fluff), and prestigious top secret 'black' projects. Dara, on the other hand, ran simulations and watched the clock tick away from the confines of her office. Another day, another set of parameters.

She wondered what the black projects were that her 'superior' work enabled. Her coworkers were anything but discreet about having these assignments, broadcasting as much by posting red 'Top Secret — Do Not Enter' signs on their office doors. Not to worry. Dara wasn't planning on it.

She ended up with the code development assignment in the first place because her coworker, John

Decker, had botched it. He was in the ex-Navy clique, which went a long way in the nuclear arena. In one of their few verbal exchanges, John told Dara she really shouldn't drink so much soda. "It's bad for you," he advised. *Thanks*, she thought. *Now I know.* Yet despite his coding failures, this guy got a black project.

"I can give you a five for written communication," Jason continued. "You have superior writing skills. That's not a given with engineers."

Dara smiled. So far, so good. Dara tried not to care about the appraisal system, but she'd been in school her entire life up until this job. The past three months were her first since preschool without being graded.

"Unfortunately, I'm not going to be able to rate you very well on the other rubrics."

Dara's eyes shifted. "What?"

"For starters, you don't take any initiatives."

Dara felt her neck stiffen as she collected her thoughts. "I developed the code we use on my own. What you had before I got here was a mess. I started over from scratch and created something that worked. Why isn't that taking the initiative?"

"Initiative means more than that. You need to show leadership."

"My assignments aren't with other people. I don't have anyone to lead."

"I don't see it that way. Maybe if you networked or joined in with your coworkers you would find a way to demonstrate those skills."

"'Joined in with my coworkers?' What does that mean?"

"Happy hour, for instance. You never go."

Dara stared at the word "Poor" on the page in front of her. "I don't drink."

"Okay," Jason said as he leaned back in his chair, his mouth curling up on one side. "Some people play on the softball team. Take Kayla Tripp — she plays, and it's been an excellent way for her to develop interpersonal communication skills with the rest of the staff. I should add it's been to her personal benefit. She and John are getting married in September."

Dara couldn't fathom how marrying John Decker could be to anyone's personal benefit, let alone why it should enhance someone's performance appraisal. "I don't see why that should have any bearing on my review," she said, forcing herself to look Jason in the eye.

"It does, Dara. I don't see you as a team player."

"My work is superior. You said so yourself."

"Dara, maybe in school you were a special cornflake or whatever they're calling child geniuses these days, but you're in the real world now. The rules are different. This goes beyond good or bad work. People try to fit in and work together, and that helps our organization function better. Accept this as constructive criticism. I'll give you one point each for the remaining three rubrics. Your total score is thirteen out of twenty-five."

Dara felt herself tremble -- lips, chin, fingers. She considered defending herself in more pointed terms, but Jason would probably just add it to his list of perceived infractions. "Does this mean I'm stuck running accident simulations?" was all she could say.

"The simulations need to be done. You have plenty of time to improve, and when you do, we can think about other assignments for you." He hit print.

Dara swallowed hard. No special assignments for her — just drudgery for the foreseeable future. With an unsatisfactory performance appraisal, there would be no escape.

Jason leaned over and signed the bottom of the printout. He handed it to Dara, motioning for her to sign as well. She stared at the number thirteen.

Her signature smeared under her hand. Dara walked back to her office without a word and closed the door.

***

Every few weeks, Avery Bouldin heard from Jane Canton, Dara's former dissertation advisor and Chair of the Nuclear Engineering Department at Chambers University. He was onto Dara's tactic of screening Jane's calls to her cell phone but could never bring himself to do the same on their shared land line.

"I haven't seen Dara in a while," she'd say, typically calling just as Avery was sitting down to dinner. "Has she thought about trying to market her climate model again? This could be a good time." She'd name drop venture capitalists, angel investors and other supposedly interested parties.

"Not now, Jane," Avery would reply, stopping himself from adding, "You rancid bitch." Things ended badly the first time Dara tried to market her software under Jane's supervision. Still, Jane never stopped trying to get her cut, insisting that she went out on a limb for Dara in supporting her dissertation research. Now Dara owed her.

This time, Avery set aside any niceties. His long-standing gratitude and deference to her for watching over Dara when she matriculated at Chambers as a 16-year-old freshman had reached its limits. "Jane, you need to face facts. Maybe it wasn't meant to be. And if it ever was, what makes you think you had any claim to my daughter's work?"

"And you do?" Jane's voice slurred a little as ice tinkled in the background. "You know as well as I do what happens to any money she makes. You've sabotaged her every step of the -"

Avery cut her off before she could finish. The screed would just devolve into Jane carrying on about how Dara was wasting time, money, her life. Any second, someone else would come along with a better model, and Dara's chances would be shot forever. Tick tock, tick tock, *boom.*

True, when Dara was finishing her thesis, the "interested parties" swarmed. Jane spread the message about Dara's research to all who would listen, referring to herself as the primary stakeholder (more than once, in case anyone missed it). Dara's success looked like a sure thing.

But the angels were fickle. Dara finished the program with Ph.D. after her name but no deal, just a deep well of debt thanks to Avery's overconfidence at the racetrack, with his broker, at the casino, with their credit cards. Of course, Dara forgave him. It wasn't the first time.

Jane Canton, on the other hand, wasn't the forgiving type. Debt forced Dara off the entrepreneurial path into government service. Conflict of interest regulations kept her out of the marketplace, which was just as well. She had neither the time nor the heart to find a buyer.

As for Avery, he was tired – tired of the drunk dials, tired of his blood pressure ticking up every time 'Professor Canton' flashed on his phone, tired of coming up with polite euphemisms for 'Get lost, Jane.'

Enough. "Get lost, Jane," he said, and hung up.

***

"Dara B.?" A large man in a Day-Glo yellow jacket pulled a flashlight from his pocket and checked for her name on a clipboard. "ID, please."

Guest list formalities were familiar to Dara, but tonight's venue was not. The arena normally hosted basketball and hockey games, with musical acts only getting booked there if they were famous enough. Jericho Wells was now famous enough.

"Okay," the security behemoth said, handing her a badge marked, 'Backstage.' He opened the door with an electronic card.

The invitation arrived by text a few days before the concert, a blink-and-you-might-miss-it: 'show sat can put u on g-list.' A second text followed a few minutes later: 'pls come-rex.' Dara fully intended to stay home, but Avery had other ideas.

"You need to get out and make new friends. Hey! Stop rolling your eyes at me." Avery tried to be gentle — he understood heartbreak — but refused to indulge Dara's snit. "Look, you're twenty-one. You can't use being younger than everyone else as an excuse anymore. Jericho is a good guy and probably your only friend. I know you love the music -- I've got the busted eardrums to prove it. Go to the concert, Dara. You might even enjoy yourself for once."

The concert, advertised as a homecoming, showcased Jericho along with his opening band, Spaceman Spiff. The openers were Jericho's label- and tour-mates on Tyrannosaurus Regina. He often spoke about wanting to thank his fans in D.C., people who knew him when. Tonight was Jericho's long-awaited opportunity.

Dara took in the cavernous backstage, complete with dressing rooms, forklifts, tool-belted crew members, headset-headed security detail. Mirrors on the walls made it look even bigger, magnifying the behind-the-scenes faces, lending a funhouse air. Aromas wafted from a fully loaded craft services table – chicken sandwiches, flatbread pizzas, vegetarian wraps.

All 20,000 seats had sold. As the sole proprietor of the label, Jericho kept a significant cut of the profits from both ticket and merchandise sales (his and Spiff's). Jericho had come a long way from playing small clubs like the Black Cherry Lounge on V Street.

Of course, this 'business end' was meant to remain invisible to fans. Jericho understood the importance of maintaining his image: poet with pentatonic scales coursing through his veins, horrified by the world the previous generation left behind, committed to saving it, never ever selling out. Still, getting his message across required cash flow. Jericho was the tree that fell in the forest heard 'round the world, and it was clear to Dara that he wasn't going to let pretentions to artistic purity get in the way of his ambitions.

Dara studied the backstage pass-holders around her -- a girl with silver lip gloss, a boy in purple combat boots, a couple that looked like Outer Space Fun Barbie and Ken — but Dara didn't recognize anyone. She overheard someone whispering about the VIP in the corner, a U.S. Senator, and the teenage boy standing next to her who looked to be the senator's son. The members of Spaceman Spiff had taken the stage, resplendent with glitter guitars and hair colors by Crayola. Dara felt the bass thump under her feet.

During their club days, she'd meet Jericho and his band mates a couple of hours before each show to help set up. A bouncer would draw a big black X on her hand for being under the drinking age. Everyone joked that she was jailbait. The Black Cherry Lounge, a little larger than a studio apartment, was what they referred to as a 'stairs gig,' in which they'd have to carry gear up two flights of stairs to get to the stage. No matter -- they felt no pain, only goose bumps and butterfly stomachs.

Dara dreaded the Cherry's wobbly ceiling fan, worried it would fly off through the audience like a rogue helicopter propeller and take everyone's head with it. She feared low attendance, despite all their efforts to promote the shows. What if a guitar string snapped during a crucial solo? What if the sound mix was off? What if the audience didn't like the new songs? Dara knew what the gigs meant to Jericho. The band was his brainchild, his heart and soul, and she was his muse.

After helping set up, Dara would sneak off and change clothes. Her favorite childhood holiday was always Halloween, the one day of the year she could be someone else besides Science Girl. Gig nights carried the same spirit. Dara didn't have much money for clothes but had a knack for adapting thrift store finds. Candy-colored hair streaks, metallic eye makeup, black satin catsuit, faux fur wrap, stilettos...she'd emerge a punk rock superhero. Even more so when she caught the glint in Jericho's eye. The guys would forget all about their jailbait epithets.

Tonight, though, Dara wore jeans, a black tee-shirt and a ponytail. No super heroics, nothing from the muse-wear section at Goodwill. Dara's cloak of invisibility was just as well, as standing out in this crowd would have been difficult. The female Dark Reverb fans had taken to airplane-gluing their hair into extraterrestrial contortions, wearing underwear as outerwear, and piercing silver and gold strands into exposed parts of their bodies. The boys favored metallic ink tattoo sleeves and the Official Jericho Wells Tee-Shirt™, which displayed eight of Jericho's handsomest mug shots from the numerous times he'd been arrested protesting social injustices. Even the senator was wearing one, her version silkscreened in neon colors like an Andy Warhol painting.

One thing was clear. The kids backstage were just that – kids. They had acne; they scrubbed at the Sharpie Xs on their hands in the rest room; they slunk off into corners to make out. They brought along their senator moms; they asked their senator moms for tee-shirt money. Kids –

something Dara wasn't anymore. Never mind the civilian attire, Dara was inherently invisible in this crowd. A pang hit the pit of her stomach.

"Dara, there you are!" Jericho smiled and kissed her on the cheek.

He stood before her, in the flesh, seemingly taller, eyes greener than she'd remembered, a larger-than-life apparition of the boy she fell in love with. She detected a whiff of the mint soap he liked to use, the same scent that lingered on their pillowcases when they used to be a couple. She gulped, struggling to recall what she had planned to say. Her cheeks flushed as each second of silent hesitation passed. Finally, she managed a raspy, "Jericho, congratulations."

"I can't believe it — we sold out the entire arena." He smiled. "I'm so glad you're here, Reg."

Just then, a willowy blonde woman appeared behind him. She wore electric blue chiffon with silver chains draped over her shoulders, a cross between Deborah Harry and the blue fairy from Pinocchio. Her hand, tattooed with tiny violets, slipped into his.

"Dara, this is Jennie."

"Hi," said Jennie, extending her free hand.

Dara only heard static.

"Dara and I used to live on the same street," said Jericho, eyeing Jennie.

More static.

"Jennie's a publicist. She's trying to help us get our message across. She's the one who got me the gigs at Senator Collins' campaign rallies, and now the senator and her kid are fans. They're here for the show tonight."

Jennie eyed Dara through azure contact lenses that matched her dress. "Networking makes a big difference," she said. "We're trying to change people's hearts and minds from the inside out."

In the mirror behind them, Dara caught Jennie's hand slipping out of Jericho's and into the back pocket of his jeans.

She could only stare. It was all she could do not to blurt out, "I'm the Regina in Tyrannosaurus Regina. Don't you forget it!" She knew the drill. Kisses weren't contracts, presents weren't promises, defeats should be accepted with the grace of an adult, not the grief of a child (or whatever it said in that stupid poem Avery taped to her bathroom mirror). But steeling herself in the face of this was another matter entirely.

Someone tapped Jennie on the shoulder, her serpentine chains capturing the light as she turned to acknowledge her minder. "Gotta go," she said, "I'm meeting up with some radio people over by the buffet table." She leaned in to kiss Jericho on the neck, then turned to Dara. "Can you believe I got Jericho in regular rotation on commercial radio? I'm still pinching myself." She floated off to the craft services table, a trail of silver body glitter in her wake.

Dara watched as she disappeared from earshot. "I'm really happy for you, Jericho," she finally said, mouth dry, eyes shifting to the now-glittery floor tiles, not knowing what else to say.

"Thanks. You know I want to be happy for you, too, Reg."

Dara looked up at him, finding his pupils through the thick eyelashes she'd known so well. "What do you mean?"

"I'd be lying if I said I wasn't concerned about you."

She stiffened. "Why? You don't need to be concerned about me."

"Dara, what happened to your computer model?"

"You already know the answer," she replied, trying to keep her voice steady. "I can't do anything with it anymore because I work for the government. The answer is nothing."

Jericho wasn't changing the subject. "I know you need your job to pay the bills, but working at AAER isn't what you dreamed of doing."

"It doesn't matter. I'm lucky to even have a job. It's a luxury in this day and age to hold out for a dream. I'm not a kid anymore, and I have to make a living."

"This isn't you talking, Dara. I know you, and this isn't you."

Dara willed herself not to tear up. This was no time for the 'grief of a child.'

"Look, I know you're paying off your dad's debts. I make money now, much more than I need. I could help you pay them off, and then you could go back to doing what you really want to do."

"I can't take your money, Jericho."

"You wouldn't have to pay me back. There wouldn't be any strings attached. I don't care about the money, anyway. I'd give it to anyone who needed it, and you need it."

Something about the last sentence made her stomach lurch.

"You could save so many lives with your program. I believe in your idea, and so do lots of other people. You were there for me when I needed someone — you believed in my dream, and look at me now."

Dara glared at Jericho. A few decibels louder: "Did you not hear me the first time? I can't take your charity."

Jericho glared back. "So, you're going to give up? Just like that? I used to admire you. You used to inspire me. Now all I see is a waste."

Waste. The word made her feel like she'd been tased.

Now other pairs of eyes, not just Jericho's, glared at Dara: the crew, radio people, Senator Collins and son, Outer Space Fun Barbie and Ken, three out of four Spacemen Spiff, Jennie. Dara's face grew hot.

"Waste?" she said. "Save your concern trolling. I'm doing the best I can. I don't want a handout from anyone, least of all you."

Then she added, "Keep your money. You're a sellout, and next year you'll be a distant memory. If you think any of these idiots care about anything you have to say, you're just kidding yourself." She shot a look at Jennie. "Especially that one."

Jericho went silent. Dara held his gaze. Finally, he said, "I'm sorry, Reg." His eyes glistened.

Dara didn't blink. "I'm not, Rex." She turned and left.

T-minus Nine

Occasionally Dara would meet with counterparts from other U.S. government organizations to update them on her work in nuclear accident modeling, typically the Department of Energy, the Nuclear Regulatory Commission, or the Environmental Protection Agency. One day, Jason Houseman gave her the heads up via a Post-it note affixed to her computer monitor to "Expect a call from an intel agency v. soon."

She wondered why someone from an intelligence agency would want to talk to her. Was it about a security violation? A terrorist plotting a nuclear accident? Avery leading a double life as James Bond? Sure enough, Dara's phone rang, and the telltale "Unknown" moniker flashed on Caller ID.

It was Alexander Fallsworth from the CIA, Special Activities Division. He wanted to meet with Dara as soon as possible.

Dara bit her lip, unsure of what the stranger on the other end of the line might want. "Do you want to discuss severe accident modeling for nuclear facilities?"

"No, Dr. Bouldin, we're more interested in other simulations you've developed."

Dara's heart skipped. "Do you mean for geo-engineering applications?"

"Yes."

Her breath tingled in her lungs. A smile came to her lips, quite possibly for the first time since the blowup at Jericho's show.

"Dr. Jane Canton of Chambers University also will participate. She signed a non-disclosure agreement since she works in the academic sector and isn't cleared."

The bubble deflated as quickly as it came. Jane had a talent for sucking the air out of a room, even when she wasn't in it.

Alexander transferred Dara to his administrative assistant who set up the appointment and gave Dara instructions for accessing the CIA headquarters site. After she hung up, Dara's cell phone buzzed. It was a text from Jane: "Next week — this is it! Try to dress like a normal person."

***

Dara knew Jane was right about dressing professionally for the meeting, although the snark-o-gram made her fantasize about showing up with green hair and combat boots to spite her. *Nope – not this time.* She opted for a charcoal gray coatdress that she'd found at a consignment shop, and black pumps. As a bonus, the long sleeves did a decent job of hiding the scars on her arm, giving Jane less ammunition for criticism. Dara wore a silver brooch shaped like a stylized atom on her lapel, pinned her hair into a bun, and applied rose-colored lipstick.

"Do I look like a normal person?" she asked, performing a quick turn for Avery as she reached for her keys.

"You look great. Don't let that witch get inside your head."

"Thanks, Dad."

"Remember, this is your baby, and a tremendous opportunity. You call the shots. Keep that in mind and you'll do great."

She needed a fight song for the drive over, and "Colors All Change" by Vitamin X on the Tyrannosaurus Regina compilation fit the bill:

I had a dream
It was a strange one
Filled with colors
I had never seen
Like none in nature
Off blue-black, green-like crimson
But then I awoke
And the colors all changed

The day, bathed in sunlight, felt like a mirage. Life in the nation's capital seemed fine, but, just in the past week, a tornado obliterated an entire community in Texas; a Florida condo building collapsed due to salt water intrusion caused by rising sea levels, killing half the residents; and twenty-six people died in Holton, Missouri, in yet another flood. Even though hurricane season had barely reached its second month, the meteorologists were halfway through the alphabet to name the storms.

The swollen Potomac splashed to Dara's right as she made every attempt to observe the speed limit on the George Washington Memorial Parkway, watching for debris on the road from recent downpours that belied the sunshine. Georgetown University's gothic spires came into view as Hoya crew teams navigated the rocky currents below. Dara recalled the famous stairs nearby where *The Exorcist* was filmed. That part of the city always looked haunted.

Dara was haunted, too, by her past, by her future, by ghosts of dreams that wouldn't rest. But this one had a chance.

I've had a life
It's been a strange one
Worlds away
From pale reality
I've climbed volcanoes,
Swam the inland oceans,
But then I awoke
And the colors all changed

The song, a three-chord distortion-fest buoyed by an almost Beatlesque bassline, propelled Dara toward her destination. Her last chance — there was no denying it. She felt like a mother summoning superhuman strength to push a car off her dying child. Or walking through fire to rescue her from certain death.

Look all around,
Curiouser and curiouser,
The life I've led
More beautiful than dreams
More frightening
Than my worst nightmare
All at once
So it seems

Don't blow it this time. She thought back to what Jericho said, the words "waste" and "this isn't you" echoing in her head.

The time has come
To set it straight
To make sense of it all
The colors change
From day to day
The point of reference gone

This could really happen.

***

"Dr. Canton, Dr. Bouldin, thank you both for coming." Alexander escorted the women to his office. "I hope going through security wasn't too onerous."

Jane laughed a bit too loudly, walking in front of Dara, her black-pantsuit-and-striped blouse combo making her appear almost as tall as General Fallsworth. Dara recognized the old pattern — Jane taking the lead, Dara bringing up the rear.

She took in the surroundings through the window. Verdant lawns, leafy trees, late model sedans and SUVs in the parking lot -- it wasn't what she'd seen depicted in spy movies, but still, CIA, baby! Dara saw another woman walk by in a sleek charcoal-colored coatdress and felt the corners of her lips turn up.

As a division head, the general had his own office which featured a small conference table where he invited the women to sit. Dara noticed a gallery of framed photographs on the credenza: a wedding picture of him and a svelte, doe-eyed woman; a present-day version of the couple at the beach with two tow-headed children; the general in an Army uniform receiving a certificate; the children playing various sports.

He closed the door.

"Ladies, please call me Alexander. May I call you Jane and Dara?"

They nodded, handing Alexander their business cards.

"Your kids are adorable," Dara said, eying the photos. "How old are they?"

Jane shot her a look.

Alexander smiled, cufflinks glinting in a sunbeam that streamed through the window. "Thank goodness they take after their mother." Pointing to the sports pictures, he said, "That's Molly on the balance beam. She's nine. And that's my little slugger, Jackson. He's six."

Jane wasn't having the small talk. "So, what can we do for you, Mr. Fallsworth?"

"Yes, we do have some business to discuss," said Alexander, his blue eyes mirror-like. "I appreciate you signing the non-disclosure agreement, Jane. When I first called you, I didn't realize that Dara works for AAER now and has a top secret security clearance. Her clearance makes our lives much easier."

Alexander continued, turning to Dara. "I understand that you've developed a simulation program to model climate change impacts after removal of geological obstructions."

Dara nodded.

"Tell me about your work."

Dara saw that Alexander had a copy of her dissertation. He'd probably already read it, but she set up a slide deck on her laptop anyway, drew a deep breath, and went through the various features of the program. She ended with a demonstration of the model using random parameters.

Dara tried not to talk too quickly. Her nerves were like butterflies in motion, in that ineffable place where panic ends and exhilaration begins. It helped that Alexander didn't treat her like a child on an audition with Jane in the role of stage mom.

"This is truly remarkable work," he said. He turned to Jane. "So, what has your department done on the subject since Dara completed her studies?"

Jane looked confused. "What do you mean?"

"When we spoke on the phone, you implied you were partners. Have you done further research in this area, or built on the work Dara initiated?"

Jane glanced at Dara. "No, we haven't. It was definitely a risk to support Dara's research. We were able to cover her fellowship. Several investors came forward toward the end, but after Dara left, the interest dried up."

"Oh, I see." Alexander looked back at Dara. "So, would you be interested in expanding on your dissertation as a black project?"

"A black project?" said Dara, aware that the designation meant the project would be top secret, but suddenly curious as to how the secrecy would play out in real life.

"Yes," said Alexander. "The administration wants to explore geoengineering as a climate change mitigator. The project would be classified as a Top Secret — Sensitive Compartmented Information project, so you wouldn't be able to speak to anyone about your work who wasn't adequately cleared and didn't have a demonstrated need to know. As you can imagine, there will be some hurdles to reach that point where we could make the project public. But we're committed to getting there."

Dara nodded. "Would I work with you?"

"The duties for this project would replace your current job description at AAER, and you would stay in the same office. I'd take over as your supervisor and drop in from time to time."

Dara stared at Alexander. "So, this wouldn't just be a research project?"

"No – that's why it's so sensitive. Our hope is to implement the program once it's fully developed. I plan to testify before several congressional committees to try and gain the necessary political support."

Then he added: "I can assure you, Dara, for me, this project is personal. I'll stop at nothing to ensure its success."

Dara beamed. "It's personal for me, too."

Jane piped up. "How much are you willing to pay us for the software?"

Dara's ears grew red. She focused on her fingernails, the buttons on her dress, anything to keep from shooting daggers at her former professor. This was neither the time nor place to argue with her, but Dara was out of practice in reeling her in.

Maintaining his composure, Alexander came to the rescue. "Jane, because Dara is a government employee, we can't purchase the model from her. That's how the system works. And if she left the government, we'd need to put the project out for bid. It would be an ethics violation and probably illegal for her to bid on such a contract for at least a couple of years."

Jane's brow furrowed. "Can we wait?"

Alexander's looked squarely at Jane. "And watch the world burn and people die in the meantime?"

"Okay. No deal, then. Thank you for your time. Dara, let's go."

Dara could only stare. Neither she nor Alexander got up. Jane beelined toward the door and once again motioned to Dara. "Are you coming?"

Dara didn't move. She didn't care about the money.

Finally, Alexander spoke up. "Jane, with all due respect, this is Dara's decision. Your department is no longer doing any work in this area, so you have nothing to add. I appreciate you coming today, but, as it happens, your opinion carries no weight."

Jane grabbed her briefcase and glowered at Alexander. Dara held her breath and braced herself, knowing that CIA headquarters was the worst possible backdrop for one of Jane's outbursts. Instead, Jane turned on her heel and stormed out of the room, muttering, "Stupid, stupid girl" to Dara under her breath.

Alexander's admin rushed after her en route to security. "I need to escort you, ma'am," he said, as politely yet firmly as possible.

Air returned to the room with Jane's departure.

Alexander shrugged, nonplussed, then laughed. "Congratulations on getting through your Ph.D. program, Dara. I sense it was a challenge, on many levels."

Dara laughed, almost as pleased with Jane's dismissal as she was with the tremendous opportunity Alexander laid out before her. "So, we'll be a team from now on?" she asked.

"You got it," replied Alexander, smiling broadly.

"Thanks so much. I promise you won't regret this," said Dara, trying without success to modulate the pitch of voice.

***

The "Top Secret-SCI — Do Not Enter" sign Dara taped to her door most days was down this morning. Dmitri kept a running tally of the number of hours she'd spent with the sign in place. Every so often, Mr. Blond Crew Cut would drop by. Dmitri already knew his affiliation, but even if he didn't, the whispers around the office about the "Culinary Institute of America" (wink, cough) fooled no one. There was a gallows humor about intelligence folks, so-called spooks, probably because the CIA-types were ironically obvious, with their padlocked briefcases, perfect posture, and shiny shoes. In contrast, the AAER scientists (the male ones at least) favored rumpled suits and clip-on ties.

Some days Dmitri would catch Dara and Alexander in the lunchroom, laughing and showing each other photos and videos on their phones. Dara had added more professional clothing to her wardrobe, mostly suits and dresses in colors other than black. Subtle cosmetics now highlighted her features, and she wore her dark brown curls ironed straight. Gone was the woman who looked like a goth high school student in dress-for-success cosplay.

As much as Dara appeared to appreciate her new assignment and supervisor, it wasn't clear that her new-found happiness extended to her home life. The surveillance logs showed that she went home to her apartment every night. She lived with her father, but usually he worked overnight shifts so their time together was limited. Few visitors came around. On weekends, Dara ran errands or went to the public library. Sometimes she took walks around her neighborhood.

If anyone was having any fun in Dara's household, it certainly wasn't Dara. Her credit report revealed major gambling debts and maxed out charge cards, but it was clear that her father was responsible since, based on surveillance, Dara never set foot in racetracks or casinos. Her rare purchases (besides groceries) were made at second-hand or consignment stores. After covering basic needs for herself and her father, Dara's paychecks went toward debt repayment.

Holding two Coke Zeros in one hand, Dmitri knocked on Dara's door with the other.

"Come in," she said.

"Hello, Dara. I appreciate you taking the time to meet with me today." Dmitri handed her one of the drinks.

"Thanks, Dmitri. However did you know I'm addicted to soda?" She smiled, something she had been doing more often in recent weeks, eying the stack of cans in her recycling bin.

"It was a lucky guess." He himself didn't like soda, but mirroring was a classic technique to establish rapport, so he held his nose and took a sip.

"I'm not into coffee," she said, "so I drink soda. Without caffeine I'd probably still be in bed."

"Somehow I doubt that. You never take a day off and look busy all the time."

Dara laughed. "That's the caffeine talking."

Dmitri wanted to tell Dara that she looked nice, but based on his cultural training, he thought the better of it. A Russian woman would be offended if a male colleague didn't compliment her appearance (especially if she had taken extra care with it), but an American woman might be offended if he did. Better to keep his mouth shut than to risk alienating his target this early in the game.

"I've been scheduling meetings with the staff to learn more about AAER's work. I know that I can't talk about any classified information with you, but perhaps there are other subjects we can discuss."

"Would you like to talk about severe accident modeling?" asked Dara. "We have an information sharing arrangement with our counterparts at RosMinAtom in Moscow, so I'm sure it would be okay."

"I've spoken to John Decker about that already. Jason Houseman informed me that he took over the project after you changed assignments."

"Yes, you're correct."

"Frankly speaking, you should talk to him about it. I think he's a bit lost."

"Poor John. He's more decorative than functional around here."

The conversation was going well. Dmitri decided that the time was right to broach the subject of Dara's climate model. "I am aware of your many publications on geo-engineering topics. Google is my friend. Perhaps we can talk about some of your climate modeling work?"

Dara hesitated. "I think it would be okay to discuss the research I did for my Ph.D. It's publicly available, so we wouldn't run into any security issues. I never made the software available to the public, but the output, analysis, and results are out there."

Dmitri smiled. "Great. Maybe you can demonstrate the software for me?"

Dara nodded. "I can show you version 1.0."

Dmitri knew not to ask about version 2.0. Instead, he took an indirect approach.

"Does your program use Markov Chain Monte Carlo sampling to estimate current distribution?"

Dara's eyes lit up, but she stopped herself from saying anything that might reveal too much about her black project. "Sorry, I'm not able to answer that." In fact, she was in the process of enhancing the probabilistic risk assessment (PRA) used in the original software, and the Monte Carlo statistical method played a key role.

Dmitri made a mental note to ask his hackers to check on it.

Several "indirect approaches" later, Dmitri had a few good leads for his support team at 'Center,' his contact point in Moscow with the Russian Foreign Intelligence Service, also known as the SVR. The infamous KGB of the Cold War era was the SVR's precursor.

"Thank you for your time today. I enjoyed learning about your model. It's impressive. You are also impressive, Dara."

"You're welcome. I'm happy to talk to you anytime, especially if you keep bringing me sodas," replied Dara, looking pleased.

"You have a lovely smile." Dmitri knew he shouldn't have said it, but there it was.

"Thank you, Dmitri." She didn't stop smiling.

***

Before Avery could switch channels, the damage was done. Morning news shows were usually noncontroversial affairs, all cooking segments and feel-good stories, typically featuring children and/or puppies. Today, however, the network decided to celebrate a musical guest whose song had just hit number one on the Billboard Hot 100. That musical guest was Avery's ex-future son-in-law, Jericho Wells.

Avery glanced at Dara, who had just tucked into a bowl of oatmeal (washed down with a tall glass of Coke Zero). He knew about Jericho's homecoming show, how Dara came home hours before it should have ended, slammed the door to her bedroom, and didn't emerge until late afternoon the next day.

But her demeanor had changed in recent days. She wore new, more office-appropriate clothes, ate regular meals, no longer cried herself to sleep. Avery surmised that her meeting at Langley had something to do with it. He knew the initial meeting was about Dara's simulation program. When asked about work nowadays, she would only smile and say, "I can't talk about it." It wasn't hard to put two and two together.

"Dara, we can switch to another channel. I don't want this to trigger any bad feelings."

She put down her spoon. "It's okay. Maybe if I watch it'll help me. I know he thinks I'm a loser. Whatever. He's a sellout."

The perky redheaded news anchor cut to commercial. Avery agreed that Jericho had changed. "He's a good guy, but you're right — a couple of years ago, he wouldn't have been caught dead on some morning show."

***

Ironic, Dara thought, her oatmeal turning cold, pretending not to pay attention to the talking (red)head. Dara had just given away her creation that should have netted millions, while Jericho sold out his music for actual millions. When they were a couple, so many of their arguments were about Dara's push to find the highest bidder. Or, more accurately, about Dara being pushed by Jane Canton and sometimes Avery to find that customer. Jericho chided Dara, called her greedy, told her she'd lost sight of her work's true objective. When potential offers rolled in, Dara couldn't even celebrate them.

At times like those, Dara heard her mother's voice in the back of her mind, long lost yet ever-present. She read Dara bedtime stories, usually little parables with morals at the end. One in particular echoed:

"A dog had a steak in his mouth, and then came across a pond. Inside the pond, he saw another dog with a steak in his mouth. He was determined to have both steaks. He went after the other dog with all his might. But it was just his own reflection and he ended up losing everything."

The story resonated. 'Having it all' — love, meaningful work, success — was an illusion, despite what glossy magazine covers purported in thirty-six-point type.

Her mother also advised her never to go to bed angry. At the time, Dara was too young to understand that arguments didn't come in discrete packages. Dara and Jericho would argue until the wee hours. Or go to bed anyway, but toss and turn all night, paying lip service to being over whatever it was that caused the fight. Either way, the nights were sleepless. No sleep = high irritability = short fuses = *boom*.

Dara stopped herself. Autopsying their breakup (yet again) wasn't going to help anyone.

After the commercial break, Perky Anchorwoman returned. Jericho sat to her left.

"Ladies and gentlemen, let's say hello to one of the brightest lights around, Jericho Wells!"

Applause from the studio audience. "Jericho, congratulations on reaching number one. How's the tour going?"

Jericho grinned in 'awe, shucks' fashion. The humble-brag came fast and furious: "It's wonderful. I'm amazed that all of our U.S. shows have sold out and touched that the fans have shown so much support."

"Clearly Dark Reverb has everyone's attention. Tell us more about your music."

Dara suspected that Perky Anchorwoman's team of unpaid interns briefed her in advance. She couldn't imagine a morning show femme bot like her anywhere near a Jericho Wells show.

"Dark Reverb is about bringing people together and giving us hope that we can make a difference. We laugh together, we cry together. We hate what's happening to our world. We hate how our environment is damaged and broken and how people we love are dying. We can change this, together. We believe this with everything we've got."

More applause. Dara wondered if he was reading from a teleprompter, complete with emojis to show which expression to use after each sentence.

"So, there's a will. Is there a way?" asked the anchorwoman.

"Yes, there is. I'd like to tell everyone about the partnership between my label, Tyrannosaurus Regina, and Senator Samantha Collins."

Perky Anchorwoman smiled. "In fact, Senator Collins is with us via satellite from Washington this morning. Are you there, Senator?"

"Good morning. Please call me Sam." She appeared in split screen, black hair relaxed, pearls in place, wearing a Jericho Wells tee-shirt over her dress.

"I see you're a Jericho fan."

"Yes, my son Antoine introduced me to Dark Reverb. Jericho and some of the bands on his label campaigned for me, and now we're joining forces to spread the word about climate change."

On cue, Jericho jumped in: "Wildfires, floods, droughts, and other natural disasters have impacted one in three American families, and by now most people understand that man-made pollution is the cause. We've been ignorant about climate change over the past several decades, and most of the ignorance has been willful. Well, I'm here to say that it stops right here, right now, with our generation."

The anchorwoman's expression morphed from perky to serious. "That's admirable, Jericho, but a tall order. We've heard so many promises. With all due respect to you and Senator Collins, some might say this is just more lip service. And to play devil's advocate, the more skeptical among us might view this as a publicity stunt to drum up votes or album sales. How would you respond to the cynics?"

"Finally," Dara exclaimed, "a real question!"

Senator Collins looked directly into the camera. "Friends, this is a serious effort. I'll stake my reputation on the outcome. Jericho is planning a series of concerts throughout the country to promote environmental education and awareness, and one hundred percent of the proceeds will go to the victims who have lost everything. I will use every bit of political capital I have to add climate science to school curricula and gain political support to fund and develop environmental technologies that could help us."

Jericho added, "Every kid in America will know that they have a voice. Those who are old enough to vote will know who their elected representatives are and which leaders or potential leaders offer a viable environmental plan. I'll make it my business to tell them and empower them to act. In places where there's nothing, we'll set up teams to mobilize young people to lobby their representatives. We'll organize peaceful protests all over America. The days of apathy are over."

The camera panned over the audience members, now on their feet and roaring with approval.

Dara caught Avery looking at her. He didn't say anything.

Publicity stunt. She let the thought sink in, surprised that the news anchor would ask an actual substantive question. Jericho never trusted politicians, yet now he was cozying up to them. This was not the Jericho she knew.

Jericho must have known it was to Senator Collins' benefit to ride his coattails and use Dark Reverb's popularity to promote her own interests. The youth demographic could make or break an election. As for Jericho, was he still using his music to promote his message? Or was he now using his message to promote himself? He wouldn't be the first celebrity to align with a popular cause for less than altruistic reasons.

Then another thought crept in from the cold: a major public relations effort would involve a publicist, someone in a position of significant trust. Someone chosen to play a key role in what was most important. That would be Jennie, the PR goddess. Dara felt her stomach knot up.

A cat food commercial blared in the background, several decibels louder than the broadcast. Even if every young person in America signed on, the reality was that ninety-nine senators not named Collins only cared about what lobbyists paid them to care about. Alexander had warned Dara that drumming up political support would be the most difficult part of their endeavor, and that she should prepare for a possible negative outcome.

At the same time, he assured Dara that her work would never be in vain. If this generation didn't accept her proposal, another generation might. Dara and Alexander weren't acting out of a desire for fame or self-promotion but for something much larger than themselves. Indeed, if Dara's program ever became reality, no one would ever know she had anything to do with it. This was not about her, which suited her fine.

Jericho's plan was all about him. Dara turned to Avery. "I'd better go catch my train," she said, emptying the uneaten half of her oatmeal into the garbage disposal.

"He's going to play his new song," said Avery. "Don't you want to hear it?"

"No," she said, grabbing her backpack, casting a final side-eyed glance at Jericho's simpering face on the TV screen.

***

Washington in late August wasn't just the figurative swamp of political attack ads, but a real-life, 100-degree puddle of muck. One morning, the Office of Personnel Management announced that nonessential employees could take leave due to the weather forecast: severe thunderstorms, torrential rains, fifty mile-per-hour winds.

So-called 'liberal leave' meant federal workers could take leave liberally and most did. Especially those with security clearances who couldn't work from home.

Dara, however, wasn't like most employees. In addition to skipping grades in school, she'd win ribbons for perfect attendance. *No wonder everyone hated me,* she thought. Still, old habits were hard to break. She showed up at AAER, commuting via Metro in black Wellies. Her old umbrella promptly turned inside out against a gale, leaving her drenched.

"You are here today," said a male voice, slightly accented. Dmitri 'toasted' Dara with his mug of tea as he walked past her office. Dara reddened, her soaked hair and clothes cold against her skin in the air conditioning.

She grabbed her hairbrush and ran to the ladies' room, taking the long way so as not to pass her Russian coworker's office.

Who else was at AAER today? The Tripp-Deckers' offices were empty. Jason Houseman was nowhere to be found. Nor were the admins, whom Dara had noticed were always ready to chat up the good (looking) Doctor Ivanov: 'Oooh, Dmitri, I'll show you where to find that report you want in the Reading Room. Sure, Dr. I, I'll make copies for you, however many you want. Absolutely, hon, I'll introduce you to that scientist in Criticality Safety.' *Those women are so ridiculous,* she thought, shaking her head.

Positioning herself on her knees under the hand dryer in the restroom, she attempted a makeshift blowout with her hairbrush. *Irony, thy name is Dara Bouldin.*

A glimpse in the restroom mirror revealed the futility of her endeavor. The frazzled mop on top of her head wasn't going anywhere, certainly not without a vat of silicone-based goop. Insult to injury, she detected a hint of *eau de* wet dog.

Reaching into her skirt pocket for an elastic, she settled on a ponytail. She washed her hands with government-issue soap, probably the same kind used in federal prison. Better to smell like clean felon than damp pooch.

A massive thunderclap interrupted Dara's pity party. A split-second later, darkness.

Dara squealed. She exited the ink-black restroom, allowing her eyes to adjust with the help of the generator-powered emergency lights before making her way down the hall.

She arrived to find Dmitri standing in the doorway of her office.

"Oh, hi," she said, feeling her cheeks flush again.

"Hi," said Dmitri, his eyes darting as he spoke. "I wanted to see if you were okay, but you weren't here."

"I'm fine, thanks." Dara's tongue suddenly felt too big for her mouth. "Looks like we've got a power outage."

Another thunderbolt reverberated, followed by what sounded like rocks pelting the roof. A woman's voice pulsed through the intercom: "Effective immediately, the agency is closed until further notice. All nonessential employees must exit the building."

The view outside the window told the story: gray-black skies, traffic lights and neon signs dark, debris flying, hailstones the size of turkey eggs bouncing on wet asphalt. Every car alarm in the city seemed to go off at once.

Dara watched as Dmitri checked his phone, his eyes widening as he read. "The entire area has lost power, and Metro is closed."

Two uniformed security guards walked by. Upon seeing Dara and Dmitri, one of them remarked in a booming voice, "You need to leave right now if you're not essential employees."

Dara stared at him. "Is it safe to go out there? I took the Metro today. How am I going to get home?"

"Not my problem," replied the guard. Both he and his colleague kept walking.

Dara shook her head. "What am I going to do?" She turned to Dmitri. "What are you going to do?"

"My car is in the parking garage. Do you need a ride home?"

She looked up at him, noticing his broad shoulders, midnight blue eyes glinting under the emergency lights. "I do."

Was this a good idea? "As long as it's not an imposition," she added.

"It's no trouble. Get your things and meet me by the stairs, okay?"

"What about your car? It'll get dinged in the hail."

"It's a lease, so I don't really care." He smiled.

She felt his eyes linger a second on her blouse, still damp from the deluge. Her body registered a shiver that wasn't from the A/C this time.

"Okay," she said. "Thank you."

***

The hailstorm came and went, but not without leaving its mark: trees felled all over the region; a body count of eight commuters who didn't survive a debris-induced pile-up on the Beltway; the power company taking its sweet time to restore service. Dara thanked Dmitri for driving her home, trying to squelch her guilt for taking him out of his way in the weather. The labored pace of the ride at least gave her the chance to learn more about his extraordinary life, with stints in London, Sydney, Helsinki. She wondered if she'd ever make it to those places.

Back on the job the next day, Dara's phone buzzed chainsaw-like against the surface of her desk. Jericho's phone number popped up, underscored by a text.

Months ago, she changed the special ring tone she'd assigned to texts from Jericho. It was her pet name for him, Rex, spelled out in Morse code. His alert for her texts was Reg, likewise encoded. When they were together, they would text each other all day — between classes for Dara; before and after gigs or rehearsals for Jericho; in the middle of the night for both of them. Her cheeks flushed as she recalled how so much depended on those dots and dashes just a short time ago.

The same electric feeling pulsed through Dara's fingertips when she swiped the phone to check the message. Love then, anxiety now — there wasn't much difference.

'Show Friday. Pls come. Need to talk to u. Will put u on g-list.'

Dara's brows furrowed. She texted him back: 'Talk about what?'

'I'm sorry about how things went down last time.'

Dara didn't know what to think. She didn't trust the new Jericho she saw on the morning show, and she trusted the pandering senator in her Day-Glo tee shirt even less. As far as she was concerned, Jericho was not only thirsty for fame but using what once meant something to both of them as a means to that end. There he was on network TV, in leather pants and a pre-ripped shirt some designer probably gave him, looking for souls to steal. A wolf in wolf's clothing.

Dara switched off her phone. She had work to do.

***

Alexander's slides were locked and loaded on the secure laptop, projector at the ready. Dara and her boss had spent the past three weeks since the storm tweaking the PowerPoint and writing his testimony to the U.S. Senate Select Committee on Intelligence, scheduled for this morning. This was where the proverbial rubber met the road when it came to reaching members of the Senate who could actually do something about the state of the environment.

Conversely, Jericho's new pal Sam Collins was a ranking member of the Senate Committee on Environment and Public Works. Since Jericho's morning show appearance, Dara had learned that climate change deniers historically chaired Sam Collins' committee, although the Senator herself was an environmentalist. This told Dara all she needed to know about how effective Jericho's campaign would be.

Due to the security surrounding the hearing along with the need to prevent leaks, only Alexander was permitted to attend from the CIA team. He had a computer science background, so Dara trained him on the software and walked him through the steps of how she developed it.

Dara started with open source, GEOS-10 Modeling Software, freely available on the NASA website to anyone, anywhere. She spent several years (blessed with the luxury of time available to an intellectually curious teenager with nothing better to do) manipulating and coupling interdisciplinary components of the NASA software, particularly its Atmospheric General Circulation Model and Catchment Land Surface Model.

Then she developed complementary software components designed to remap land surface given variably defined parameters. Still another program she coded determined the number of kilotons of explosive necessary to eliminate various geological obstructions and modeled the impacts of fission products and blast effects for above ground detonations.

Next came the fun part. Dara and Jericho spent hours virtually blowing up Mount Everest, Denali, the Matterhorn, anything massive and obstructive. Afterwards, they'd watch what their imaginary destruction had wrought — shifts in the Jet Stream, temperature drops, rainfall, floods, mudslides, desert-like conditions, permafrost, nuclear winter. Committing crimes against nature was endlessly entertaining.

Alexander proved to be a quick study. Dara noticed that he, too, was running experiments, entering parameters to find sweet spots. The coordinates were locations of geological obstructions that, when eliminated, 1) could solve given climate problems, and 2) would meet the least political resistance to being eliminated, since whatever they decided to bomb would ultimately become a giant crater.

One thing was certain: nuclear science was a cakewalk compared to politics. In recent years, NIMBY, 'Not in My Backyard,' had given way to BANANA, 'Build Absolutely Nothing Anywhere Near Anything.' Previous administrations spent billions of dollars on the Yucca Mountain Nuclear Waste Repository, yet the project still ended due to political problems. The public decided that contaminating little-used desert land in Nevada outweighed the potential public good of having a final disposal site for spent nuclear fuel. This was despite the fact that the material remained "IMBY," cooling in spent fuel pools and languishing in dry casks at reactor facilities and interim storage sites throughout the country. The fact that nuclear energy didn't spew greenhouse gases into the atmosphere barely registered.

On the other hand, Americans were more than happy to 'drill, baby, drill' and otherwise tear up the Arctic National Wildlife Refuge in Alaska when it came to oil. They felt the same about fracking for natural gas in other states. No one cared about the home where the buffalo roamed anymore. The desire for cheap energy turned nearly every man, woman, and child into a militant pragmatist, climate change be damned.

Clearly, it was all about the political will and capturing the hearts and minds of the voting public. Their hearts wanted what they wanted, and what they wanted was economic development.

They also wanted freedom. Everyone wanted the problems solved, but no one wanted to change their behavior to get there. This was America, the land of having your star-spangled cake and eating it, too, while staying thin and avoiding cavities. The theme dovetailed perfectly into Alexander's sales pitch.

***

"Members of the Select Committee," Alexander said, voice steady and composed, "I urge you to consider what is already happening due to our environmental challenges."

The photos on his slides told the story. They depicted images of smoke billowing, not just from wildfires but also from tear gas cannons; scenes of civil unrest and organized looting after national disasters; ordinary citizens standing on porches, openly protecting whatever they had left with firearms; a man beaten and left for dead after being relocated to a less-than-hospitable part of the country; protesters turning violent against slow-to-react state and federal authorities.

Alexander distilled the photos to grim statistics captioning them. Pie charts showed economic degradation over time in key cities, followed by graphs of crime statistics that directly correlated to environmentally-induced economic impacts.

"We have seen the results of our disastrous environmental conditions. At best, they are destroying our economy and inimical to our national security interests. At worst, they are leaving people helpless and hopeless. We are showing the world our vulnerabilities and weaknesses, including our enemies who would exploit them. It makes you wonder why we sacrificed so much blood and treasure fighting the wars of the past while ignoring the ticking time bomb sitting right in our laps."

"We all know that people are not going to change their behavior," he added, solemnly shaking his head. "And even if they did, little could reverse what's already been done. But we have options."

Shifting gears, Alexander ran through several simulations using a variety of parameters, showing that it was indeed possible to use technology to undo the damage. He surveyed the room, gauging the expressions on the faces of the senators and their aides. They didn't blink, look at their notes, or fall asleep. In fact, when the Q&A session commenced, the barrage of questions made it clear they wanted more.

"Is it safe?" they asked. "Is it legal?"

"It's safer than the impacts of climate change. The radioactive fallout would soon decay, dissipate, or break down. In any case, most of the detonations would occur underground, and hardly anyone lives in the remote areas we're talking about. The wildlife population would eventually make a comeback as evidenced by other contaminated places on earth, Chernobyl and Fukushima being prime examples."

He continued: "Legally speaking, the U.S. only *abides by* the Comprehensive Test Ban Treaty. We never ratified it. So it's legal. My answer is yes to both questions."

More queries followed. "Now I'll show you which obstructions when eliminated would give us the most bang for our buck, if you will," he said. Alexander had them where he wanted them.

***

Dara ran up the Metro stairs toward the AAER building, bounding on nervous energy. Alexander had called, expressing confidence that the hearing went well. There was still the matter of getting the president on board, not to mention the public, but at least Congress was listening.

Reaching her floor, she noticed her coworkers had congregated around the elevator banks, staring at the TV screens tuned to CNN. The sound was on mute, but the

"Breaking News" chyron and closed captioning told the story.

"Flash fire overnight devastates Argus, CO. Eleven firefighters dead. Hundreds feared dead or missing. 80,000+ to be evacuated. Water trucked in due to severe drought conditions."

A girl in pajamas, probably ten or eleven years old and clutching a stuffed rabbit, spoke to a reporter. "I can't find my mom. I don't know where she is. Please help me," read the caption. Her dark, puffy eyes shifted as she spoke, scanning and re-scanning the faces around her in the shelter.

Dara stared at the screen, dropped her tote bag and purse. Tears welled up, burned into her cheeks. Jason Houseman, watching the broadcast seconds before, brushed past her in his haste to get back to his office. The others shrugged and walked away as well, seeing but pretending not to see Dara. Another day, another disaster.

Someone, probably Kayla Tripp-Decker, whispered, "She's making everybody uncomfortable." But Dara heard only the sounds in her head of roaring flames and people screaming. Those sounds were always there, but at times like these they muffled everything else.

Finally, someone picked up her bags, extended a hand. "Dara, come with me. It's better you don't watch that." The hand felt strong, yet gentle. It didn't make her feel self-conscious that her own was rough with scars.

"Will you have some tea?" Dmitri asked, leading Dara into her office. He set Dara's bags and jacket on a chair. Dara shook her head, covered her face with her hands.

Dmitri got a cup of tea anyway from the kitchenette across the hall. Dara looked even smaller trembling behind her desk. "I wish I could help you," he said. "If there is anything I can do, please tell me."

He set the Styrofoam cup in front of her and took a neatly folded handkerchief out from his pocket. "You might need this, too."

Dara looked at the handkerchief through her tears. "Thank you," she said, momentarily distracted by the gesture.

"It is a terrible situation, what's happened in the United States," said Dmitri. "I heard that the soil in some places has become like sand after so many years of drought. Every time I turn on the news, I see another story about uncontrollable fires. Where there's no fire, the water is the problem, with whole families dying in floods or storms."

Dara dabbed at her eyes with the handkerchief, quiet for a moment. She folded the handkerchief back into a rectangle, her eyes focusing on everything in the room except for Dmitri. Finally, she said, "I'm so embarrassed. I don't want people to see me like this. I'm from Colorado, and my mom died trying to save me from the wildfire in Granger City ten years ago."

"I'm so sorry, Dara." Dmitri already knew what had happened. The tragedy's repercussions on Dara's life were clear: her unquestioning loyalty to her father, her willingness to give away her climate model, her relentless work ethic. All in the service of undoing the damage, however Sisyphean the pursuit.

"Tea is very important to Russians," he said, gently pushing the cup of tea in Dara's direction. "Sometimes all you can do is have some tea and try to feel better, even if it's just temporary."

Dara took a sip, this time looking at Dmitri. "I tried so hard to keep it together, but then I saw the interview with the girl, the one with the stuffed bunny. I had one when I was a kid. My mom got it for me for Easter when I was three. It was my favorite toy, but like everything else we had, I lost it in the fire."

"My mother died when I was nine," said Dmitri. He reached under his collar and pulled out a rose gold chain with a crucifix pendant on the end. "She gave me this, and I wear it every day. It's all I have left of her." He focused on the shining memento, glinting under the fluorescent office lights. "Not many people in life are ever going to love you more than your mother." The sentence caught in his throat, and then he noticed tears re-emerging from Dara's eyes.

"God, I say such stupid things — I'm sorry, Dara. Please forgive me."

"It's not stupid, it's the truth. Here, I think you're going to need your handkerchief back."

"It's okay. I can use my sleeve." He smiled sheepishly.

"I guess we should probably do some work."

"I'll come by and check on you later, okay?"

"Okay," said Dara. "Thanks for being so nice to me."

"It's my honor," said Dmitri. And it was. Dmitri shuddered at their coworkers' sidewise glances, sharp elbows and barely hushed commentaries, not to mention his own powerlessness to make other people care.

***

The few people who did care demonstrated as much via text messages that lit up Dara's phone. First from Avery: "thinking of u — love, dad," then from Jane, of all people: "Saw the news and wanted to make sure you were ok — JC."

Then Jericho: "sad news from CO. r u ok, reg? sorry about the show, sorry about everything -- rex"

Dara typed Jericho a reply: "i'll be ok. i'm sorry too." But she backspaced over "i'm sorry too" and just sent the first sentence.

***

The fiscal year in the federal government began on October first, and with it came Dara's second quarterly performance appraisal. This time Alexander did Dara's review, giving her 'Outstandings' on each of the rubrics. It was all she could do not to make photocopies of the signed appraisal form and wallpaper Jason Houseman's office.

"We should celebrate," Dmitri said to Dara when she told him over a cup of tea – *chai* time, as she called it, using the Russian word for tea that Dmitri had taught her. She couldn't remember the last time she drank soda, and her stomach reaped the benefits.

Tea soothed her. Maybe Dmitri did, too. He offered to take her out for a proper Russian dinner at Kalinka, a restaurant in D. C. popular with diplomats and Russian members of Washington's hockey team.

"I don't know anything about Russian food," Dara said, looking into Dmitri's dark blue eyes. What she really wanted to say was, 'Do you mean for this to be a date?'

"I will teach you. Food is very important to Russians. Friends break bread together, and you are my friend," he said, adding, "That's *padruga* in Russian."

"So that makes you my *padruga*?" she asked.

"No," he said. "I would be your *droog*. *Padruga* means girlfriend." He reddened, remembering that English didn't treat the world 'girlfriend' the same as the phrase, 'friend who is a girl.' "I mean female friend, as opposed to male friend."

Dara blushed in sympathy, pretending not to notice his flub. "Yes, *droog*. I'd like that."

***

Dara wondered why subordinate employees didn't get the opportunity to rate their superiors, at least in the federal workplace. Alexander proved to be an outstanding manager and supervisor. He stayed out of the way, let Dara do her job, gave her kudos and encouragement at every turn. Moreover, he showed genuine appreciation for her efforts, not only by giving her positive marks on her performance appraisal, but also by insisting that she teach him the finer points of climate modeling, the tricks of her unique trade. Jason Houseman, conversely, couldn't have cared less about Dara's efforts, only about taking credit for anything she did that made him look good.

As much as Dara enjoyed working with Alexander, she recognized that he wasn't her friend, he was her boss. Management always instructed staff to discuss career-related issues with their supervisors, but Dara wasn't comfortable with that prospect, particularly since her main question was whether or not it was okay to date her Russian coworker. There were formal policies against sexual harassment, of course, but this was not that.

Dara decided to keep her feelings from her superior — not for the first time, by any stretch. In graduate school, she noticed that Jane Canton, her dissertation advisor, would make snide-sounding comments about social science not being a 'real science,' 'liberal arts types' siphoning funding from 'real majors that actually get people jobs,' and business majors being mostly in the 'business' of partying. She even dubbed industrial engineering, a STEM major she'd deemed insufficiently rigorous, as 'IE, imaginary engineering.' Despite following up with, 'Just kidding!' or, 'You know I'm joking, right?' the comments always set Dara on edge.

But telling Jane off could have cost Dara her fellowship, a risk she couldn't afford. At the time, she didn't even realize questioning her supervisor was an option. So she prioritized keeping her personal and professional lives separate, which meant not telling Jane about Jericho. If Jane was in fact a Philistine, Dara didn't want to be on the receiving end of any nasty comments about her poetry-loving musician boyfriend.

And yet, complicating matters, Jane could be kind. She knew that Dara marked the anniversary of her mother's death every year by donating blood. Jane would accompany her to the Red Cross on these occasions, donating her own blood in solidarity. She'd also send Dara texts and 'Thinking of You' cards after news broke of particularly devastating wildfires, knowing they would trigger unspeakable memories.

Jane also believed in Dara's modeling program from the start. She convinced the dean to authorize fellowship money to finance her graduate studies, served as her dissertation advisor when no one else would take her seriously and always encouraged her to up her game.

It was hard to know what to do about someone like Jane, except to refrain from confiding in her about anything too personal. But if not Jane, who? Not Avery — asking him for advice about Dmitri was not the sort of father-daughter conversation she felt comfortable having. Dara's mother was gone, and she didn't have any close female friends, one of the downsides of starting college only a few years into her teens and taking on a male-dominated major.

Not even Jericho's mother, who almost became her mother-in-law, remained her friend. She had liked Dara well enough, but when she realized her baby boy wanted to marry a girl with a gambling addict for a father and massive debts, a palpable deep freeze took hold. Dara wondered if Jericho had introduced his mother to Jennie. If Jennie's designer outfit and aura of privilege were any indication, she'd easily curry Mrs. Wells' favor.

Jennie. Dara cursed herself under her breath for thinking of her, for the self-inflicted reminder that Jericho had moved on to someone new. Someone like Jennie, no less -- Dara's one hundred and eighty-degree opposite.

All signs pointed to keeping her "*padruga*-ship" with Dmitri to herself for now. He was just a *potential* romantic partner anyway — no kisses, no contracts, no promises. Dara clenched her fists — that awful poem that Avery had forced upon her after her breakup with Jericho would echo in her head every so often, despite that she'd torn it off her bathroom mirror months ago. If she ever ran into the poet Jorge Luis Borges in a dark alley, she'd have at him for inflicting "Comes the Dawn" onto the world.

A text buzzed on Dara's phone. Perhaps there *was* someone in her life who could know about her budding relationship with Dmitri. The message said: 'need confirmation re g-list sat. u coming?'

Dara texted Jericho back, her heart ten paces ahead of her brain, 'yes. can i bring a +1?'

T-minus Eight

The White House Situation Room: mahogany paneled walls, screens at every turn, Top Secret — SCI LEDs ablaze, numbers flashing – 11:00, 13:00, 16:00, 18:00, 21:00 – representing hours in time zones around the world. Everyone seemed to be wearing a dark suit/American flag lapel pin combo – including the most powerful man in the free world, President James Donahue, who sat at the head of the table. A cadre of stone-faced Executive Branch types led by Victor Rawls of the National Security Staff flanked him.

Alexander was keenly aware that this was probably the most secure disclosed location on the planet. He tried to focus on the leather armrests, his breathing, the wedding band he kept twisting around his finger, anything but the gravity of situation in the room. *Ha — the situation in the room.* Alexander drew in a breath. *Whatever you do, Fallsworth,* he thought to himself, *don't, under any circumstances, laugh.*

No note-taking or electronics, either. His laptop and smartphone waited for him in a safe elsewhere in the building. Alexander felt every synapse compensate for the lack of technology, his mind memorizing, storing information, analyzing at light speed what the man he voted for had to say.

President Donahue opened the discussion. "General Fallsworth, I understand you've met with my staff in advance of today's meeting. This latest disaster isn't going away. Members of Congress can't keep up with the demands from their constituents to do something, and my polls are way down. The protestors aren't just hippies anymore. They're a lot less peaceful than they used to be. The Intel Committee has been after us for a while to talk to you about the code your staff developed."

Alexander nodded, wishing he had a bottle of water.

"Tell us more about it." Donahue leaned back in his chair, arms crossed. Rawls' arms were folded in similar fashion.

Clearing his throat, Alexander delved into his pitch, parroting back everything Dara had taught him about the use of nuclear weapons to eliminate geological obstructions (most likely a mountain range in Alaska), the corresponding shift in the Jet Stream and the projected environmental turnaround as demonstrated by the climate simulation software.

The CIA lawyer seated next to Alexander then explained why the plan wasn't illegal and how Congress hadn't ratified any treaties that would prohibit them from moving forward.

"Moreover, we've done the cost benefit analyses," Alexander added, "and climate change is infinitely worse for the ecosystem than what we plan to do with the weapons. As our environmental impact analysis shows, most of the damage will occur underground, and, in a few years, the flora and fauna will rebound."

The CIA attorney chimed in: "It's true, Sir. There might even be a hormetic effect. The organisms that received lower doses from the fallout could end up stronger." The factoid came courtesy of Dara, who got it from her middle school science project entitled, "Hormesis with Ionizing Radiation."

Donahue went silent. Alexander wondered if it was a thoughtful pause or — as rumors would have it — it was because he was out of his depth when it came to scientific discussions.

"Do you have the numbers on that, General Fallsworth?" asked Rawls. His lapel pin was a "Don't Tread on Me" flag.

"Yes."

"We would need to procure an impartial contractor to review the code," Rawls added, "but this type of expertise would be hard to find on short notice. Our intention is to act quickly."

Alexander's thoughts swirled, landing on the realization that a solution was at their disposal: "Chambers University has the expertise. We could sole-source the bid." Score — he knew Jane Canton would jump at the opportunity.

The president nodded. Finally, he spoke again. "How far along is the software?"

"We're moving into the beta testing phase. I believe we sent you our study on potential coordinates for detonation."

"Yes. The Governor of Alaska is a personal friend of mine, so that helps. I think with enough PR we could get the public onboard. Still, it's going to be a hard sell to most of the Congress."

Alexander lurched into Army mode. "Sir, I'll do anything in my power to ensure the success of this mission. The United States is on the brink, and I've dedicated my entire life to the service of our country. This we'll defend."

President Donahue smiled when he heard the U.S. Army motto. He relished his role as Commander-in-Chief, despite the fact that he had never been anywhere near the armed forces during his own career prior to taking office. "Thanks for your service to the nation, General," he said, "I appreciate your dedication to the task. We'll move forward. My staff will be in touch with next steps."

"You're welcome, Sir." Alexander beamed, unable to keep his elation in check. No matter — a win was a win, and this one would ultimately benefit everyone on many levels. He wasn't worried about convincing the American public. Over the decades, they'd accepted nuclear weapons, space exploration despite high profile catastrophes, mass vaccination programs despite the lack of data on long term side effects, war upon war upon war. With Donahue onboard, Alexander could focus on persuading the rest of the Congress. When safely back on the Metro, he high-fived his attorney and wondered whom he should call first – Dara or Jane.

***

Saturday night — show time. This time, no invisibility cloak. Dara entered the backstage, arm in arm with her plus one, Dr. Dmitri Andreevich Ivanov.

The venue was packed, all shimmering girls, shambling guys, and everyone in between. Dara outshone them all in sliver skinny jeans and a white handkerchief blouse, diaphanous where it counted. She'd streaked her hair with temporary dye, silver on black, and painted tiny stars with phosphorescent shadow around her eyes. A jingling sleeve of silver bangles camouflaged the traces of her past traumas, and black stiletto boots added at least 5 inches to her height. *All the better to look you in the eye, my droog*, she thought.

Dmitri was the one in the invisibility cloak tonight: black jeans, black shirt, black jacket. His job had taken him to many strange places, but a Jericho Wells concert would have been strange on Mars.

Three paces in, there he was. Jericho's gaze cut through the sea of extraterrestrials. "Dara," he said, green eyes wide, unblinking.

She drew in a breath, the cologne in the air a witches' brew of esters. "Jericho," she said. "Thanks for the invitation. This is my friend Dmitri Ivanov. Dmitri, this is

Jericho Wells." She turned to her escort. "Jericho and I grew up together."

Jericho visibly stiffened.

"Hello," Dmitri said, shaking Jericho's hand.

Silence. Finally, "Um, Dara, I need to talk to you." Jericho glanced at Dmitri. "In private, if it's okay."

Dara's eyes shifted from Dmitri to Jericho then back.

Finally, Dmitri piped up. "Dara told me about your 'straightedge.' I'm Russian, and we don't have that. I'll go find a drink while you talk."

As Dmitri retreated to the bar, Dara, despite her own straightedge stance, thanked all that was holy for alcohol. She followed Jericho to his dressing room.

***

As far as rock star dressing rooms were concerned, Jericho's was Spartan — a few grooming supplies, his beat-up Martin guitar, a vinyl couch that had seen better days, a full-length mirror that had no doubt seen its share of backstage debauchery.

Dara noticed that Vitamin X and Spaceman Spiff had much "spiffier" accommodations, as evidenced by furniture without any stuffing popping out and copious bowls of green Nerds (Tyrannosaurus Regina's version of Van Halen's anything-but-brown M&Ms). Dara smiled. It was just like Jericho to let the other bands have the better digs.

"Dara, look at you," said Jericho, closing the door.

She reddened, hoping he wouldn't notice. "Thanks."

"Have a seat. I remember those boots pinch your toes."

Dara laughed. "I'm okay. The pants pinch even worse. I don't think I can sit in them."

He motioned to the edge of the couch. "Maybe you can lean?"

"I'll take you up on that." Shifting places, Dara caught a glimpse of her reflection in the mirror and tried not to stare. It had been a while since she had seen herself like this. She'd left her jacket at the coat check. Jericho was well acquainted with her look in show clothes -- not to mention various stages of undress — but things were different now. She felt exposed. Everyone who saw her had to know that her outfit came with an agenda.

"I read that Total Static Head got a major label deal," she said, trying to change the subject.

"Yeah," said Jericho. "Their new label bought them out of their contract with me, so they had to drop out of the tour. I liked those guys."

"Me too. Remember how I named them?"

"Right, one of your nuclear terms."

"I wanted to save them from 'Monster Bucket.'"

"You did them a great service."

Noticing that Jericho was staring at her reflection in the dressing room mirror, gooseflesh formed on Dara's wrists. "Hey," she said, crossing her arms in an attempt to cover herself, "I saw you on TV."

"Yeah, I wanted to talk to you about that."

"Oh?"

"That senator I partnered with said she heard a rumor that someone at your agency was coming up with a way to reverse climate patterns. One of the senate committees is working on getting a program greenlit. Do you know anything about it?"

Dara didn't know how to respond. This was Jericho, not a stranger. But she had a compartmented security clearance that didn't care about love, history, or trust. She was only permitted to discuss her project with cleared people who demonstrated a need to know.

Every synapse in her brain wanted to tell him. She wanted him to be proud, to erase whatever doubts he had about her. But if anyone found out, someone else would probably take over and get all the credit. Or worse, she'd lose her security clearance and the project would end. The last thing she wanted was to pour ice on the one thing that was working in her life. She stared at the pointed ends of her boots.

"I don't know anything about it," she said, eyes remaining in a downward and locked position. Visions of her own look-at-me foolishness, her ruminations on Jericho being a sellout, and the scene she'd made at Jericho's homecoming show flashed through her head like a bad movie. She certainly wasn't redeeming herself from the trifecta of ill-conceived behavior by telling an outright lie.

"Okay," said Jericho. "Do you want me to tell her about you?"

Dara's stomach fluttered. "Um, it's probably better not to. My thesis is on the Internet. She can find me if she needs me. I'm easy to find."

"Okay." Jericho's eyes shifted back to the Dara in the mirror. "Being easy to find sucks, by the way. People are starting to show up at my doorstep."

"You have a number one song, Jericho. Goes with the territory."

"You know what I did? I set up a trust with my lawyer and bought some land out in the middle of nowhere. Remember how we always said we would buy a place like that?"

Dara's heart skipped. "Yes." When she and Jericho were a couple, they'd spend hours fantasizing about the hypothetical house they'd build, purchased with hypothetical money.

"I've got a cabin for the time being, and I'm converting the barn into a recording studio. All vintage, with real tape."

Dara's eyes shone. "Your next album's going to sound amazing." She recalled what a revelation it was to hear digitally recorded music after transferring it onto analog tape. The richness, the warmth, the fullness of each signal — sounds that had been gated and compressed opened up, transformed.

"It's worth it. Recording when you have actual money makes a huge difference."

"I can't even imagine." The trials and mostly errors using ProTools software to get a decent sound in the Wells' musty basement flickered through Dara's head.

"Remember how you used to make me lay vocal tracks in the bathroom?"

"I do. Nine times out of ten, the take wouldn't sound anything like it did in my head. But that tenth time, something magic would happen."

"Now we don't have to worry about studio time or how much tape costs." Jericho turned from the mirror to in-the-flesh Dara. "It's not the same, you know. It's lost something."

Dara looked away. Jericho's "something" apparently wasn't shaded by memories of their near-constant arguments. Music itself wasn't always better in the abstract, but in Dara's experience, most other things were.

Dara breathed deep. "Is Jennie here tonight?"

"Jennie?" Jericho looked at Dara, his brows quizzical. "I'm not seeing her anymore."

"Oh." Dara noticed a shadow passing over Jericho's face.

"Jennie 'leveraged' her experience working with me to get a sweet offer to do PR with the Simpson Harding

Agency. That was the end of that." Jericho punctuated the statement with air quotes around the word "leveraged."

"I'm sorry," said Dara, at a loss for what else to say.

"Now, I ain't saying she a gold digger, a gold digger..." Jericho chanted the chorus from the old Kanye West song, bitterness dripping from each syllable. He stopped himself. "I shouldn't fault her; she's got bills to pay. That seems to be a trend."

There was a knock at the door. Opening it a crack, Dara felt a draft. A stagehand brandishing a clipboard said, "You're on in ten, Jericho."

"Okay." He reached past Dara to close the door.

"I should go," she said.

Jericho touched her arm, looked into her eyes. "Reg, that guy you're with?"

"Yes?"

"I hope he's good to you."

Dara reached up, stroking Jericho's cheek, the face she knew so well. "Break a leg, Rex," she said, then exited the dressing room before she did something stupid.

***

Dmitri had started on his third brandy by the time Dara returned to find him in the corner. "Are you finished talking?"

"Yes," said Dara, as he took her arm and pulled her closer to him.

"I want you to tell me something," he said, wrapping his arms around her waist.

"Yes?" Her heart pulsed under the thin material of her top.

"Did you bring me here to make him jealous?"

Dara's cheeks grew hot. Before she could deny it, Dmitri put a finger over her lips. "Don't lie," he said.

Her eyes shifted downward, catching a glimpse of Jericho past Dmitri's shoulder as he took the stage. The chords to "Break the Skin" rang, bass line spilling out, reverberating from the stage to floor, then inside Dara's body. She tried and failed to reply.

Dmitri pulled her closer and kissed her, his breath hot. "I don't like you right now," he said, his forehead pressed to hers.

Dara's voice returned in a stammer. "If you don't like me, w-why are you kissing me?"

"Do you have eyes, *padruga*? Everybody here wants you. Especially him," he said, glancing back at Jericho.

Electrical shocks jumped up Dara's spine. "It's okay," said Dmitri, his kisses shifting from her lips to her neck.

She could still taste the brandy inside her mouth from the first of Dmitri's kisses. And still feel the rough stubble from Jericho's cheek lingering on her fingertips.

"I want a woman in my bed, not a girl in a costume. You Americans are teenagers forever. Russian women don't play games like this."

"I'm sorry," she said, knees buckling.

He enveloped her in his arms, whispering in her ear this time, "Let me take you home and we can wash off all this paint. And I will do a lot more than kiss you."

The pounding music, the brandy kisses…Dara caught another glimpse of Jericho, framed in Dmitri's leather collar. She steadied herself in his arms. Nothing added up anymore. Except leaving, which made all the sense in the world.

"Let's go," she whispered back.

***

Dmitri wanted to say that it was a mistake, but it wasn't. He wanted to say that he had had too much to drink, got caught up in the moment. So many things he could have and probably should have said. But he would be lying. He tried not to think about the absurdity of wanting to be truthful in his real life versus the lying he did on a daily basis as part of his job description.

He studied Dara's face, pallid in the moonlight that shone through the window, her hair still damp against the pillowcase, back to its original brown. Dara had no idea about Dmitri's real identity, and yet she knew everything — what brought a smile to his face, what kept him up at night, what troubled his heart. "It must be hard, going from country to country," she said. "Do you even have a home anymore? What do you want out of all this?"

Dmitri's parents were long gone, his country an ocean and a continent away. His life, by design a mystery, even to himself. Everything — his triumphs, his problems, his views — was secret and of no consequence to anyone except his employer. Dmitri was a chess piece in someone else's game, and he knew it. He hadn't desired anything or anyone in a long time.

"It's best not to tell anyone at work about us," he said.

"I was going to say the same thing."

He glanced at the clock. Five a.m. No sleep for either of them. Both excited, both ready for a new chapter in their lives. But now, back to Earth. Dara mentioned to him that her father's shift would end soon. If she didn't beat him home, her outfit would make for an awkward entrance on a Sunday morning.

***

"So, are you going to tell me?" Avery grinned as he twirled spaghetti around his fork.

"Tell you what?" said Dara, texting rather than eating.

"What's keeping you from my creation? Perfect red sauce takes half the day."

"I know – you slaved for hours over a hot stove, the tomatoes were blessed by the Pope himself, and you stirred it with unicorn horns."

"Okay, have your little secret. I know it's that Russian guy."

Dara put down her phone. "Oh, do you?"

Avery laughed. "I do now! Your face matches the sauce. Don't ever play poker."

Dara sighed. She didn't want her father to know about Dmitri, at least not until she figured out where Pandora's kisses would lead this time. A couple of weeks had passed since the show, and she still wasn't sure how to characterize their…friendship?

She rolled her eyes. "If you must know, I wasn't texting him this time. It was Jane."

"The wicked witch of the Mid-Atlantic? What does she want?"

"She saw the news about the wildfire the other day and thought of me."

Avery wrinkled his brow, sprinkling extra Parmesan on his pasta. "She must want something."

Dara shrugged. "Of course she does. But she's always been sympathetic about things like that. And she did apologize for being such an idiot with Alexander. She asked if I would meet her for lunch this week."

"Tell her you can't make it. You're busy. She's the one with the grad student flying monkeys to do her work for her, not you."

"It's just lunch, Dad. Maybe she needs someone to talk to. It's not like she has any friends."

She rearranged the strands of spaghetti in her plate. Dara didn't have any flying monkeys, but she didn't have any friends, either. Boyfriends and fathers didn't count. As much as Dara hated to admit it, she and Jane Canton had much in common.

Dara picked up her phone. "c u Friday," she thumbed onto the screen.

***

The local news carried the announcement, which then made the national news, which then dominated the social media outlets. In light of recent events, Senator Collins would host a March on Washington against Climate Change. The event would start with a march from the White House to the Capitol, followed by a day-long rally featuring speakers including Nobel-prize winning scientists, famous actors, and political figures.

At night, there would be a concert. Tickets would be free, but all proceeds from the television broadcast of the show would go to charities to aid disaster victims. Jericho Wells had top billing, and the Tyrannosaurus Regina website crashed immediately from all the traffic.

There was a special section on the site where people could light virtual candles for loved ones who had died as a result of climate-related disasters. Thousands had been lit. The discussion boards jammed with comments, the collective unconscious pouring out:

"Why won't they do something?"

"My family got killed."

"I had to start a new life a thousand miles from home."

"WAKE UP!"

When Dara finally got through on the website, she marveled at the sheer number of hits. "proud of u Rex," she typed into her phone. But she backspaced over it, stopping herself from hitting send.

So much water under this particular bridge. Jericho and Dara had a running debate when they were Rex and Regina. She believed that technology was the answer to the world's problems, but he insisted that art was the only way to get through to people. The sparring started out as a goof: "Folk music inspired workers to join the labor movement," he'd say. "Robots made the work safer and more productive and led to better working conditions," she'd retort. And so on.

It was all fun and games until things got real. Debates morphed into fights, which colored in dark markers outside the lines, seeped into other aspects of their relationship.

Rather than admit he felt lonely or envious, Jericho would complain about Dara spending less time with him, caring only about work. "All you want is success for yourself," he'd say, refusing to look at her.

"You're jealous that you haven't had any success for *yourself*," she'd say back, glaring.

Now that Dara's work finally experienced a degree of victory, she couldn't even tell him. Not that it mattered anymore. In the end, all those arguments were so much wasted breath, misplaced emotions. Dara felt something sting her cheek, realizing it was a tear.

The true measure of success was not in ego gratification but in the number of lives saved. That number was currently zero, but Dara knew that between what she was trying to accomplish with her climate model and what Jericho was working toward with the march, they might get somewhere. She wished she could share it with him.

She re-texted, "proud of u Rex," this time hitting send.

***

Alexander invited Dara to CIA headquarters to help smooth out technical glitches that had popped up on his version of the software. He was forever tinkering with it, trying out different coordinates and parameters. Documentation wasn't his strong suit. Dara tried to convey the importance of proper documentation, especially since programs like theirs were almost certain to be audited by the Government Accountability Office.

"You worry a lot," Alexander replied. "I need you to focus on the positive. Don't forget, we're changing the world." That was Dara's cue to drop the subject.

Dara didn't enjoy being a subject-dropper, but work was work. "That's why they call it a job," her father would say when Dara's previous life under Jane Canton's thumb grew unbearable. She put up with Jane's nastiness, knowing – because Jane reminded her all the time – that none of the other professors at Chambers wanted anything to do with her climate change research.

Personal insults weren't the only issues she had with Jane. Dara also fielded her ego-driven marching orders to nowhere, relegating Dara to the sidelines while Jane took the lead in presenting software Dara had designed, or forcing Dara to recode sections of software her way, which would inevitably turn out to be incorrect. Jane had let her graduate students do the thinking for her for so long that she'd barely get through technical discussions. But she'd yell and make threats if Dara corrected her, no matter how wrong she was.

Still, the grant money flowed, the kudos – contrary to Jason Houseman's "poor" assessment of Dara's work – mounted, and, every so often, Jane would show kindness, remembering significant dates in Dara's life or taking her off-campus for frozen yogurt.

A pang hit Dara's stomach. *The sell-out isn't Jericho at all,* she thought, *not by a long shot.*

She poured tea from the thermos she carried in her tote bag, the ideal antidote to thoughts of Jane. Her switch from soda had stuck. It was either that or brandy, given what Dmitri kept around his apartment. The tea's calming effect worked wonders on her anxiety, and she felt silly for corroding her insides all those years with fizzy drinks.

"I prefer brandy's 'calming effect,'" Dmitri would say, making her laugh. Jericho had always demonized alcohol, telling her he didn't want to go through life numb. Dara wasn't interested in booze, but Jericho's comment did make her think. Things that were so important to her just a year ago might not have been such a big deal after all.

"Want some tea?" she asked Alexander.

"I'm all set," he said, pointing to his coffee mug emblazoned, "Best. Dad. Ever." in bright green lettering. "I bought this cup myself."

"Hey, did you hear about the March on Washington? It's in a couple weeks."

"You mean the one Samantha Collins talked about at the press conference yesterday?"

"Yes."

Alexander rolled his eyes. "You know I call her Senator Sam-I-Am."

"Like from Dr. Seuss? Why?"

"Because she 'does not like it.'"

"As in Green Eggs and Ham?"

"Yep – but instead of green eggs and ham, she doesn't like nuclear power, nuclear medicine, or nuclear research. And definitely not nuclear weapons, even the ones that could reverse climate change."

Dara sipped her tea. "I think the rally could help us."

"I doubt it," Alexander said, fumbling with the laptop's touch screen.

"Why?" she asked, eyebrows raised.

"She's just trying to get the youth vote. As far as the march is concerned, it's just a bunch of punk rock kids who know nothing about what we're trying to do and probably don't care. They'll get excited for a week or two and then move on to the next shiny object."

Dara was acquainted with at least one punk rock kid who knew all about using nuclear weapons for geo-engineering purposes, but of course she couldn't tell Alexander. Association with that scene was not the image she wanted to portray, at least not to superiors with a degree of control over what she could and couldn't do professionally.

She tried a different tack. "Music gets through to people. Art can change the political will. Think of all the great songs from the 1960s and how they impacted the civil rights and anti-war movements. You might just be surprised."

"I wouldn't call anything that's going to be on that stage 'music' or 'art.' I'll take whatever political will I can get, but I don't have a lot of faith in Sam-I-Am Collins. You know she rides her bike to Capitol Hill every day from Fort Washington? She thinks all it takes to reverse climate change is wind farms and getting rid of cars."

Dara braced herself, having heard Alexander's dreaded 'On the Pointlessness of Renewable Energy' stump speech in the past. He continued: "Or maybe solar panels. And if the sun isn't shining or the wind isn't blowing? She pretends that baseload power isn't important. I don't know who's worse — Sam-I-Am or the climate change deniers. She never went to war to protect our freedoms and way of life. Watching our enemies get ahead while we're struggling over the whims of nature makes me wonder what was the point of it all?"

Dara said nothing, not that she could fit a word in edgewise. She focused on her tea and the patch she was coding. In her head, she gave Alexander a piece of her mind. But workplace relationships were another story, all about the grip and grin.

***

"Oh, God, Samantha Collins? That's hilarious that your boss calls her Sam-I-Am." Jane Canton chortled as she ladled dressing over her salad.

Dara took a bite of her sandwich, immediately regretting that she ordered the chicken which dripped with sticky-sweet honey mustard. She tried to wipe off the offending sauce without anyone noticing.

Not that Jane cared. She signaled to the waitress, using her outdoor voice even though they were inside, "I'll have another IPA."

Dara looked at Jane, nonplussed.

"That's for India Pale Ale. Still no alcohol in your life, sweetie?"

"It's not my thing," Dara replied. Examining the premature wrinkles on Jane's face, it occurred to Dara that the straightedge lifestyle might have benefits beyond those originally intended.

"Suit yourself. Cheers!" She took a swig.

Dara hid her now mustard-covered napkin inside a clean one, hoping she didn't get any drippings on her blouse. No matter. If she did, Jane would be the first to tell her.

"So, Dara, I hear that handsome boss of yours is looking for someone to do an independent analysis of your project."

There it was. Avery was right. She only contacted Dara when she wanted something, and this was what she wanted. A consulting job.

"I think you need a security clearance for that," Dara said, hoping to close the subject.

"Guess what? I was able to get one for myself and my team through a contract at Chambers. We're doing safety analyses for defense nuclear facilities. They could transfer our clearances — it's pretty routine."

Treading as lightly as she could, Dara made every effort not to give away that there was a ton of independent analysis work on the horizon for the right consultant. In fact, Alexander had mentioned Jane as a possible candidate, but Dara, thinking quickly, pointed out that her lack of a security clearance could delay the project. No such luck now. "Just get in touch with Alexander and tell him you want to bid on whatever he has."

"Can you put in a good word for me?" said Jane, oozing saccharine.

Dara refused the bait and instead served up a bit of her own treacle. "Jane, someone of your stature wouldn't need a recommendation from little old me. You're the quantum mechanic, remember? I'm just a gearhead, messing around."

Jane's smile remained plastered on her face. She gulped her IPA, stared back at Dara. "Hey, you got some mustard on your shirt," she said. "Put some club soda on it before it sets."

***

Dmitri regarded the items that arrived that morning, couriered via diplomatic pouch: badge, electronic keys, green contact lenses, uniform, encrypted flash drive. He decoded the USB, finding a list of instructions and a series of numbers: forty-nine, twenty-five, thirty-six. Alexander

Fallsworth apparently favored squares. Either that or he was imagining a particularly well-endowed pin-up when he set the combination for the Class 6 file cabinet in his office.

Dmitri himself had discovered the combination, having spotted the numbers on a Post-it note on Dara's desk the day the power went out, partially hidden under her keyboard. The note remained until one afternoon when she left work early for an offsite meeting. His counterparts on the surveillance team confirmed she had gone to Langley. The Post-it must have gone with her, as it was no longer anywhere on her desk, nor was it in either of the wastebaskets in her office (*Thanks, janitorial mole*). All signs pointed to the Post-it numbers being the correct combination.

He wondered about Alexander. Surveilling Dara's boss around town revealed nothing but family man *bona fides*, but perhaps something more lay under the surface. So many in the intelligence business led secret lives, the logical consequence of lying for a living. Politicians were of the same ilk, but life in the public eye meant they would get caught (and make no mistake, they always got caught). Spooks, conversely, carried on with impunity. In Alexander's case, Dmitri and his colleagues were surprised not by a hard drive full of outlaw porn or cell phone numbers of on-call dominatrices, but rather the absence of such trappings.

To get a better read on Alexander, Dmitri drew Dara out, increments at a time, as per his training. After all, he had a professional need to know if Alexander had eyes for women other than his wife, and, more to the point, if Alexander's special interest in Dara extended beyond her coding abilities. Or perhaps Dara had developed a crush on her mentor? This was not unusual when colleagues spent long hours together.

He recalled the conversation he'd had with Dara the previous day in the coffee shop near AAER. "You were working late last night. Are you afraid to be at the office when no one else is there?"

"It's a little scary after hours, but I was with Alexander. He used to be a soldier. I'm sure he could break some heads for me if it came to it."

"I used to be a soldier, too, you know," Dmitri said, laughing. "And I sleep with you," he added, *sotto voce.*

"Yeah? Well, if you'd like to keep doing that, *droog,* you'll need to stop asking me silly questions," Dara replied, not so *sotto*-ly.

Dmitri stifled the urge to snap back in retort, but the red tint he felt forming on his ears gave away his *modus operandi.* Perhaps he wasn't as subtle as he'd hoped. He'd be more careful next time.

Dmitri turned his attention to the first page of his instructions. He salt and peppered his hair using the temporary dye in the disguise kit and affixed the fake beard. Looking at his now transformed visage in the mirror through the contact lenses he'd inserted, he practiced his American accent. He'd been working with a dialect coach, jokingly using it on Dara when the mood called for levity, invariably resulting in peals of laughter. Her laugh was like music to him, sometimes loud but always sweet. He longed to call and make her laugh again. Not that his security guard drag was a joke he could share.

Dmitri memorized the driving directions to the site along with the floor plan of Alexander's building. His counterparts at Center had laid most of the groundwork remotely.

The embassy staff, on the other hand, made Dmitri's job far more difficult. There were many words he could use to describe them, but 'detail-oriented,' 'on the up-and-up' and 'competent' were generally not among them. Still, he enjoyed being around other Russians when he'd stop by, usually under the pretense of 'visa purposes.' Everyone there, from the ambassador to the cafeteria ladies, was Russian, unlike other embassies in Washington that occasionally hired locals. The embassy also employed its own doctors, and many of the diplomats and their families even lived on the premises in embassy housing.

Any given stroll around the Glover Park section of Washington where the Russian Embassy was located revealed small slices of Russian ex-patriot life: slim, fashionably-dressed moms pushing fair-haired babies in prams; preschool-aged children toddling along, gurgling in Russian baby-talk; visitors in double-eagle festooned military uniforms lunching at the cafes along Wisconsin Avenue; diplomats toasting each other in the bars. Slavs, like himself, trying to fit in but fooling no one.

Dmitri had a temporary office within the embassy that overlooked the parking garage. The Russian appreciation for flashy cars made for an often-amusing view. Today's white Corvette Stingray stenciled with red and orange flames said it all.

Alas, in the guise of 'Wayne Carlson,' American security guard, Dmitri got a Nissan Sentra, complete with non-new car smell inside and pockets of rust outside. At least the radio worked. Dmitri found the classical station, in part to calm the chatter in his head, but mostly to distract from his increasingly sour stomach. The uniform pants came with padding to make him look pot-bellied, but at times like these he'd have preferred a hot water bottle. Maybe he'd suggest it to the tradecraft people next time.

He switched off the radio upon his arrival to the gates at Langley headquarters, as the Venn diagram of CIA security types and fans of Prokofiev's "Symphony Number One in D" overlapped by a sliver, at most. The multitude of guards onsite rotated posts and changed shifts regularly, so

Dmitri felt confident that he wouldn't arouse suspicion. Still, his pulse quickened when he, ostensibly arriving for the third shift, handed over his badge. The guard checked the picture, waved it over the sensor, and the green light appeared. "Thanks," Dmitri said, trying not to exhale too loudly, remembering his dialect coach's reminder to pronounce the 'th' in 'thanks.'

"Take it easy," the guard replied, eyes already looking past Dmitri at the next vehicle in line.

Approaching Alexander's building, Dmitri a.k.a. Wayne activated the tiny infrared camera hidden in his hat. The camera was designed to emit a tiny electrical pulse when another graveyard-shifter came within a certain perimeter. The closer a warm body got, the stronger the pulse. Dmitri knew the building layout by heart by now, and therefore where to duck for cover if needed. His hacker colleagues at Center replaced the surveillance video in real time with a CGI-altered mashup of videos of the usual guards from previous nights.

Dmitri felt a tiny pulse from the infrared camera, estimating that the 'real' guard was two floors above him. He proceeded to make the rounds, going through the motions of a security guard's assigned duties, checking all the safes and file cabinets to ensure that all the locks were locked.

A dull thud made the temporarily salt and pepper hairs on Dmitri's neck stand on end. A *whoosh* sound followed. Just the HVAC system. Exhale.

The pulse grew. Elvis was in the building, a bit closer this time, and Dmitri needed to hurry. Alexander's office was in the crosshairs. Dmitri side-eyed the wall which was papered and plaqued with framed evidence of Alexander's ego, the top of the credenza decorated with trophies and pictures of his wife and kids.

He beelined toward the safe. Forty-nine, twenty-five, thirty-six, a few other manipulations, click — there was the laptop. Computers like this one typically weren't encrypted since they lived in a Class 6 cabinet. Dmitri was thankful -- the pulse was growing. He photographed the contents of the drawer, then plugged in and started up the computer.

The USB stored software was designed to copy what was on the laptop, then erase any evidence that a copy had been made. Dmitri cursed the spinning hourglass under his breath. The growing pulse was starting to irritate him.

While the icon spun, he installed an integrated circuit, about the size of a bead, into the motherboard of the laptop as per the directions he'd memorized. Alexander's every keystroke would be captured.

Dmitri felt around for a spot for another bead, this one containing a camera, right behind the desk just under one of the diplomas. Signals and images captured on these beads could be activated at will and downloaded from afar by a cognizant recipient. They came complete with their own signal jammers and encryption.

Dara would have finished the tiny soldering job with time to spare and probably would have wanted to hack into someone else's computer just for fun. She was much smarter than he was, and he knew it. Dmitri smiled.

Then the pulse went haywire.

Adrenaline -- heart pounding, stomach in a wringer, hands trembling, he put the laptop in the drawer, checking its placement against the photo. Shut the drawer, wind the combination lock…thirty-six, forty-nine, twenty — *damn it!*…forty-nine, twenty-five, thirty-six. God, whoever it was coming toward Dmitri was just yards away…steps away. He pocketed the tiny soldering iron, the tiny camera, the USB.

Where to hide? He could see the guard's shadow. Behind the door -- there was no other choice. Dmitri shimmied between it and the wall, silently praying for invisibility.

The guard wandered in, zig-zagging to the Class 6 file cabinet. The swimsuit photo of Alexander's bottle blonde wife probably had something to do with his short detour to the credenza. Dmitri willed himself not to breathe, willed the guard to get on with it, willed every deity he could think of for bodily assumption into the great beyond. Or at least an electromagnetic pulse to stop the infrared camera's infernal pulsating from boring into his brain.

The guard reached up, checked the lock. *Please God, don't let it open.* Dmitri listened for a damning click...nothing. He exhaled a tiny bit of air. The guard took another look around, then turned toward to door to exit. Dmitri exhaled a bit more. *Go, please just go.* Then the guard reached for the doorknob.

Every axon in Dmitri's body went rigid. The guard pulled the door, an eternity from start to end. Finally — the door clicked shut.

Dmitri remained still as the pulses became more tolerable, one second at a time. Exhaling more — Dmitri promised his lungs he would never take them for granted again. The throbbing barely registered now. Time to leave. Dmitri exited the office, slipping into the moonlit parking lot, hiding inside a specially-designed seat built into the Nissan Sentra. He set his watch to quitting time. Eventually, he'd drive out with the others from the overnight shift. Dmitri lay with one eye open, oblivious to the crickets, wishing for brandy, Prokofiev, Dara...something, anything to snap him out of his nerve-addled state.

***

If the media saturation of recent weeks was any proof, Jericho had learned a thing or two about marketing from Jennie, the not-so-dearly-departed PR maven. Dara caught Jericho several times on podcasts and local morning radio shows during her commute, yukking it up with the A.M. shock jocks but quickly turning serious and asking listeners to pick up tickets to his upcoming Rock against Climate Change concert on the National Mall in Washington.

Dara knew how much Jericho hated the morning zoo shows, especially the 'inane D.J.s,' as he referred to them. Yet, there he was in the hot seat, at the other end of the notorious D.J. Fat Frank Esposito's microphone.

Fat Frank started off with a compliment. "A guy with your face oughta coast through life on his looks. If I were you, I wouldn't bother making the world a better place. Why is this cause so important to you?" he asked. "Seriously, all I care about is bacon."

The other jocks on Fat Frank's team of sycophants shrieked with laughter in disproportionate measure to the punchline.

Jericho could only muster radio silence.

Another D.J., probably accustomed to guests not taking Fat Frank's bait, filled the dead air with a treasury of bathroom humor sound effects.

Dara cringed in sympathy with Jericho from her seat on the Metro.

Several fart noises later, Jericho found his composure, along with a response for the poor players strutting and fretting their hour upon the airwaves. "All kidding aside, I'm glad we have you guys to make us laugh during these dark times and help promote the cause."

"Aw, thanks, man," said Fat Frank.

"I've seen too many people lose everything, and that's why I'm fighting."

One of the minions chimed in. "My brother's family got flooded out of East Levitt a couple years ago. His son almost got swept away." Another jock described a childhood friend's memorial service after she had died in a freak tornado.

"Have you lost anyone, Jericho?"

"No, not due to climate change, but someone I care about did. Half the town where she grew up burned down in a wildfire. The drought was so bad that there wasn't enough water to control the fire. Her mom didn't get out alive."

"That's rough."

"It was. Still is. It's hard to watch someone you love deal with a memory like that. That kind of pain never goes away. We promised each other that we'd fight for change, and I have every intention of seeing this through till the end."

Fat Frank's nice-guy timer must have gone off, as he decided it was time to embarrass Jericho again. "Hmmm…and who might this person you 'love' be? Is this an exclusive reveal? Because you know we're not going to let you out of here without finding out who you're dating."

"I'm not seeing anyone," said Jericho, in earnest.

"He's blushing! Spill!" Laughter from Frank's entourage reverberated.

"Sorry, guys, I got nothin'."

"C'mon, you're famous and, let's face it, real 'purty.' We're old, married, and obese. Give us a crumb. We wanna know what it's like to live the rock star life."

The minions followed up, chanting: "Spill! Spill! Spill!"

Several of Dara's fellow commuters visibly guffawed, giving away what streamed through their earbuds. Dara turned to the window, attempting to hide her glowing cheeks, only to face her reflection.

Jericho broke through the chants, sounding as flustered as Dara felt. "It's someone I broke up with. She's with someone else now. Seriously, there's nothing to spill."

The minions hushed, then emitted a loud, "Awwwww!"

"Jericho," said Fat Frank, "you're breaking my heart."

"Not as much as she broke mine."

At this point, the sycophants switched to fake sobbing. The sound effects guy played soap opera-style organ music in the background. Amid the theatrics, Frank called out, "Hey, are you still straightedge? In times of despair, I highly recommend the chemical route, if you catch my drift."

"Nah. My dad died of alcohol poisoning when I was little. Don't think I'll go there."

Record scratch. The studio went silent.

"You're killing me, dude," said Frank. "Read my lips: We. Are. Having. A. Good. Time."

Another jock jumped in, taking his cue to shift the mood back to party before his boss blew a capillary: "If you break the skin, you'll see the state he's in!"

Peals of laughter resumed.

Jericho sighed, ultimately interjecting, "Look, I know I'm beyond saving, but there might be hope for the environment. We're spreading the word. It's time President Donahue listened to us."

Frank's ears pricked up upon hearing the President's name. "Donahue? Speaking of fat SOBs, 'nuff said. That guy wants to change the design of the American flag to say, 'Your Ad Here.' Screw him and the beast with seven heads he rode in on. Jericho Wells, best of luck with the march."

The studio erupted in applause.

Dara's train emerged from underground, flooding the car with sunlight that stung her eyes. "Am I a prop to get sympathy?" she wondered. Still, her heart jumped when she realized Jericho was talking about her.

Days later, it leapt again when a text popped up: 'g-list for the march sat? please come —rex.'

She stared at her phone. The answer had to be no. Her heart may have been in Jericho's corner, but her body had taken up residence in Dmitri's bed.

'thx, will watch on TV this time. Rooting 4 u.' She hit Send.

***

Dmitri had a comprehensive dossier on everyone at AAER, so he already knew that Dara's birthday was on Sunday. Of course, he didn't let on until she broached the subject.

"Twenty-two is much better than twenty-nine, believe me, *padruga*," he said, brushing the hair out of her eyes.

"How so?" Dara looked up at him through mascaraed lashes, her body sleek in a navy silk shift and matching stockings. Dmitri smiled.

"Less worry, less responsibility, more time," he said, his head moving from side to side for emphasis as he spoke. Conversations like these reminded Dmitri that Russian was far more precise a language than English. He wanted to tell her that twenty-two-year olds had more time to try and err, to slouch toward whatever they were meant to become. But despite his stellar English, the right words eluded him.

"God, I can't imagine having more worries," said Dara. "I'm in panic mode all the time."

"It's not worth it. The world keeps turning if you worry, and it keeps turning if you don't."

She nodded, reaching for Dmitri, her head at just the right level to hear his heart beating. His hands lingered along the back of her dress.

"I'm always worrying, too," he whispered. "Don't tell anyone."

She leaned closer as Dmitri's heartbeat quickened. "What do you worry about?" she asked.

He hesitated, breathing in Dara's jasmine-scented hair. "Many, many things," he said, but got quiet again.

"You don't have to tell me. I can't find the words to describe half of what I'm thinking."

Dmitri decided it was best to change the subject.

"You know, we have a different 'Happy Birthday' song in Russia. It's from a cartoon. The singer is a crocodile named Gena, and he wears a red overcoat and plays the accordion."

"Crocodile?" she asked, eyebrows raised. "Please tell me he doesn't eat the children on their birthday."

Dmitri's dark eyes twinkled. "Eat the kids? Absolutely not. Gena is a very respectable crocodile. He smokes a pipe and works at the zoo. Very distinguished."

"That's a relief," Dara said, laughing. She glanced over at the massive bouquet on the dresser. "Does he bring his *padruga* twenty-three pink roses on her birthday?"

Russian tradition called for an odd number of flowers, hence the extra rose. "Perhaps," he replied, "But the cartoon doesn't focus on Gena's romantic life, so I'm not sure. Do you like the flowers?"

"I love them, *droog*," she replied, reaching up to stroke Dmitri's cheek.

"I'm glad."

"You know what would make my birthday even happier?" she asked, a mischievous grin lighting up her face.

Now Dmitri was the one grinning. "I have many, many ideas."

"Can you sing Crocodile Gena's song for me?"

"No way! I am terrible singer," he said, stumbling uncharacteristically over the article.

"I wanna hear it. Please?"

Dmitri sighed. "Okay, birthday girl." He cleared his throat, mumble-sang the first verse, then burst into laughter before he could finish.

"You're not a terrible singer! It sounds too sad to be for a birthday."

"Gena's saying it's a pity that birthdays only come once a year. But, you know, everything in Russia is sad." Dmitri shrugged.

"Oh, I don't believe that. I doubt Crocodile Gena meant for his birthday wish to get lost in translation."

Dmitri shook his head, realizing the folly of trying to explain Crocodile Gena, the Russian soul, or the suffering inherent to his countrymen's psyche to his American *padruga*. Instead he said, "Language is never enough. I admire your friend Jericho. Everybody understands music."

He felt Dara flinch at the mention of her ex's name, so he kissed her before she could say anything. Almond eyes, fox-like cheekbones – up close, Dmitri's features illustrated Napoleon's saying, "Scratch the Russian and you'll find the Tatar."

"It's okay," he said, "I'll shut up. I'd rather kiss you again."

Dara met his gaze, lips still parted, electric. "I like that idea," she said, catching her breath.

***

"My fellow Americans, welcome to the March on Washington against Climate Change!"

Senator Samantha Collins of Massachusetts greeted the million or so marchers, a speck onstage to all but the thousand or so who had camped out in front the night before. Everyone else crowded around Jumbotrons placed in strategic areas on the National Mall. Millions more, including Dara, watched the broadcast on network TV from their living rooms.

In real life, Sam Collins was anything but speck-like. At least six feet tall with ebony skin, she carried herself regally, even in her Day-Glo shirt emblazoned with Jericho's mugshots. Today she wore a white pantsuit and bright green blouse, her hair corn-rowed for the occasion. The high definition view on TV revealed that the beads at the end of her braids were shaped like tiny planet Earths.

Dara spotted the Senator's look-alike son, also corn-rowed, cheering her on from his spot at the edge of the stage along with various Tyrannosaurus Regina band members. Others in the crowd – teens, twenty-somethings, families — bounced beach balls, waved homemade signs and did the wave, while the hardcore Dark Reverb fans in attendance stood around in extraterrestrial punk regalia, too cool to make any sudden movements.

Senator Collins knew how to command an audience. She didn't stand in place and read her speech from the teleprompter like so many others. Instead, she worked the crowd, wireless microphone in hand, like a cross between a tent revivalist and Oprah Winfrey.

"Friends, I'm curious. How many of you have heard an elected leader promise you the moon on climate change? Let me hear you."

The crowd erupted. She nodded. "Uh huh. And then what happens? You all know the answer as well as I do. Say it with me, friends, on three. One, two, three: Nothing!" A million voices joined her as she yelled out the word.

The Senator surveyed the crowd. "One more time, folks. This time, I want you say it so loud and so proud that President Donahue could hear you from his soundproof panic room in the White House — and you know that's where he's hiding today, because he sure as heck isn't here. So, let me hear you. One, two, three..." She held her hand to her ear.

"NOTHING!"

Dara laughed, not just at Sam Collins' image of the president hiding out in the White House, but also at the irony of it all. Dara herself was hiding, her spot on the couch in front of the TV serving as her own private 'panic room,' her solution for avoiding in-the-flesh Jericho.

Dara's amusement was short-lived. This was the biggest concert of Jericho's life, and she wasn't there. She tried to distract herself watching the bands, focusing on the music —Vitamin X, The Green Flash, Spaceman Spiff, Trigger Happy, Jericho -- all playing songs she loved. But it just sank in further that she was home on her couch. The kids moshed, filled out voter registrations, listened to scientists who spoke between sets, and lived what would probably become a memory for them as Woodstock and Live Aid had been for previous generations.

Day turned to night to the tune of the million voices raised in support of a cause so dear to her, brought together by the man so dear to her. When Jericho finally took the stage as headliner, he opened with a new song called, "Water."

And I felt my heartbeat like the sun
Could not even count to one
With pulse like cuffs around my hands
I've never understood
I'll never understand

And all night I heard the faucet drip
All day I heard my Seiko tick
Moves so fast but still I stand
I've never understood
I'll never understand.

Jericho's hair had grown since Dara had last seen him. She named his new do "The Stylized Bedhead," knowing this was something they would have kidded about together. With Dmitri, she found herself explaining her jokes half the time, like how she'd refer to John and Kayla Tripp-Decker from the office as "The Triple-Deckers." Language, idioms, humor—any expression with cultural overtones was hit or miss, and the more time Dara spent with Dmitri, the more she realized that everything had cultural overtones.

The song reminded her of a poem she discovered when they were a couple called 'One Ordinary Evening,' by Virginia Hamilton Adair, about the poet's husband's self-inflicted death. It read, 'Later that year, you were dead by your own hand, blood your blood. I have never understood, I will never understand.' Jericho must have taken the poem as inspiration. They had always compared the willful neglect of global warming to suicide, with ordinary life moving forward while death and despair lay in wait, just under the surface, ignored.

Take me to the water's edge
Hanging by a spider's web
Can't you hear blood course my veins?
Why am I still here, the same?
Every now and then I can't breathe
And I just float away

After the chorus, Jericho tore into a blues solo that poured like liquid into the audience. Senator Collins and her son danced together from the side of the stage, the cameras panning to various celebrities in the crowd. After the solo, the song got quiet:

And I thought I'd tell them what was wrong
But I turned around and they were gone
No trace of footprints in the sand
I've never understood
I'll never understand

It's like I bleed internally
Cry so hard I cannot see
Dreams slip like tears right through my hands
I've never understood
I'll never understand

Poetry was a lot like humor in that language mattered. Dmitri rhapsodized about the Russian poet Alexander Pushkin, but English translations barely scratched the surface of what Pushkin was trying to say. Dara would have loved to discuss poetry with Dmitri, but there would always be an impasse.

Music fared better, but even so, Dara knew that Dmitri mostly tolerated her All-American musical preferences, while he favored opera and classical. Maybe musical incompatibilities weren't the problem. Was there even a problem? Dara wondered. There was something fundamentally unknowable about Dmitri. Sleeping together brought them physically closer, but even Dara in her early-twenties naiveté understood that physical and emotional intimacy were entirely different things.

Maybe he just didn't want anyone, not even Dara, to truly know him. After all, his assignment in Washington would end at some point. He'd return to Russia or get sent to some other foreign research institute or technical support organization, thousands of miles away.

Dara felt a pang. Mystery was a language she had hoped to learn. Perhaps she'd read too much into what little she knew of her new love. Unlike Jericho, the proverbial open book, Dmitri seemed to favor solitude, sometimes with Dara at his side, but often not. The pile of empty brandy and vodka bottles in his recycling bin spoke volumes about how he spent his 'me time.'

Just as she overlooked his drinking, she was grateful to him for closing one eye to the remnants of adolescence that roughened her edges. Every so often she'd paint little stars on her cheeks and play dress up in her punk show outfits, binge-watch online videos of Jericho's performances, or spend entire afternoons with the blankets pulled over her head, trying to remember her old life that got lost in the fire. She knew she needed to work on herself, smooth herself out, grow up.

Dara turned to her ex on her TV screen, he in command of countless millions of fans, in full control of himself, his emotions, his actions. She wished she had that kind of self-mastery.

And a little water pulls me right up to the edge
Wonder where it all will end?
Water, water everywhere
How did I get here from there?
Every now and then I can't breathe
And I just float away

Tears filled her eyes, dripped through her hands. She had a long way to go.

T-minus Seven

The holiday season approached. It was a green Christmas, unseasonably warm. "Unseasonable is the new seasonable," as one journalist put it. Dmitri worked on Thanksgiving Day at his Russian Embassy office, which remained open. In fact, the embassy was even open on Christmas. Dara didn't realize that Russians celebrated Orthodox Christmas, which takes place thirteen days after December 25th, following the Gregorian calendar. In any case, New Year's Day was the premier winter holiday for Russians, a holdover from the Soviets' ban on religious celebrations.

"Did you see what Jericho sent us?" Avery asked Dara. He motioned to the card on the shelf. It featured a photo of Jericho and his band posing with a department store Santa, grinning, mugging for the cameras, guitars and drumsticks in hand.

"Cute, huh? There's another one on the table that's addressed to you," he added.

The scrawl gave it away. Dara often joked that if Jericho ever had his handwriting analyzed he'd be outed as a serial killer. This card displayed a dog Nativity scene. She wondered what the atheist Soviets would have thought of that.

Reg,

Got your card after the march — thanks! Glad you liked the new song. It's going on the next album, but who knows when that'll drop since I'll be touring for the foreseeable future. Touring is boring — did I ever tell you that? Oh yeah, all the time. So tired. Missing my own bed, missing everyone back home, missing you.

Band and crew's personal hygiene has gone South, which sucks when it's just you and them in a bus for hours at a stretch. Okay, I'll stop whining now.

Hope to see you soon! I have something for you.

Have a merry one,

Rex

xoxo

There was little difference between Jericho's holiday message to Dara this year versus any other message he'd ever sent her, including during their engagement. Only this yuletide season, it would be just Dara and her father at home, with Avery cooking far too much food for two people and *It's a Wonderful Life* blaring in the background. The first Christmas in ages that Dara wouldn't celebrate with her ex-fiancé.

Jericho unabashedly loved Christmas, joking every year that he was a 'cafeteria atheist.' Dara traditionally agonized over what to give him. Musical gear didn't carry a sufficient personal touch, so one year she tried to knit him a sweater. It devolved after multiple tries into a nubby, uneven scarf. Winter didn't get cold enough for him to wear a scarf that year (so he said), so it ultimately took up residence in his guitar case along with a wallet-sized picture of Dara, cut into the shape of a heart.

Dara had no idea what became of those mementos. Regardless, she wasn't his fiancé anymore. If Jericho got her a gift, she wasn't under any obligation to give him anything in return.

Living with Avery now meant not having a Christmas tree, as Jericho retained custody of the ornaments after Dara moved and her current budget didn't allow for new ones. Besides, casino work meant in-your-face holiday décor and a continuous loop of carols over the sound system starting the day after Halloween. Avery had little interest in repeating the theme at home.

A smattering of holiday cards decorated the shelf along with Jericho's. One featuring a decorated McMansion came from the realtor who helped with the short sale of their house. One, sent by their dentist, depicted the elf from *Rudolph the Red-Nosed Reindeer* practicing dentistry on dolls rather than making toys. Another card stating 'Season's Greetings' in white font against a red background, signature stamped on, came from a far-off relative who remained distant thanks to Avery's one-too-many requests to borrow money. Other cards, equally impersonal, arrived from former neighbors in Colorado whom Dara barely remembered. With both sets of grandparents having passed away years ago, it was a lonely time.

Dara focused on reading a holiday letter that aggressively touted the family's prior-year triumphs: straight A's for the teenage daughter, the mom's three-and-a-half hour marathon finish, the family vacation building houses for the poor in Honduras, even the dog's third place finish in a Frisbee competition.

She wished she could warn the daughter about the dangers of accomplishment. It amounted to precious little, if in fact the girl was studying for those A's for herself. If she was doing it to please others, well, that was just pathetic. But as false a promise as achievement was, failure was even worse. The industrialist Thomas Watson famously claimed that the recipe for success was to double one's rate of failure, but Dara was onto him. He probably just said that to sabotage his competition.

Regardless, she knew it was fundamentally useless to warn anyone about anything. As Jane Canton used to remind her, Dara herself was the Queen of Deaf Ears. A person could only learn lessons about success or failure the old-fashioned way, through experience, and even that was a fifty-fifty proposition.

There was a bright spot, though — Dara would celebrate New Year's Eve this year, thanks to an invitation from Dmitri. The Russian Embassy planned a gala, and Dmitri's superiors cleared her to join him. New Year's Eve had always been a work night for her since Jericho's band usually headlined gigs, typically in other cities. Dara would tag along, but mainly to lend her audio engineering skills. Even when the band got someone else to do sound, Jericho was on the clock all night while everyone else counted down. It wasn't exactly a party for one's plus one. Dara closed her eyes, imagining herself all done up, dancing the waltz to Tchaikovsky, gliding along in Dmitri's arms. This year would be different.

***

Washington became a ghost town during the holidays. Members of Congress returned to their districts on recess, the Supreme Court ended its session, and the president went back home to Texas. Thousands of federal employees made sure to 'use or lose' their excess remaining annual leave, lest they be unable to carry it over into the next year.

Dara ended up donating her leave to an AAER employee whom she'd never met whose son had a brain tumor and needed significant care. She wasn't planning to take any time off and knew that helping someone on the leave recipient list was the right thing to do. It was just as well, since Alexander intended to work through the holidays in hopes of getting a jump on the software's beta test. Dara would remain on hand to do the lion's share of the work.

The office stragglers, small in number, brought in a disproportionate quantity of trays laden with cookies, cakes, fudge and chocolate Santas. A Viennese dessert table it wasn't. The items appeared to be leftovers from holiday parties – leftover for a reason. The Santas tasted like cocoa flavored wax, cake frosting called to mind glue mixed with food coloring and the cookies were mostly stale. Keeping with the tradition of second-rate sweets, Dara brought in a bag of Nerds candies. They were an impulse purchase, prompted by a sense of nostalgia since Nerds were always on Jericho's gig riders. Dara ate a couple, but then the bag sat around for weeks. It was time to put them out of their misery.

Alexander dropped by that afternoon. "Dara, here are the coordinates I've been studying. Your mission, should you choose to accept it, is to run tests on all of them. I'd like the results as soon as possible after the new year." He smiled and handed her a document of at least fifty pages, its cover emblazoned "TOP SECRET" in red. The coordinates were in 8-point type, listed in columns on each page.

Dara felt her eyebrows knit together. The majority of the longitude and latitude coordinates weren't serious candidates for implementation. Some would even cause more environmental harm than good. Still, as Alexander had stressed, she needed to test them in order to develop a full picture of the potential results, at least as far as probabilistic methods would allow. More samples meant a more complete picture and ultimately, a greater chance of getting the president to agree to detonate a nuclear weapon and obliterate several mountains in Alaska. It remained a monumentally tall order.

There wasn't time to question the process. President Donahue's confidence in Dara's thesis – previously referred to by everyone at Chambers U. except Jane Canton as "that crackpot dissertation" – was miraculous, especially given the throes of rejection Dara experienced only a year ago. Dara inspected the parameters, silently calculating how little sleep she'd get over the next two or three weeks, and resigning herself to days and nights of painstaking analysis.

But this was her baby, as Avery called it. Of course she would accept the challenge, fueled on week-old Christmas cookies and caffeine, but mostly on fear of blowing it. "Thanks, I think," she said.

"I feel like Ebenezer Scrooge," said Alexander.

"I'm getting more of a Grinch Who Stole Christmas vibe."

Alexander nodded. "Yep — that's me. Only I'm green and scowling on the inside, where it counts." He chuckled, coaxing a smile from Dara. "I know I'm asking a lot of you, but you're the only one who can do it. I want the president to bring up climate technologies during his State of the Union speech, so it doesn't give us much time."

The State of the Union address would take place on Tuesday, January 27 — indeed, not much time. Alexander advised the National Security Staff of the importance of the public's buy-in, which, given the project's controversial nature, warranted revelation in baby steps. They'd need focus groups, grassroots outreach, educational campaigns — anything and everything to win the public's acceptance, as soon as possible. The other key component of the process would be to instruct supporters to contact their respective members of Congress and urge them to authorize, fund, and implement the program. Will, meet way.

Alexander pulled a laminated certificate from his briefcase. "Dara, I appreciate all you're doing. Federal rules don't allow me to give you a decent Christmas gift, but I think you'll be pretty happy with your performance bonus. Here's a certificate of commendation for all you've done." He handed her the token, grinning broadly.

"Thank you. That's so generous." Dara eyed her certificate, regretting her less-than-positive attitude with a twinge of guilt. All she ever wished for every Christmas since high school was a shot at saving the broken planet, and Alexander came through for her with the opportunity. Working extra was a small price to pay.

New Year's resolutions were in order. Dara would do everything in her power to complete the beta test over the holidays, deliver the results to Alexander, and work on a public communication plan. No getting distracted by Dmitri's presence on her floor. If anything, they were careful to avoid each other at work now that their relationship had blossomed beyond friendship. Jason Houseman may have told the staff when Dmitri arrived that he had been vetted 'nine ways from Sunday and should be treated like any other coworker,' but Dara stuck to her mantra to keep her private life private.

Above all, she would remain positive. Early on, Dara promised Alexander that he wouldn't regret working with her. She had every intention of following through on her commitment.

***

Gala night – last day, last hours, last seconds of the year. Not an ideal start to the end for Dara because it was a workday, one that demanded her full concentration. Given the late hours she'd been devoting to the beta test, every cell in her body begged for a decent night's sleep. Instead, she'd brave the crowds on the Metro, rush home, shower, do her hair, change clothes, spackle the dark circles under her eyes, and otherwise pull out the stops to try to look like a normal person. Better than normal, actually — the Russian women, mostly diplomats' wives or diplomats themselves, all looked like supermodels. Some even were supermodels. Tonight's gala was the event of the year for the Russian community in Washington. As one of the few Americans on the guest list, Dara felt she needed to represent, or at least not embarrass her date.

Dmitri said he'd pick her up at eight. Dara tacitly understood that she'd chauffeur the return trip home, since 'champagne-ski' would be a significant part of Dmitri's night. That meant bringing along a pair of sneakers, since she wasn't comfortable driving in stiletto heels.

Shoes, dress, hair, makeup…thrift store finery wasn't going to cut it this time. A couple of weeks before the event, Dara found online images of the previous year's gala, which made clear she was in over her head. Black tie all the way -- men in tuxedos and women in designer gowns that spared no sequin, yard of silk, or embroidered trim. Beyond the gowns, the women dripped in diamonds and even furs despite the incongruous weather.

Dara was in no position to bust her budget on an outfit worth more than her car, having already accrued enough debt for a lifetime. The irony about debt was that in order to obtain and keep a security clearance and therefore a federal job — which would provide a salary to pay down the debt – one couldn't have bad credit in the first place. A few weeks into her tenure at AAER, Dara had to prove to a government adjudication board that she was actively chipping away at what she owed, just to get cleared. Maintaining her security clearance meant living as frugally as possible, and, of course, never again sharing a credit card or cosigning a loan with the likes of Avery Bouldin.

So, tonight's outfit meant Dara needed to improvise. She owned a floor-length black satin skirt, slit up the side, and decided to re-engineer something into a top. The best she could do was to cut up a silver lamé miniskirt and fashion some silver chains into spaghetti straps. To tie the look together, she bought a black satin remnant from the fabric shop and cut it into three pieces, reasonable facsimiles of a choker, sash, and wrap. She didn't own a strapless bra, so she'd have to go without. It was just as well. Maybe that would keep people from staring at the rest of her do-it-yourself formal wear.

Her go-to sleeve of silver bangles covered the scars on her arm, and sheer black stockings, black satin pumps and a matching clutch from the budget shoe warehouse completed the look. She found some dangly silver earrings in her jewelry box and pinned up her hair, loosening a few tendrils to frame her face. Dara stifled the urge to get too creative with her makeup, settling for smoky eyes with frosted silver shadow on her brow bone, shimmery pink lipstick, and rose blush. A thick application of concealer cream was the best she could do for her stubborn under-eye shadows. The makeup took a few tries, but eventually Dara was ready to inspect her efforts in the full-length mirror.

She gaped. The woman glaring back at her looked like an R-rated Cinderella, only wearing a dress designed by the mice with the stepsisters' most risqué castoffs, barely held in place using safety pins and double-sided tape. The missing bra was obvious, the slit was higher than she'd remembered, and her waist looked alarmingly tiny in the sash. Probably because it *was* alarmingly tiny, as the long hours at the office typically had her crawling into bed after work, too tired for dinner.

Adjusting the tie around her waist, she felt her stomach rumble but, alas, it would have to wait. Food options tonight meant caviar and goose liver paté--her least favorite food, followed by her second least favorite food. She considered wolfing down a sandwich, but her makeup took an hour to get right and she didn't have it in her to start over in case anything smeared.

Nerves and flushed embarrassment setting in, she vowed to hide in the corner all night under her satin remnant. No glory, but then again, no guts puked all over the ballroom floor. At least she could take solace in the fact that her year of "interesting times" from the Chinese curse was coming to an end. Her Russian prince arrived on schedule to take her to the ball.

Dmitri stood before her, tall and wolfish in his tux, bow tie askew, hair slicked back. He gasped when he saw Dara, barely checking himself, consuming her through dark blue eyes. "*Padruga,*" was all he could say.

Then he reached for her sash. "Let's just stay here tonight."

Dara detected the scent of brandy, probably the Armenian cognac she got him for Christmas. Dmitri apparently had gotten a jump on the festivities at home. "Did you drive here? Please tell me you didn't."

"I took taxi. Where's my new year's kiss?"

She pulled his hand away from her sash. "I'm sorry, *droog*, my outfit is going to fall apart if you untie me, and my lipstick is going to end up all over both our faces if we kiss. We should to go to the party. They'll put us on a watch list if we don't show up."

"But you look like princess." Dmitri pouted, stumbled a bit then laughed at himself. "I am Russian stereotype tonight."

Dara sighed and straightened his tie. Her tipsy prince, magnificent if a bit rumpled in his tuxedo, cut quite a figure in her vestibule. The gleam in his eye gave away that he was still a young man wanting to party, wanting the woman in front of him. Dara had spent so many years with Jericho, paragon of self-control, that she didn't know quite how to respond to Dmitri's insistence. But calling him on his behavior would probably start an argument, and Dara didn't want to be the New Year's Eve spoiler.

So, she resigned herself – to driving, to holding her nose and downing the fish eggs and goose liver, to making the most of her night on the town with her drunken *droog*.

It had to be better than twiddling knobs all night, doing sound for the Tyrannosaurus Regina crowd, practically begging for a kiss when the clock struck twelve. At least it felt like progress.

"Let's go, sweetheart," she said. "You can untie me later."

"Okay, deal. Hey, did I tell you you're beautiful? Look at the time -- it's later." With that pronouncement, he tried to pull her sash again.

Dara smacked his hand.

She changed into sneakers for the drive, feeling ridiculous with her pumps in a grocery store bag. Dmitri guffawed at the sight of her, his hands running up the slit of her skirt as she drove. Dara found a parking spot on Wisconsin Avenue in front of the embassy and reached for her shoes. Dmitri wouldn't let go of her thigh.

"Sweetie, I can't change my shoes if you won't give me back my leg."

"Sorry. Did I make you mad?"

Dmitri's eyes were like a baby basset hound's, not those of the steely, focused man she knew from work. Finally, she reached for his hand, deciding it was best to fess up. "*Droog*, I'm not mad. I want this night to be perfect, but I've never been to a gala like this before. I don't have the right clothes and I don't know how to act. I'm already going to stand out for being American. I don't want to make you look bad." She lowered her head, hoping that Dmitri wouldn't make fun of her.

He straightened up in the passenger seat. "*Padruga*, look at me. Of course I can't stop touching you. You made yourself into this glamorous shiny thing. I promise, everyone in there will love you. Like me." He held her gaze.

Dara stroked his cheek. In the morning, Dmitri would have no recollection of anything he just said, but she appreciated the sentiment. "Let's go inside, okay?" she said.

Security check completed, they queued up with several hundred other partygoers, filing into the venue. The ballroom took up the entire upper level, with a floor-to-ceiling two-headed eagle emblazoned on the doors to greet guests at the entrance. Inside, twinkling snowflakes hung from the ceiling, chandeliers and candelabras lit up the space, and a full orchestra played Tchaikovsky's greatest. Tables festooned with white poinsettias, silver holiday trees and confetti flanked each wall. On closer inspection, the majority of the tables were actually well-stocked bars. Servers roamed the floor, offering glasses of champagne and buttered crostini flecked with black beluga.

So many glittery women, legs and/or décolletage on display as would have made Jessica Rabbit blush. Dara needn't have worried about her attire — she fit right in. A man with broken capillaries around his nose started speaking to her in Russian just as Dmitri stepped away to find the restroom.

When he discovered that she was American, he exclaimed, "We need to make you into proper Russian woman!" He grabbed a shot of vodka and shoved it into her hand.

"Um, thank you," Dara said, hoping it didn't sound like a question.

"Our embassy is like really being in Russia, so that's real vodka. Vodka you have in United States is vodka we give children and sick people." The man chortled, downed the shot he poured for himself.

Dara craned her neck in hopes of finding Dmitri, her face growing hot. Mercifully he appeared before things got awkward, since Dara had no intention of drinking alcohol not meant for kids or the infirmed.

Dmitri said something in Russian to Broken Capillary Guy, who laughed, kissed Dara's hand and took his leave.

Safely out of the man's view, Dmitri took Dara's glass and drained it. "I don't know him, so I told him you just found out you were pregnant. Congratulations, *padruga*. Let's dance!"

He maneuvered her onto the dance floor. Dara had been practicing the waltz with Avery, hoping not to embarrass herself. Fortunately, Dmitri had his wits about him enough to take the lead, guiding her to the music, one-two-three, one-two-three...

The ballroom spun around like the inside of a snow globe, an enchanted planet inhabited by *Ded Moroz*, known in English as Grandfather Frost, and *Snegurochka*, the Snow Maiden. The bizarro version of the extraterrestrial Dark Reverb scene tonight was all about beauty in the classical sense. Just before midnight, a pre-taped video appeared on the monitors featuring the President of the Russian Federation giving a short address — brevity sorely lacking in President Donahue's repertoire. A few champagne-ski toasts later, the countdown began.

Dmitri held Dara as the crowd counted down in Russian — "*Decit, devit, vossim...*" Dara joined in.

"Dara, you know the numbers in Russian!"

"I checked out a phrasebook from the library."

"*...sem, shest, pyat, chetire, tri, dva, adin—S'novim godom!*"

Dara didn't quite understand how Happy New Year translated from '*s'novim godom*,' which literally means "with New Year," but she was too busy kissing her now *tri*-sheets-to-the-wind dance partner to care. Echoes of 'Everyone in there will love you. Like me,' reverberated in her head. She didn't want to let go.

Dmitri motioned for her to follow him to a corner of the ballroom, pulled a tiny box from his pocket. "I have surprise," he said.

"For me?" Dara remembered that Russians give each other gifts on New Year's just after midnight.

"Please, open it."

Dara tore off the gold paper, revealing a blue velveteen box. Her mouth agape, she found a diamond pendant inside, dangling from a white gold chain. The jewel, round and flawless, the size of Dara's thumbnail, competed with the Mylar snowflakes, holiday trees, and bedazzled female guests in capturing the light that strobed through the ballroom. A booming fireworks display over Red Square crackled through the video screens.

Dara threw her arms around him. "*Droog*, it's beautiful. Thank you so much – *spacibo*!" She stared, saucer-eyed, at her first-ever diamond. Even her engagement ring from Jericho had been a simple platinum band.

Dmitri took the pendant out of the box and clasped it around Dara's neck. Stroking her face, he said, "You were worried that you didn't have any diamonds to wear tonight like the other ladies, and now you do. Will you think of me when you wear it?"

"I'll think of you whether I wear it or not."

Dmitri smiled, gave her another champagne flavored kiss. "Time to go home, *padruga*?"

"Yes," she said, taking his hand. The diamond around her neck, the handsome prince by her side, Dara felt a twinge of hope for the coming year. All still in the abstract, all merry and bright. She didn't want to sleep anymore, just float inside her Russian fairy tale as long as it would have her.

***

Late January. You'd have thought it was a Super Bowl party, what with the giant-screen TV and copious spread of nachos, home-made burritos, chocolate chip cookies, and assortment of craft beers. Instead, Alexander opened his home on a Tuesday night to his CIA comrades-in-arms, not for football but to watch President James Donahue give his State of the Union address.

Donahue's speech warranted celebration, as it contained a segment that represented the culmination of all that Alexander, Dara, and company had worked toward last year. The text read: "I've consulted with my advisors and am convinced that there is a direct way to address the devastation Mother Nature has inflicted on our beloved nation. I stand before you tonight with a vision of hope. My idea is to counter environmental threats with measures that are truly proactive, utilizing the very technological capacities that have brought forth the exceptional standard of living we as Americans enjoy."

Alexander himself crafted the Reaganesque excerpt. The words that followed outlined the plan in brush strokes, downplaying the role atomic weapons would play, glossing over potential geological consequences, ending with an appeal for every citizen to reach out to their Congressional representatives with behests to support the program.

Dara wasn't keen on parties, especially parties where everyone knew everyone else except for her. Still, she appreciated Alexander's invitation. There was never much to look forward to in January after the holidays, so she latched onto the prospect of visiting Alexander's home for the first time. Not that she cared to hear President Donahue, subject matter notwithstanding. Outside of work, she sometimes referred to him as President 'Duh-nahue.' Jericho came up with the moniker early in Donahue's presidency and it stuck. Childish, yes, but Dara knew full well that the president continued to harbor doubts that climate change was real. His interest in her model was largely about boosting his sagging poll numbers.

Alexander's house was in McLean, Virginia, a tony Washington suburb. Curb appeal, redwood wrap-around deck, swing set…what, no picket fence?

Dara rang the doorbell, and the woman last seen smiling in the framed photos on Alexander's office credenza answered.

"Hi, I'm Carmen." Mrs. Fallsworth wore a starched blue-and-white striped apron over a red shirtwaist dress. A star-shaped pendant dangled from a chain around her neck. She extended her hand, French manicure (freedom manicure?) capturing the light.

"I'm Dara Bouldin. Nice to meet you." Shaking hands with her hostess, she took in the straight-from-the-Ethan Allen-catalog surroundings. "You have a lovely home," she said, realizing that each and every 'advisor' referred to in the speech populated the living room. Dara had changed into jeans and a black sweatshirt after work, but everyone else wore business attire.

"Thank you. Let me take your jacket. There's a ton of food and the gang's all here." Dara noticed U.S. flags on the table, a large arrangement of red and white roses, and a sprinkling of metallic blue confetti. Carmen Fallsworth, with every strand of hair in place, each morsel of food artfully arranged, and all corners of her house spotless, personified perfection.

Alexander caught Dara's eye. "Welcome!" he exclaimed.

Reminding herself to smile, Dara walked toward him.

Alexander let out a loud whistle that cut through the din. "Everyone, this is Dara Bouldin, the woman behind our success tonight."

Dara felt every corpuscle in her body rush to her cheeks. The partygoers spontaneously broke into applause. "Thanks," she said, eyes darting around the room, not knowing what else to say.

A guy in a houndstooth suit approached Dara with an equally well-dressed gent following in his wake. "Hi, I'm Randall Swanson. This is my husband, Ron. I'm one of the folks on the other end of your beta test."

Dara stared. She had never met any of the so-called 'wizards of Langley' and assumed that the beta testers were artificial intelligence bots. "Nice to meet you," she finally replied. "I'm sorry if I seem taken aback. I just figured the beta tests were automated."

Randall, eyebrows raised, said, "Really? Didn't anyone tell you about us?"

Ron looked away.

Dara hesitated. "Um, I guess not. Alexander doesn't talk much about what you guys do, and I generally don't ask."

"I think I'm going to get a burrito," said Ron.

"Me, too," Randall agreed, brows now furrowed. "Excuse us." The Swansons beelined toward the buffet table.

Dara may as well have reverted back to high school. The youngest, the most socially awkward, hopelessly clueless – it felt all too familiar. God, her sweatshirt wasn't even black, it was off-black, having faded after too many wash cycles.

Just then, she felt a tug on her pant leg. "Hi, what's your name?" said the small boy doing the pulling.

She smiled. Maybe she wasn't the youngest, after all. "I'm Dara. And I know your name. It's Jackson, right?"

"Yeah." He held a deck of cards. "Come with me," he said.

"Sure."

Jackson took Dara's hand and led her down the hallway into a brightly lit, pastel-hued bedroom.

A girl in striped leggings and a sunflower-appliquéd sweatshirt sat on the bed with Barbies, doll clothes, and several pairs of the family's bedroom slippers strewn around her. "Hi," she said, barely acknowledging her visitors as she styled a brunette Barbie's hair into an up-do.

"You must be Molly. Your dad has pictures of you and your brother all over his office. I'm Dara."

On the bedside table, she noticed a stack of tween magazines that drew her eye up to the large poster taped over Molly's headboard. A familiar face winked back at her. It was all Dara could do to keep from doubling over in laughter. "Well, look what we have here!"

Molly eyed Dara, her expression serious. "I'm in love with Jericho Wells," she said, "and when I grow up, we're going to get married."

Dara smiled. She debated telling the sweet-faced girl that she could probably arrange for Jericho to at least sign her poster.

"Too bad Daddy hates him!" Jackson shouted, playing Go Fish with a stuffed panda on the floor.

Molly nodded, sighing. "Our dad thinks Jericho is a bleeding-heart limeral."

Oh. With that, Dara pulled the plug on Operation Autograph. Poor Molly. At least when Dara was planning to marry Jericho, she had her own father's blessing.

The girl stared at Dara intently. Finally, she asked, "Do you think I'm pretty enough for Jericho to like me?" Dara caught the pleading look in her crystalline blue eyes and immediately felt terrible for trivializing her feelings.

"No!" yelled Jackson.

Life as an only child wasn't all bad, Dara reckoned. "Jackson, that's not true. Your sister is very pretty."

"But am I pretty enough?"

"Of course you're pretty enough, but I'll let you in on a secret. I have it on good authority that Jericho wants someone who's more than just pretty."

"Do you mean beautiful? Like a princess?"

"No, I mean he wants someone strong."

"Like a body builder?"

"No. It's good to be physically strong, but I mean strong on the inside. Like a strong person. Somebody who's confident, who stands up for herself, for her friends, for what she believes in. Someone who can take care of herself."

"Oh, like somebody who doesn't need help?"

Dara hesitated. "It's complicated."

"Would he stop loving me if I stopped being strong?

Dara thought of many possible replies, but instead just repeated, "Love is complicated." She looked away.

"How can I get strong?"

"Sometimes you have to go through hard times to get strong. You learn that way."

"Yeah. Don't be such a crybaby, Moo-ly," chided Jackson, demonstrating thorough mastery of the bratty little brother role.

Dara rolled her eyes. "Don't listen to him. It's okay to cry. It shows you care. Just don't let the sad things turn you into a sad person."

"Okay, thanks," said Molly, as she positioned the Barbie dolls inside the slippers and pushed them around on the bed.

"What are they doing?" asked Dara.

A toothy grin took over Molly's face. "The slippers are cars!"

"Clever girl." Dara took one of the dolls and began braiding her hair.

"Ooh, I like your sparkly necklace," said Molly, moving in for a closer look. "Is that a real diamond?"

"Yes, it is. I got it for the holidays."

"From Santa?"

"No, from my boyfriend."

Jackson chimed in. "You know what's the only thing that can scratch a diamond?"

"No, what?"

"Another diamond!"

Dara nodded at the little face peering up at her, so proud of his factoid. "That's absolutely correct."

Apropos of nothing, Jackson yelled, "Fifty-two pickup!" and flung the deck of cards at the ceiling.

Alexander entered just in time for the card shower.

"Welcome to my world, Dara," he said. "Come on, kids, I think you've bothered our guest long enough. Time for bed."

Molly and Jackson bear-hugged Dara, then scrambled off to brush their teeth.

"They weren't bothering me at all. Your kids are wonderful. Even Jackson."

"Really?" said Alexander. "You want him?"

By the time the kids went to sleep, the State of the Union was in full swing. As a bonus, Dara didn't have to suffer through awkward conversations with the adults who watched the President in rapt attention. Everyone stood and cheered when he brought up the geo-engineering proposal – not just the high-fiving staffers in Alexander's living room, but also most of the representatives and senators in the chamber on TV.

Except for Sam-I-Am Collins, that is. She remained in her chair, arms crossed, silent.

T-minus Six

"Rex?"

"Reg!" Jericho grinned at Dara via Facetime, his hair now in baby dreadlocks. "So, did you get it?"

Dara held up Jericho's belated Christmas present, sent from the road, all smiles. "Yes! Thank you!"

It was a photograph of Jericho, a proof actually, black and white, autographed. On the back was a note scrawled in Jericho's trademark chicken scratch: "Just for you, Reg, an advance copy of the cover art for my next album — XOXO, Rex."

On closer inspection, Dara noticed that draped around Jericho's neck was the scarf of Christmas past that she had knitted for him, the one she assumed he'd hidden in his guitar case so as not to hurt her feelings.

"So can I name you as my wardrobe mistress in the liner notes?"

Dara laughed. "Nah. How about Edith Head?"

"The ghost of Edith Head would be more like it."

"Perfect." Dara felt her face redden, hoping her knockoff phone's camera would wash out her complexion.

"So how are you?"

"Busy, like you."

Jericho hesitated. "I heard Duh-nahue on TV the other night."

"Yeah?"

"I think I know what you're busy doing."

Dara looked away from the phone. "Rex, there's a lot I can't talk about."

"Security clearance, right?"

"Yeah. I'm sorry."

"It's okay. Just know I'm proud of you. People are going nuts."

"I heard."

"Some of the radio stations want to throw 'Let's Get Bombed' parties if it happens. They're asking me to play."

"That's crazy. Talk about coming full circle."

"I'll say."

"Did you speak to Senator Collins?"

"I didn't get a chance. Don't worry. If she mentions it, I'll pretend I know nothing."

"She's anti-nuclear. I don't think we'll get her support. She might fight us." Dara wanted to say more, but the words caught in her throat. Samantha Collins was a rising star in Congress with a national following. Moreover, she relied on Jericho to rock the vote. In turn, Jericho's alliance with her helped transform him from punk rocker to social justice warrior-poet.

"I'll always support you, Reg."

Dara found herself doubting him, but just said, "Thanks." Best to change the subject. "Did you do anything special for the holidays?"

"I had dinner with my mom and my aunt's family, then I went home for a few days. The studio's mostly set up, so I did some recording."

"Did you make the band come find you in Boonieville?"

"Aw, it's not Boonieville – the town I'm in is probably smaller than that. And yes, I did make the band come out. They hate me more than ever now, but we got some decent tracks."

"I can't wait to hear them."

"You will. Did you do anything special?"

"Work. Lots of overtime. Had Christmas dinner with my dad. He made roast beast." As she spoke, Dara grew conscious of the diamond pendant scratching against her chest. She decided to wear it inside her shirt, keeping it under wraps for Facetime purposes. Too conspicuous, too bourgeois, not punk rock. Not to mention Jericho would ask who gave it to her.

"I hope that slave driver you work for is treating you well."

"Oh, Alexander's great. I finally met his family, they're awesome, too. His wife is like a Latina Martha Stewart, and their kids are adorable."

"Alexander the Great, huh? I think you have Stockholm Syndrome."

"You may be right."

"I hope you come visit me when he finally gives you time off for good behavior. Maybe in the spring?"

"I'd like that."

"It gets cold here in Boonieville. You should bring me another scarf."

"What would the ghost of Edith Head do?"

Jericho cracked up. As he laughed, Dara noticed the dark circles under his eyes, crinkles in the corners, hollows under his cheekbones. Life on the road was taking its toll, emotionally and physically. She recalled a documentary they had watched together on the Beatles, how the group, fed up, decided that their last tour would be in 1966, several albums before they actually disbanded. Not that Jericho was more popular than the Beatles — indeed, saying that Jericho was bigger than the Beatles was like John Lennon saying the Beatles were bigger than Jesus Christ. Still, there was something unwholesome about touring, about so many people wanting a piece of him. There had to be a better way.

"Rex, please take care of yourself. Eat healthy food, sleep, take vitamins. I worry about you."

"I'll try. It's hard to do. Lots of moving parts on my end."

"You've come so far. Just make sure you don't lose yourself."

"Success means trade-offs. You lose, you gain. You'll see."

Dara nodded. Life just a year ago may as well have been life on another planet. There was no way to prepare for the reality that unfolded that bore such little resemblance to the life they'd planned. After they said their good-byes, Dara set off to find a frame for the photo Jericho had sent her, along with a spot for it on her dresser.

***

"Chairman Willoughby, Chairman Chu, Ranking Member Lynch, and Ranking Member Collins, distinguished members of both subcommittees of the Joint Committee on Appropriations, it's an honor to appear before you to discuss today's topic."

Alexander shuffled his notes, military posture in full effect, jaw set. Today's topic was the deployment of nuclear weapons to reverse global warming trends. The Office of the President had wasted no time in crafting the proposal into a bill, now before Congress. After a month of sleepless nights, Alexander and his advisors pulled together his testimony before the Joint Subcommittee, elaborating on potential environmental consequences and financial implications, ending with a thorough cost-benefit analysis.

The hearing room in the Dirksen Senate Office Building dwarfed his usual digs back at the Agency. Paneling, wainscoting, marble fixtures in the bathroom — everything Alexander saw declared, "You're out of your league, son." But he arrived, spring-loaded. A Senate staffer handed out copies of the independent safety evaluation, procured courtesy of Dr. Jane Canton, LLC. Cost projections displayed in purple, blue, and green infographics accounted for every red cent. Beyond the props laid Alexander's secret weapon, his knack for explaining technical information to lay audiences. It was theater, and he was the master thespian, or so he kept telling himself in the mirror this morning as he shaved.

Everyone knew full well that Alexander's only real antagonist was Samantha Collins, the minority party senator from Massachusetts. The ranking member of the subcommittee from the House side, Daniel Lynch, hailed from Kansas, a state that had been to hell and back several times over thanks to years of harrowing tornado activity. His constituency was all for the proposal, and so was he.

So were the multitudes from environmental action committees large and small that showed up on the Capitol steps to rally for the cause. Busloads from Missouri, Arizona, Texas, Florida, and other states demonstrated their support, waving "Let's Get Bombed" signs and yelling out "Hi, Mom!" to the throng of reporters. Online, a video from a group called Planet Plan It went viral, featuring sound bites from school-aged children.

"If you had a treatment that could cure cancer and save thousands of lives, would you let people have it?" asked Jimmy from Omaha, seated in a wheelchair, bandana tied around his head.

"If you had a car that could withstand any crash, would you let people drive it?" inquired Sabrina from Portland, prosthetic leg in view, entering an SUV.

"If you had a way to keep kids safe from crime, would you keep it to yourself?" posited Raul from Chicago, flanked by gang members, en route to school past a graffiti-covered wall.

Then the three children appeared with several others against a backdrop featuring iconic scenes from recent natural disasters. An older girl that Alexander's daughter Molly identified as popular tween actress Sailor Angelo announced, "You have a way to save us from the ravages of climate change. Use it, or we all lose." At the bottom of the screen was a link to the Planet Plan It website where constituents could find instructions on how to contact their elected leaders and let them know they favored the bill.

The closed hearing room was windowless and cell phone-less, showing no signs of the hullabaloo on the Capitol grounds outside. One couldn't even hear what was happening in the hallway immediately outside the room, only flipping pages and Alexander talking inside. He tried not to sound like a robot, having practiced in front of his wife, kids, and a menagerie of the kids' stuffed animals the night before, projecting his voice, breathing from the diaphragm, trying to keep gesticulations to a minimum. Finally, having read the entire testimony, he concluded with, "Thank you for the privilege of testifying on this most important subject. I would be happy to answer any questions and provide more detail as requested."

Chairman Chu thanked him, looked around the chamber, and then said, "I would like to recognize Senator Samantha Collins."

"Thank you, Mr. Chairman. I'm pleased to be here. I have several questions for the witness."

Alexander steeled himself, pictured Molly and Jackson in the crowd in an attempt to set himself at ease.

"The Regulatory Flexibility Act requires the evaluation of the impacts of proposed rules. I appreciate that you have provided environmental and safety studies by Dr. Canton, and my staff is working through the specifics of the software. In the meantime, I'm sure you're familiar with the line from the Hippocratic Oath that says, 'First, do no harm'?"

Alexander swallowed hard. Actually, he'd heard that was a popular misconception. The oath said no such thing. But in the interest of picking his battles, Alexander nodded.

"General Fallsworth, I'll be frank. You're proposing blowing up a chunk of our 49th state. How do you reconcile that with doing no harm?"

"Thank you for your question, Senator. We have provided a complete cost-benefit analysis, including a study of all regulatory impacts. As I mentioned in my testimony, we estimate that if we move forward, over the next decade between 50,000 and 100,000 lives would be saved, along with hundreds of billions of dollars in infrastructure restoration, disaster relief allocations, and medical costs. However, if we don't take action, we'll remain on our current trajectory of damage, loss of life, and fiscal waste. Based on the calls that are flooding your switchboards, the public rejects staying the course."

Sam Collins, cool as ever in her gray-skirted suit and silver choker, said, "I just received a letter against the bill signed by chiefs of all 229 recognized Native tribes in Alaska. What about them?"

Alexander was aware of the letter, which would be published as a full-page ad in Sunday's *New York Times*. He disagreed with the premise but chose his words carefully in his response: "We have full support of the governor of Alaska, and we've determined that the Native tribes in the state would not be impacted, at least from an economic perspective. The proposed detonation coordinates are located in uninhabited, untraversable parts of the state. No roads, no airports, no industry in these locations – only mountains. In any case, the detonations will be conducted underground, limiting the release of radioactive fallout to nearly zero. We've calculated that you'd get more exposure flying in an ordinary airplane than you would from what we've proposed, even if you lived within 20 miles of the detonation site. We have every right to do what is best for our country within our own territory and doing so is not at odds with any international convention."

"General Fallsworth, with all due respect, I'm not convinced we should fund this program," replied Senator Collins. "What about the long-term impacts?"

"The long-term effects after the bombings at Hiroshima and Nagasaki showed no genetic abnormalities to future generations. And nature continually renews itself, at least over the course of centuries and millennia. Take volcanoes, for instance. An eruption will kill everything in its path, but within a couple of years, the plant and animal life makes a comeback."

Senator Collins glared at Alexander, arms crossed in front of her. Finally, she said, "Thank you for your responses. My staff will continue to review what we received and get back to you."

"Thank you, Senator." Alexander exhaled, glad that the interrogation was over, at least for now. He moved on to the remaining questions from the other Joint Committee members. Softballs, thankfully. Chairman Willoughby provided closing remarks, struck the gavel, and adjourned the hearing.

As for Senator Collins' staff reviewing the software and impact reports, Alexander wasn't worried. The best scientists worked for industry, universities, national labs, and, of course, organizations like AAER. Capitol Hill staffers were political operatives first and foremost. He smiled to himself. *Bring it on, Sam-I-Am.*

***

Dara knocked on Dmitri's door at the residential hotel where he had been living during his stint at AAER. The week before, they had planned to get together for Thai food. She hadn't seen him at work in a couple of days and her texts went unanswered, but without a firm cancellation, Dara assumed their plans were still a go.

She debated asking Jason Houseman if Dmitri had called in sick but decided against it. Their relationship still wasn't public. At times like these, Dara would wonder if she could even call what they had a relationship. In any case, she didn't want to be one of "those" women who needed to know where their boyfriends were at all times. She banged harder on the door. No answer.

She went to the parking lot to look for the car Dmitri had leased, but it was nowhere to be found. Maybe he turned it in for an upgrade?

Not knowing what else to do, Dara found a sofa in the lobby of the building. 'i'm here. where are u?' she texted. She attempted to read the book she'd downloaded onto her phone, but too many unsettling thoughts encroached. *Was he sick? Or just rude? Maybe he was picking up groceries or gasoline? Maybe he forgot about their plans? Maybe he was seeing someone else?*

She sat for at least an hour, staring at her phone, not reading emails or websites, waiting for a reply. Wondering about Dmitri's whereabouts soon shifted to assessing what she might have done or said to cause a rift. Getting stood up sure felt like some sort of division. But then again, 'rift' presupposed that they were a couple, that there was a bond between them. Maybe there wasn't.

Tears stung Dara's eyes. She knew this feeling, the sense that someone was slipping away. But she also knew, deep down, that there was only one remedy, at least for tonight. Leave. *Whatever he's going through isn't about me*, she told herself. And even if it was, all he needed to do was tell her he didn't want to see her, that he had other plans, that he had someone else, that he needed space.

Perhaps just for tonight, or perhaps for the foreseeable future — she would accept his wishes. What else could she do? Other people's feelings were not within her control, only her own. She got up and walked toward the exit.

Before she could take her leave through the glass doors, a dark apparition materialized —Dmitri, only not her Dmitri. Disheveled, ripped tee-shirt poking out under his leather jacket, stained jeans, bed head, several days' worth of stubble covering his now haggard-looking features. He reeked of smoke, alcohol, body odor.

Dmitri stopped in his tracks. "Oh," he said.

Her eyes involuntarily panned up and down, registering shock at his appearance, alarmed at how bloodshot his eyes were. "Don't worry, I'm going home," she said, shaking her head, moving as fast as she could out the door, toward her car.

As she reached for the car door handle, she felt a hand grip her arm.

"I said I was leaving. Let me go."

"No, I need to talk to you."

"Not like this." Adrenaline masked how roughly he had grabbed her. A red welt developed, coloring the scar tissue on her forearm.

Dmitri only dug in harder, then started dragging her toward the lobby.

"No!" Dara yelled, and pushed him off as hard as she could with her free hand.

Inebriated and unsteady, he fell to the curb.

Every muscle in her body contracted at the sight of all six feet two of him splayed out on the pavement.

Dara scanned the parking lot, then turned her attention back to Dmitri when it was clear that no one else was there. The last thing she wanted was to attract attention, as if witnesses would render what just happened true. Without them, there was still a chance that it was only a nightmare.

But the pain from the welt grew. This was no dream. "Are you okay?" she asked, concerned that she might have seriously injured him.

"I-I'm okay," he said, slurring.

She sat down on the curb next to him, but changed her mind and stood, worried he might try to grab her again. "Look," she said, peering down at him, voice quavering, "you need help."

Dmitri's eyes remained fixed on the ground. "You don't know anything about me."

"I know an addiction when I see one. My father has a problem. He gambles. We lost our house because of it. He told me a month ago that he started going to a support group. It's called Gamblers Anonymous. It's free and he doesn't even have to give his real name."

"I d-don't need anything like that."

"Well, I think you do. I care about you. Your drinking is going to ruin your life and your health. Alcoholics Anonymous could help you."

Then Dmitri glared at Dara, brows knit. "My problem isn't drinking. My problems make me drink."

"What problems?" she asked, voice softening, recalling analogous conversations with Avery.

He continued to stare at her but said nothing.

"You're young, you're smart, and when you're not killing yourself with booze, you're healthy. You have an amazing job, and people respect you. I don't understand what's wrong."

As Dara spoke, Dmitri's head bowed. At first, she thought he was laughing at her, but then she realized he'd broken into sobs. Finally, he wiped his eyes with the back of his hand, and, with considerable effort, got up off the curb. "I need to go inside."

It was all Dara could do to stand her ground. "I'm not coming with you," she said, "I only want to talk to you when you're sober."

Dmitri eyes were pleading now. But he just said, "Do what you want."

She wanted to stay, to understand what he was going through. To hold him in her arms and say it would all be all right. But she knew from experience that coddling an addict would only hurt him—and herself in the long run.

"Take care," she said, avoiding eye contact. Dara got into her car and drove off. When she knew that she was no longer in Dmitri's field of vision, she pulled over and dissolved into tears.

***

Breaking news: the Climate Action Act (CAA) passed in the House. Dara, watching the evening broadcast with her father over baked tilapia, fully expected the bill to clear its first hurdle. Avery knew it was a triumph for Dara but pretended he didn't.

She smiled. "It's okay, Dad," she said. "I can't say much about it, but I think you've probably guessed."

Avery recalled his daughter just a few years ago, green streaks in her hair, braces on her teeth, presenting an early version of the software at a national high school science fair competition. She won first prize and a full tuition scholarship to Chambers. And now this. "I'm proud of you, sweetheart," he said.

"Thanks, Dad."

The anchorman segued to various talking heads, each providing commentary. "Representative Lynch, please share your thoughts."

"I'd like to thank my colleagues in the House on both sides of the aisle for supporting the bill," he said in his trademark Southern twang. "We've had some rough years, but now we have hope for the future."

"Thank you, sir. I hear you're planning a countdown party if the bill gets through the Senate."

"You betcha," he replied.

"And now we turn to Dr. Jane Canton, an expert in geo-engineering from Chambers University. Dr. Canton, thank you for joining us today."

"Thank you for having me," she replied.

Avery rolled his eyes. "Good lord, are we going to have to see her on TV every time they talk about this bill?" He squinted at the screen. "What the hell did she do to herself?"

Noticeably nipped and tucked, Jane now looked like a younger yet more severe version of herself. "Face lift, probably," said Dara. "That line between her eyes from scowling all the time is gone, so I'm guessing she also drank a jug of Botox."

"Tell us about the plan, Dr. Canton. Critics have grave concerns about potential damage to the ecosystem. What do you have to say to them?"

Jane apparently received media training in addition to the facial overhaul. She smiled broadly, looked into the camera. "John, I understand the tendency to fear big ideas. People were afraid of the telephone, television, the Internet, space travel, everything we take for granted today. Marconi got referred to an insane asylum when he requested funding for wireless transmission. Can you imagine life without radio nowadays? Geo-engineering is just one more technological breakthrough that could help us as a society. Given the dire straits we're in, we'd be foolish to ignore it."

Avery had enough. "I agree with her and I still would rather cut off my ears than hear her talk. Could we please change the station?"

"Sure," Dara said between bites of tilapia.

Subsequent channels showed different perspectives on the day's breaking story. In one, a group of college students discussed their upcoming plans for Spring Break – a trip to Florida where a massive 'Let's Get Bombed' pre-party was being planned. The promoters had already printed tee-shirts for the occasion depicting a silkscreened mushroom cloud with the words, 'We've Got This' emblazoned underneath. The back of the shirt read, 'Let's Get Bombed! Daytona Beach, FL.'

Another news clip showed schoolchildren writing letters to their senators as part of a civics lesson, asking them to pass the CAA. Still another featured an interview with a corporate executive who claimed he was kicking himself for not investing in the modeling technology when he had the opportunity. Dara knew exactly who the man was, recalling her trip to Chicago last year to pitch to his company — with fresh hell in tow in the form of Jane Canton. Jane barely let Dara talk, and the CEO soon lost patience with them. He apparently forgot that part, but Dara hadn't.

The entire day felt surreal. A quick text of congratulations arrived from Jericho. Alexander suggested a celebratory lunch to mark their victory in advance of the next round of hearings before the Senate. Dara's father bought lemon custard frozen yogurt for dessert, her favorite.

But overall, the proceedings felt...anticlimactic. Radio silence from Dmitri, although he eventually returned to the office looking a bit more like the Dmitri who gave her the diamond necklace. Dara didn't have the heart to wear it given what had happened the other day, at least not until he explained himself. That seemed unlikely. He might never speak to her again at this rate.

***

After the CAA successfully passed in the House of Representatives, the majority party of the Senate, led by surrogates for President Donahue, had every intention of ramming the bill through their own house of Congress as quickly as possible. A favorable vote appeared likely, since senators on both sides of the aisle enthusiastically supported it. Sam-I-Am Collins was the holdout.

Senator Collins made every attempt to rally others in her party and stage a filibuster. Appearing on the Sunday morning talk shows, her message filtered through: 'This is a bad idea.' But there were thousands of lines of code, millions of permutations of potential results depending on which coordinates they selected for the detonation. There simply wasn't enough time for an independent review of the independent review.

"What exactly are you worried about, Senator?" queried a blow-dried talk show host. "In the last century, the United States government tested and detonated nuclear weapons in many parts of the world, including Alaska. The ecosystem survived. There were no long-term repercussions. In this century, instead of wiping Bikini Atoll off the map for military purposes, we would eliminate geological obstructions to restore our environment. The benefits are spelled out in the independent analysis." He held up a paper copy of the study as if Senator Collins had never seen it.

In the classified version of the study, five sections of the Alaska Range, part of the American Cordillera, were named as potential targets. The land belonged to the government, so the government held all the cards. Still, the atmospheric scientists who understood the movements of the Polar Jet Stream and other weather patterns weren't well-versed in the intricacies of probabilistic risk analysis, at least not at the levels required to extrapolate the long-term results of geo-engineering applications. Sam Collins knew that the person who wrote the software developed a brand-new approach to climate simulation, something analogous to Beethoven's Symphony No. 9 or Mozart's Symphony No. 41 in its inventiveness, integrating atmospheric science, nuclear physics, seismology, and advanced PRA. The programmer obviously devoted many years to the task. Senator Collins surmised that deciphering it would be akin to translating the Rosetta Stone.

Indeed, her science advisor had been working non-stop in an attempt to reverse-engineer the data, but there was no way he'd beat the clock. Sam Collins voiced her frustration live on TV, her trademark cool nowhere in sight.

"Have you lost your damn mind?" she replied to the talking head. "We need to debate this initiative. We need time to fully understand what we can expect long-term. I don't care what the Chambers University team had to say. That's just one viewpoint."

"But facts are facts," he replied. "The study thoroughly covers all possible scenarios."

"With all due respect, you only know what's public."

"It's good enough for the vast majority of your colleagues in the Senate."

'Well, they've lost their damn minds, too." Sam Collins was in no mood to be patronized.

The reporter's eyebrows were halfway up his forehead by the time the interview was over. Minutes later via social media, Senator Christopher Willoughby, one of the bill's sponsors, demanded an apology from Senator Collins. But all he got was a curt message saying, "I stand by what I said."

Sam-I-Am's TV exchange made for spirited water cooler talk Monday morning. Dara wished she could reach out and explain her methods but knew Alexander wouldn't allow it. His team at CIA worked on the Congressional inquiries; she just played the grease monkey back at AAER.

Indeed, programming was lonely work — even more so now that Dmitri was avoiding her. Not that she could talk to him about her triumphs, anyway. Ultimately, the bill sailed through the Senate virtually unopposed. The final step would be for President Donahue to sign it, a foregone conclusion.

From her desk, Dara could see Dmitri at his, talking to one of the other scientists. The afternoon sunlight filtering through the window brought out the reddish glints in his hair. Dara wished she could run her fingers through it and hear him say her name again.

A knock on the door snapped her out of her daze. Kayla Tripp-Decker stepped into her office. "Hi, Dara," she said, giving the room the once-over. Thanks to Dara's now-entrenched tea habit, she wouldn't get a lecture about the dangers of Coca-Cola this time.

"Hi." Dara tried to find an out-of-place hair, chipped fingernail, or stray thread on Kayla's person, to no avail. "What can I do for you?"

"I'm collecting money for a going-away party we're planning for the end of the month. Can you contribute? The suggested donation is five dollars. We're getting cake, a card, maybe a small gift. But don't say anything. It's a surprise."

"Sure," said Dara, reaching into her purse and finding five singles. "Who's it for?"

"The Russian guy, Dr. Ivanov."

***

The signing of the Climate Action Act into law may have been a foregone conclusion, but President Donahue knew that without involving the fourth estate, implementation might lose steam. The public needed to know and the media needed to keep reminding them. The President would use the CAA and the 24-hour news cycle to his — and his poll numbers' — advantage, starting today.

Alexander surprised Dara, along with several members of his staff, with passes to watch the signing in the Rose Garden at the White House. They'd stand anonymously in the background in secret celebration, the ghosts responsible for the machine.

Dara recognized members of Alexander's team in the security line: his administrative assistant, tech officer Randall Swanson, and a few others from the State of the Union party. She went through each checkpoint, feeling her stomach tighten at the sound of German shepherds panting behind a screen at the penultimate gate.

Brisk weather today, but at least the sun was out. The White House Rose Garden was more of a tulip and daffodil affair this time of year. March had gone out like a lion in Washington, with wintery temperatures lingering into April. The children bundled up in winter coats for the annual Easter Egg Roll on the White House lawn just one week prior. Dara tried to get away with a wool suit jacket, but now against the elements she wished she had followed the kids' lead.

There were other familiar faces besides Alexander's party guests, recognizable not because Dara knew them personally but because they were Nobel Prize-winning physicists and climate change scientists. President Donahue's handlers invited them because they registered support for the program.

Alexander walked over to Dara, all smiles. "Congratulations. It's like a mini-Manhattan Project in here."

"Can I be Madam Curie?" she asked.

"But of course, *mon chéri,*" he replied in a goofy French accent.

Dara laughed. "You can be Robert Oppenheimer."

"I'll need to brush up on my Sanskrit," he said, referring to the father of the atomic bomb's polymath proclivities. Turning a bit more serious, he added, "You realize these laureates are here because they want in, right?"

"What do you mean, 'in?'"

"If the administration is going to start admitting that climate change is real, these folks want a piece of the research money. They'll have you to thank."

It wasn't clear if Duh-nahue would publicly embrace climate change as a real phenomenon vs. the will of the people, but signing the bill was as close as anyone from the majority party had ever come. That was progress. Dara smiled at the thought.

But not for long. In the front row, decked out in a hot pink suit, Dara spotted none other than Jane Canton, the original scientist who wanted "in." Oh, well, at least Dara didn't have to stand next to her.

After his press secretary's introduction, the President emerged, a beige and navy blue blur from Dara's vantage point. Glossy salt and pepper hair, American flag lapel pin, shiny shoes — the image soon came into focus. Camera clicks broke through the white noise of DC traffic. Showtime.

The President thanked the press secretary, then joked, "Given the chilly weather today, maybe we should call the whole thing off." Everyone laughed.

He delved into his speech: "My fellow Americans, we're here today to sign the Climate Action Act into law, a historic bill that passed almost unanimously in both houses of Congress." The crowd broke into spontaneous applause before the President could even complete his sentence.

Donahue smiled, allowing the interruption. "Bipartisan support is definitely something to applaud in this day and age. It speaks to the importance of this bill and what it stands for."

With every cheer from the audience, Dara allowed the victory to sink in. Her idea, her creation, her triumph. Whatever happened, no one could take this away from her, not even the woman in shocking pink down in front.

"We will work with the Congress to select a Detonation Day. My hope is to declare it a national holiday so we can always remember the day we made our country great again." He turned to his flack. "Let's do this."

She handed him the ceremonial pen, which he used to sign the act in his trademark loopy script. Photographers swarmed as the Nobel laureates gathered around the President and the EPA Administrator, mugging for the cameras, patting each other on the back. Mission accomplished.

The show ended, and Dara hurried to catch her train back to AAER headquarters. As a bonus, she got onboard before Jane could spot her. Safely on the Metro, a couple of texts popped up on Dara's phone. One said, "Proud of you, sweetheart! Love, Dad." The other one said, "Now I get to watch u on tv – go get 'em reg!" Silence from Dmitri, but Dara wasn't going to let that spoil her extraordinary day. She had every intention of remembering it for the rest of her life.

***

*B*oom.

Huh?

Boom, boom, boom. The sound of a demented heartbeat invaded Dara's sleep.

Still dark. Still sleeping. Maybe dreaming? Not sure.

Buzzzzzzzzz. The doorbell rang, sounding more like a power tool. Dara half-opened her eyes. Three twenty-eight a.m. according to the clock radio. Did Avery forget his keys? His shift didn't end until seven. But he would have called.

Buzzzzzzzzz. The neighbors? Maybe the building was on fire and the smoke detectors weren't working.

The thought bolted Dara upright. Wearing a Tyrannosaurus Regina tee-shirt, she found some sweatpants and hoped whomever it was wouldn't notice the dried zit cream on her face. "Yes?" she asked without opening the door.

"It's me," said a deep voice in a half-whisper.

Dmitri. No calls or texts for weeks, avoiding Dara at work at every turn – and now he shows up on her doorstep at 3:28 a.m.

"I'm sober, I promise."

Dara wasn't having it. "Look, tomorrow's a work day. I can't just show up when I want, like you. I'm going back to bed, and you should go home."

"I need to talk to you. It's important." The half-whisper morphed into a pleading half-growl.

Be firm. Don't cave. "No, Dmitri. The time to talk is not during the middle of the night. Next time, you call first."

"I'm going back to Russia."

Dara's hands clenched. "I already knew that."

Silence for a moment. Finally, the half-growl morphed back into a whisper, catching part way in Dmitri's throat. "Dara, please let me in."

She sighed. He wasn't leaving. He didn't sound drunk, at least. She opened the door. The lamp would stay off — too bright for this time of night. And she really didn't want a good look at him given what his motives might be, knowing her own weaknesses in the face of them. The nightlight would suffice. "Okay. You can come in for a just for a minute, but then you'll have to go."

He entered the apartment, arms crossed, warding off the dead-of-night chill. Dara motioned for him to sit on the sofa. "I won't stay long," he said. "My flight leaves at ten o'clock. I still have to finish packing."

What? Kayla said his departure was at the end of the month. Dara didn't want to let on what she knew, but, then again, what did it matter?

"I thought you were leaving later this month," she said. "Did you tell Jason?"

"The embassy will. Nobody knows yet, just you."

"Why are you cutting your assignment short?"

Dmitri stared at the floor, silent.

Dara's voice sharpened. "You've been ignoring me. You didn't even call me to tell me you were coming tonight, let alone leaving the U.S. all of a sudden. Why?"

Dmitri's head fell into his hands.

Dara relented. Everything about Dmitri's demeanor looked broken, even in the darkness. It wasn't like him to slump in despair, certainly not when he had his wits about him. "Dmitri, I'm sorry I said you were an addict, but I was worried. I still am. I still don't know if you have a problem or not. Is that why you're going back to Russia?"

"Dara, I'm not addict. I swear."

She could see the pleading look in his eyes. "Please tell me what's wrong."

He reached for her hand. Dara pulled it back. She hadn't touched him in what felt like eons but knew precisely where one touch could lead. No. She needed answers first.

Finally, Dmitri whispered, "I know something. I am not supposed to tell you. I don't know what to do."

"If it affects me," said Dara, "you need to tell me."

"It does." He looked away.

"Tell me."

Dmitri hesitated. After a long silence, he finally said, "Dara, do you trust your boss?"

"You mean Alexander?"

"Yes."

Thoughts raced through Dara's mind. Did Dmitri even know Alexander? Why would he mention him? "What does my boss have to do with anything?" she asked.

"Everything," he said.

"Everything, how?"

"It's about your climate simulation program."

She stiffened. "I can't talk to you about anything that's classified. You know that."

"I know." He continued speaking in a whisper. "I found out something, something bad. Your boss is manipulating your software."

Dara stared at Dmitri. "What are you saying?"

"Alexander is using different coordinates than the ones you recommended."

Dara continued staring, her words not catching up to her thoughts.

"Someone named Swanson is running tests using alternate longitudes and latitudes for detonation. If they use those coordinates, the results would be devastating for sections of Asia, half of China, and much of Russia."

Dara grasped for words. "What do you mean, 'devastating?'"

"Land would become uninhabitable. Part of my country would become...wasteland."

She shook her head. "Alexander is a good man. He wouldn't do that."

"He would. I'm sorry, but he would."

Nausea swept over Dara's body. She got up from the couch, realization sinking in. "You expect me to believe you? Your country roots for America's failure. Is this some scheme to keep us from succeeding?"

But Dara wasn't finished, a quaver coming to her voice as she continued. "And is that why you decided to be with me? Did you target me for information? I opened myself up to you — my body, my heart. How dare you do this?"

Dmitri looked up at Dara, his face contorted. "I'm sorry I hurt you. I --"

"No wonder you drink so much. You're a professional liar. How do you live with yourself?"

"I'm sorry."

"Does anyone know you're here?"

"No. That's why I haven't been calling you, to protect you."

"Protect me? Don't do me any favors."

"It's treason for me to be here. I'm not supposed to tell you."

"I don't believe you. Not a single word. You're a snake. Did you personally do the analysis?"

"No, my government did."

"Sorry to break the news to you, but the Russian Federation isn't a paragon of integrity. Do you honestly trust your government?"

Dmitri was glaring at Dara now. "Do you honestly trust yours?"

Bile crept up her esophagus as she struggled to keep her voice down. "Well, one thing's for sure, I don't trust you. You need to leave."

Dmitri could only shake his head. "I'm sorry."

"Stop apologizing," she said through gritted teeth. "I don't care, and I don't believe you."

He stood up, tried to take Dara's hand, but she yanked it away. Tears now streamed down her face, stinging over the benzoyl peroxide. "Don't touch me," she snapped. "God, how could I be so stupid? Dmitri's not even your real name, is it?"

He walked toward the door to let himself out, but not before turning back to her. "You're right. It's not," he said, his eyes brimming over.

As the door closed, Dara crumpled to the floor, shaking, shell shocked.

T-minus Five

Holed up in her room for several days, little interest in food, calling in sick to work, loud sobs, louder music — it was clear to Avery that something bad had happened to Dara. The dirge-like nature of the songs blaring through the walls suggested heartbreak. Strange — it wasn't her usual punk rock but classical music in a deathly minor key. Dara hadn't been with 'that Russian guy' for very long, but based on the giant rock around her neck, Avery surmised the relationship had grown serious.

Since joining Gamblers Anonymous, Avery had read up on psychology, specifically Elisabeth Kübler-Ross's five stages of grief – denial, anger, bargaining, depression, acceptance. After Avery's wife Anne died, he hovered between stages one and two for years, gambling away his feelings. Dara became the adult in the family, making sure the house was clean and getting herself to school on time. She didn't have the luxury of grief during her tween and teen years with a barely functioning father around.

That changed when she lost both her relationship with Jericho and her dream of finding an investor for her software within the space of a year. Dara fell into a depression, one that only recently had lifted. Avery worried that she'd fall back into old patterns since her heart hadn't fully mended from the first time it had broken.

What to say? He had no idea, so he decided to say it with soup. Dara's favorite was beef barley, and Avery's version was the very definition of comfort food, made with zero shortcuts. He crafted his own broth with bones from the butcher plus snippets of vegetable ends, peels, onion skins, and anything else he could throw into a pot for several hours and then strain away for maximum flavor. He cut up and slowly simmered the meat, soaked the barley, sliced and sautéed celery, carrots, and onion, poured in tomatoes he had canned himself during the summer; and added his special combination of bay leaves, garlic, and seasonings, plus the secret ingredient, sriracha, just enough to bring out the flavor without being overpowering. After the lengthy prep time, the soup required at least two hours on low heat for the barley and vegetables to get tender.

The beef and tomato aromas wafted through the apartment, through the halls of the building, and into Dara's bedroom — but still no sign of Dara. When his creation was ready, Avery decided to serve it in his special soup tureen and bowls, the ones with lion head handles. Cloth serviettes, napkin rings, candles – why not? Anything to make his daughter feel better.

But she still wouldn't emerge from her room. Time to take action. Avery tapped on her door and said in a quiet voice, "Dara, I made beef barley soup. Come have dinner."

He heard only the sad blast of music for what seemed like minutes, until a small voice responded, "I don't think so."

"Come on, sweetheart, I'm worried about you. Please come out."

Dara just sniffled.

Avery sighed. "Do you want to talk about it?"

"No."

Her 'no' was final — that much was certain. Avery knew better than to push, remembering last year when he asked her why she'd stopped wearing her engagement ring from Jericho. That line of questioning didn't end well.

"You don't need to tell me anything, sweetheart. Just come out and have some soup. It's your favorite, and you have to admit that no one makes better beef barley soup than your old man."

No response.

He continued, cajoling in a singsong: "I guarantee you'll feel better with a little comfort food in your stomach. Please?"

To Avery's surprise, Dara turned off the stereo and opened the door. She stood before him in pajamas, eyes red, skin blotchy and tear stained.

"That's my girl! Come on. I even got you sourdough bread from the bakery."

She started sobbing, covering her face with her hands. It was all Avery could do not to tear up in sympathy. He pulled her into his arms. He had served as both her mother and father for so many years now, usually poorly, and still felt he had no idea of what he was doing in either capacity. "You cry as long as you need to," he said. "You'll be fine. I promise."

"I don't think so, Dad. Not this time."

"I know it feels awful right now. But you're young, you're smart, you're pretty, you have your whole life ahead of you. Whatever happened, don't worry about it."

She gulped, nodded.

"Right now, you've got your favorite soup waiting for you. Dry your eyes and let's focus on that."

"Okay."

Avery led Dara into the kitchen, noticing a hint of smile on the corners of her lips at sight of the table he'd set.

"Now that's more like it," he said, filling her bowl with soup, hoping for her speedy return to the land of the living.

***

Dara resumed her day-to-day activities, although a couple of weeks passed before she removed Pyotr Tchaikovsky's

Symphony No. 6 in B minor from her playlist. Known as *Pathétique*, Dmitri told her the story of how Tchaikovsky dedicated the symphony to his nephew, with whom he carried on a secret love affair. Loneliness and regret pulsed through every note. Dara knew how the composer felt.

On her commute to AAER headquarters, Dara dismissed any notion that Alexander was in some way manipulating her data, as Dmitri had claimed. Music was always the answer to blocking out unpleasant thoughts, so Dara fired up the iTunes app on her phone. Spaceman Spiff's song "Fall of a Sparrow" overtook Dara's consciousness through her earbuds:

> *Concrete hard beneath her feet*
> *It's all she can do to cross the street*
> *The sun starts to fade*

> *Starting home again she thought*
> *Once again she tried for naught*
> *Start over again*

The song's beat was tightly controlled, pinned down by a good, old-fashioned riff oozing from a Marshall stack. Deep down, Dara knew what her next move should be: get back to her beta test at work, resume her routine. Maybe call Randall Swanson? Perhaps he could tell her what — if anything — Alexander was doing.

> *No you cannot*
> *Have what you want*
> *Won't matter a bit*
> *So get used to it*

> *No you cannot*
> *Change how you feel*

Or change what's around
So change how you deal

Since signing the CAA, President Donahue proposed tentative detonation dates, all of them in August. The 'Let's Get Bombed' party-planning was underway. Dara didn't have time to waste. But then again, confronting Randall or Alexander for information could backfire. Dara didn't want to bring suspicion on herself.

Door is closed, the windows locked
Curtains drawn, the sun is blocked
The feeling creeps in

Ride it out, take it slow
Feel it all so that you know
How it comes, how it goes

So much for music as a distraction. Paralysis, helplessness, uncertainty — Dara was the one who felt *pathétique.* She wondered what ulterior motives Dmitri had for telling her such a ridiculous story, that the U.S. government wanted to turn other countries, some of them allies, into wastelands. She remembered reading about hacking scandals of the past, allegations that foreign governments had attempted to start pandemics or promote divisive presidential candidates in order to weaken the United States. Was Dmitri trying to pull the plug on the CAA so the U.S. would continue to suffer due to climate change? From Dara's vantage point, it didn't seem like much of a stretch.

Does anyone care what she knows
Or if she falls or where she goes
Her eyes start to burn

There's a special providence
In the fall of a sparrow, so it went
The leaves start to turn

God, why did she let herself fall for Dmitri? She felt used on so many levels, like a fool to trust him, to fail to see through his deception. But as with Tchaikovsky, the secrets made it worse. Hidden problems meant no one could console her. As sympathetic as Avery had been with his TLC and homemade soup, it wasn't the same as being able to share exactly what had happened, to have another human being commiserate and to feel less alone with the awful truth.

Watch the leaves swirl in the wind
Sparrows fly away but then
They come back again

Someday soon the winds will still
You'll find a way to calm the chill
Just hold on until

Chalk it up to experience. The princess had to kiss a few frogs before her prince finally appeared. Not that kisses were contracts to begin with. As that terrible poem said, you learn, you learn.

***

"Dara Bouldin?"

"Speaking." Dara wasn't used to receiving calls on the secure line from anyone other than Alexander. The unfamiliar voice startled her.

"I'm Chase Tucker, Senator Samantha Collins' science advisor. I have some questions about your climate modeling program."

Dara felt her heart rate quicken. "I have a secure email address," she said, her voice betraying the lump in her throat. "Could you please send me your questions? I'll reply as soon as possible."

"I'd rather speak with you now. We've identified several problems."

Dara hesitated. She hoped the staffer couldn't hear her pulse against the receiver. Finally, she choked out a repeat of her instruction: "Please email me your questions. That's our protocol." She read him her secure address, thanked him for his call, and hung up before her voice could give out.

She braced herself. Why were they calling her? Alexander's office handled Congressional inquiries. She could already hear Alexander chiding her, as he generally did when she expressed any doubts. "Focus on the positive," he'd say. "No one understands what you're doing — certainly not some pissant Congressional staffer."

It was already June, and they were rapidly nearing the detonation date, now set by Executive Order for August 14th. The giddiness was palpable, their own and that of the public, which had fully embraced the event as a festive celebration. Eat, drink, and be merry, for tomorrow we might not die after all. Everyone seemed convinced that the "stronger, brighter tomorrow" President Donahue promised was on its way.

Soon after the call, the questions from the "pissant" landed in Dara's inbox. Right away, she saw that he knew much more about programming than Alexander would have assumed.

***

"Rise and shine, America!"

Fat Frank's sonorous voice rang through the airwaves, never once betraying his hangover, back pain, lack of rest due to sleep apnea, GERD, or the many other physical ailments he'd complain about on the show. He was like the *idiot savant* of the obesity epidemic, falling apart in every way except his one area of proficiency.

"Today on Fat Frank's Morning Zoo we've got Kenny Jameson and Chris Singh from Total Static Head. They're going to be headlining the 'Let's Get Bombed' festival on August 14th on the Mall in DC. Guys, welcome to the show."

Frank and his team of sidekicks applauded America's newest rock and roll heroes, who recently hit number one with their psychobilly-punk song, "Iceberg." In unison, the minions broke into the chorus:

I-I-Iceberrrg, I-I-Iceberrrg
Ice so cold, it's blue like me
Ice so blue, it's cold like you!

"Pretty catchy," said Frank.

"Thank you," replied Kenny. "And thanks for having us on your show today."

"My pleasure. Congrats on your success. Now that you're number one, I can only imagine the groupie situation."

"Ooooooh" from the peanut gallery echoed through the studio.

The band mates stared at Frank, nonplussed. "Sorry to disappoint you," replied Kenny, "but we have wives at home. Chris has a brand-new baby. No groupies here."

Frank sighed. "Well, that was a trick question. We knew you were married, but we thought we'd try to trip you up. Looks like you passed. Lots of sad young ladies out there. How could you do that to them?"

Boos from the sidekicks this time, followed by guffaws.

Fat Frank continued: "So is TSH straightedge like the other bands in the Dark Reverb movement?"

"You could say that."

"I see. Well, good for you," said Frank. "We, on the other hand, are a Work Free Drug Place."

"And proud of it!" shouted one of the jocks, to raucous cheers.

Dispensing with the fluff, Frank segued to his real question. "So, we understand that you guys left Jericho Wells' record label last year. And now, Total Static Head is headlining the biggest 'Let's Get Bombed' party in the country. But Jericho and his label mates aren't playing anywhere on Detonation Day. In fact, our moles tell us not a single band from Tyrannosaurus Regina is booked. What gives?"

Kenny and Chris hesitated. Finally, Chris said, "We don't know."

"Oh, really?" said Frank. "My B.S.-o-meter thinks maybe you do know."

The sound effects crew jumped in with canned flatulence and jack-in-the-box music. "That's the sound the B.S. detector makes," said Frank, his voice wry.

Kenny and Chris remained silent. They were new to media relations, and Fat Frank had every intention of exploiting their naiveté.

"Oh, come on, you're not going to tell us? Can't you see we're trying to do some real journalism here?"

"Well, I…" Chris stopped himself.

The fart noise/jack-in-the-box music combo kicked up a notch, signaling that Fat Frank wasn't finished with the hapless young men in his studio. "You know, Jericho was here a few months ago. His lifestyle choices are even more boring than yours, by the way. He was promoting the 'Rock against Climate Change' concert on the Mall."

"Yeah, we know."

"He partnered on that cause with Senator Sam Collins. Last year, he campaigned for her election."

"And?" asked Kenny, registering his impatience.

"I read that the Senator was against the Climate Action Act. Do you know anything about that?"

"You'll have to ask her."

Fat Frank pressed on: "Do you suppose Jericho isn't playing any 'Let's Get Bombed' gigs because of his support for Senator Collins?"

"You'll have to ask him," Kenny said. "Look, we haven't seen much of Jericho since we left Tyrannosaurus Regina. TSH crossed paths with him a few times on tour, but that's it."

"Did you guys leave the label on good terms?"

Chris chimed in. "Our new label had to buy out our contract with Jericho's label, so he made a ton of money off us. That cash came out of our advance. It seems the only people making money are Jericho and our new company. Not us."

The sound effects guy rang a bell in the background: "*Ding-ding-ding-ding!*"

"Now we're talking!" shouted Fat Frank. "So, is your sellout pal Jericho toadying up to the politicos? Thinking he's Wyclef Jean? Putting politics over progress?"

"We never said that!"

"Oh, I think you did. You heard it here first on Fat Frank's Morning Zoo. Senator Sam Collins is against the CAA, and Jericho Wells is her lackey and won't play any of the Detonation Day celebrations. Well, screw him. We're getting bombed and taking our country back!"

The studio sycophants cheered, but Kenny and Chris weren't having it. "This interview is over," said Kenny. "Goodbye."

"Hey, why so serious?" Frank yelled as the band mates walked out on their interview. "We didn't even get to ask you about your original name, 'Monster Bucket!'"

Shrieks of laughter shot through the studio. "Like the popcorn?" asked one of the jocks. "God, that's terrible."

"Now I'm hungry."

"You're always hungry, boss."

"True, dat," said Frank. "Time for a commercial break, kiddos. When we come back, we're going to talk about how we can boycott Jericho Wells."

***

Dara tried to remember what she'd practiced in the mirror at home. Square your shoulders, stand up straight, project, breathe. Alexander rarely stopped by AAER headquarters nowadays, so Dara needed to make the most of today's visit. The message from Chase Tucker shook her to her core — especially given what Dmitri had said – and she wanted to clear the air.

"Alexander, we need to discuss these questions from Senator Collins' staff," she said, dispensing with her usual pleasantries about weekend activities or his kids' soccer results.

He regarded Dara from his chair, then asked her to close the door and put up the TS-SCI sign. "So, what do they want?"

"Here's what they sent," she said, handing him the printout, flipping back the red cover marked, "Top Secret."

"And?" Alexander ignored the pages in front of him.

"The coordinates for the detonation aren't where we originally discussed. I didn't participate in the congressional testimony, but you and Randall Swanson did." Dara looked Alexander in the eye. "Did you decide on different coordinates?"

"Maybe." He grinned. "What of it?"

Dara's eyebrows furrowed. Why was he smiling? "The science advisor wrote a second program extrapolating the model using your coordinates."

"I repeat, what of it?" Alexander barely kept his eye rolls in check.

"If you use those coordinates, you'll solve America's climate problems, but you'll turn sections of Asia into deserts. Parts of the northern countries would turn into Antarctica, and parts of the southern half would turn into Death Valley. Half of Russia alone would become uninhabitable, as would huge sections of China. We talked about this. Do you remember?"

"Calm down, you're overthinking again."

"No, I'm not!"

"Dara, there's no need to raise your voice."

"Are you kidding? What's going on? We can get decent results with the coordinates we discussed. What good would it do to use these? You'd ruin the lives of millions if not billions of people."

Alexander rose from his chair. "I know you're young and idealistic, and I appreciate your passion for your work. We think the coordinates we selected will do us the most good, and you need to accept that."

"What are you talking about? They won't do anybody any good," said Dara, shaking her head.

"Quite frankly, I think Sam Collins sent you bogus program results. She's against the CAA, and I wouldn't put it past her to make her team exaggerate the results to achieve her own ends."

She glared at Alexander. "I went through their extrapolation. I know what I'm talking about. I invented the software, remember? What you're planning to do would bring other countries to their knees. I think *you* need to accept *that*."

Alexander snorted. "You'll need to check your insubordination. With all due respect, this matter is above your pay grade. I fought for this country and know a thing or two about what other countries have done to us, both directly and indirectly. This conversation is over."

She stared at him, eyes wide. No. She was not going to let the matter stand. She stood up, words blurting from her mouth before she could stop herself: "If you don't stop this from going forward, I'll file a complaint with the Inspector General."

Alexander burst into laughter. "So you'd have your little say, and after a long, drawn-out process, the record would show that no one did anything unethical or against the law."

"We'll see what Senator Collins has to say about it."

"Sam-I-Am is in the minority party, so don't go running to her. She can't help you. But hey, if you want to go the whistleblower route, be my guest." His eyes shifted as he spoke.

"Okay, then," she said, folding her arms in front of her chest. "I'll leak it to the press."

"Really?" said Alexander, a bemused expression on his face. "You'd divulge top secret information? You're as good as ruined if you do that. You'd probably go to jail, or at least lose your security clearance and then your job. You'd wind up on the street. Who would hire you in this economy if you got fired? And you and I both know your dad couldn't help you."

Dara's hands balled into fists. "Leave my father out of this."

"Look, you have nothing. You have no one. I gave you a chance to make something of your life and do something for your country. You wanted to change the world, right? Well, as the leader of this program, I make the decision on which coordinates we propose. You need to get over yourself. No solution is going to be perfect. I guess it's better you learn this now rather than embarrass yourself when you're older and the bleeding heart routine isn't cute anymore."

Dara glowered. She'd had enough. She walked over to within inches of Alexander's face, not breaking eye contact. "You get the message out or I will," she said, shocked by the menace in her own voice. "It's true. I have nothing. That means I have nothing to lose. I don't care what happens to me, and I'm not backing down. I won't stand by and let you destroy millions of lives. I mean it."

Alexander's smirk disappeared. The room went cold. Dara remained in place, unblinking, knowing that if she moved even a millimeter, she'd lunge at him.

Finally, Alexander averted his eyes, shoved his papers into his briefcase. Before taking his leave, he turned toward Dara.

"You'd better think carefully before you do something stupid," he said. "Very carefully."

T-minus Four

Boycott — not ideal when an artist is on the cusp of releasing a sophomore album. Jericho Wells had been living off the grid in his West Virginia paradise, with Wi-Fi signals intermittent at best. Not that he spent much time online — his hipster accountant/office manager Jamal Roche and team of college student interns back in D.C. dealt with Tyrannosaurus Regina's finances, fan relations, and media inquiries. Jericho didn't realize a boycott was underway until several days had passed.

Since Tyrannosaurus Regina staffers wouldn't be caught dead listening to Fat Frank Esposito, Jamal didn't realize it either. Even the interns charged with tracking social media found the likes of Fat Frank too uncool and distasteful to acknowledge. The message went unnoticed and unheeded for days.

But then the record and merchandise sales for both Jericho and his label mates suddenly plummeted. Was everyone on vacation? Were they victims of rampant illegal downloading and tee-shirt pirating? Journalists started calling.

"Tyrannosaurus Regina, this is Amy speaking," said an intern, bright-eyed and rat-tailed.

"This is Dennis Cordon from the *Washington Post*," replied the baritone on the other end of the line. "We'd like a statement from Jericho Wells about the boycott."

Out of her depth, Amy transferred the reporter to Jamal, whose face fell upon hearing the B-word. "No comment," he said, hung up, and silenced the phone. A quick Internet search revealed that not only was a boycott in progress, but that petitioning against Jericho and Senator Collins had gone viral.

Jamal called Jericho, knowing full well that eight thirty a.m. was going to be a bad time. "Jericho, I'm sorry to call you this early, but something's up."

"Hmph?" replied Jericho, still half asleep.

"Fat Frank from that morning show is out to cancel you." Jamal quoted the latest sales figures and directed him to the website the D.J. had set up for the express purpose of shaming Jericho.

Where was Jennie the gold-digging publicist when you needed her? thought Jericho in a state of twilight sleep. *Oh, right — making a fortune at her new job, probably representing dictators and arms dealers.* Visions of Jennie in punk sugar plum fairy guise danced in his head.

"Jericho, you've got to wake up," said Jamal, this time with palpable urgency. "You need to make a statement to the press as soon as possible. Your revenue's down to a trickle. I don't think we can afford a pro to do PR unless you want to go through your savings."

With that, Jericho's brain processed what Jamal was trying to tell him. He bolted upright. What about the other bands? Would he be able to pay them? What about his partnership with Senator Collins? He believed in the CAA but respected her desire for further review and debate. He didn't think the two options were mutually exclusive, let alone reason to stop working together.

What to say? Whom to contact? Jericho looked around. The cabin he'd renovated, the studio he'd built in the barn just outside, the views of the mountains through the windows. Peace and quiet came at a steep price, beyond monetary. It also meant he was completely alone. Jericho thought he needed the solitude in order to duck his fans and create his art, but right now, it just felt empty.

He told Jamal he'd get back to him. Time to call Sam Collins.

***

That morning, Dara drove to work because the annual AAER All Hands Meeting had been planned, and she had promised to bake cookies. She wasn't much of a baker — in any case, Avery offered to do the job — but Kayla Tripp-Decker was a master at rallying her coworkers to participate in work events.

There was no escaping Kayla. Organizing committee, birthday party, or bake sale, she was on it like white marshmallows on Rice Krispies treats. Dara learned it was best just to put her head down and do whatever Queen Bee Kayla asked.

The aroma of chocolate chip cookies, several dozen arranged just so on a giant platter emblazoned with the Yellowstone National Park logo, permeated through Dara's Hyundai as she navigated through rush hour. The sweet scents bonded to the upholstery, her clothing, her memory.

The tray was a relic from her mother, a souvenir from a long-ago vacation they had taken as a family. Most Friday nights her mother would pull out the tray and go on a cookie-baking spree – usually oatmeal raisin, but, at times snickerdoodle. Dara recalled her mom, smiling and apple-cheeked in her red checkered apron. The tray survived the fire because Anne Bouldin stored it in the oven's built-in drawer.

Dara wished she'd had more pictures of her mom. Most of them succumbed to the flames. In any case, there weren't many to begin with, either on paper or online, since Anne usually was taking photos rather than posing for them.

Dara hadn't smiled much since yesterday following her confrontation with Alexander. Didn't sleep much, either. What to make of it all? Was Chase Tucker serious? Maybe Alexander was right and Senator Collins ordered her staff to manipulate the data to suit her own purposes.

But maybe he was wrong. Dara wondered if she should ask for a transfer to another assignment. Still, the prospect of entire countries turning to dust demanded action. But what?

She knew that calling the Inspector General or leaking information to the press might result in zero changes and at worst, get her into trouble. Alexander was right about the fate of leakers. Some went to jail. Some left the country. All ended up with ruined careers, despite lip service that the government protected allegers. The ghosts of whistleblowers past came to mind: Snowden, Manning, Silkwood. Dara wanted no part of that graveyard.

Then again, Dmitri expressed the same concerns as Senator Collins. He was the last person Dara wanted to consider, but she had to, in hopes that retracing steps would yield answers. After all, Dmitri mentioned Randall Swanson's name. Dara only knew of Swanson's involvement because she had met him in person at Alexander's State of the Union party. If Dmitri had unearthed that information, he likely knew the rest of the story. None of this could have been a coincidence.

That settled it. It wasn't enough to request a transfer. The program had to be stopped, and people needed to know the truth. Dara's stomach clenched at the thought, realizing what she had to do.

She tried to calm herself. Reporters were always looking for tips. Isn't that what happened so many years ago during the Watergate scandal? Bob Woodward and Carl Bernstein succeeded in bringing down President Nixon, and history remembered them as heroes. Decades later, Nixon's election hijinks seemed like a fraternity prank compared to what amounted to Climategate, the weaponization of the environment.

Reporters went to jail to protect their sources, so maybe she could remain anonymous, or at least plausibly deny any accusations that she was responsible for the leak. The stakes were simply too high to remain silent. She resolved to track down and call the right people in the media, today. She entered her building through the parking garage, formulating in her mind what she'd say.

Tossing her jacket and backpack on her desk, Dara brought the tray of cookies to Kayla to take to the auditorium. The assembly started in a half hour, so in the meantime she pretended to check her work email while sneaking glances of online newspaper mastheads on her phone. *The Washington Post, New York Times, Politico...*

When the time came for the All-Hands Meeting, she started for the auditorium. Blurred images came to mind — her mom at Yellowstone, her dad in the kitchen last night, the last look from Dmitri before he walked out. She approached the door of the auditorium, flanked by other AAER staffers, shiny plastic ID badges draped around their necks.

"Ms. Bouldin?" A young man Dara didn't know stopped her before she could enter the meeting.

"Yes?" He carried a walkie-talkie.

"I'm William Lopez. There's an urgent meeting you need to attend. Follow me."

She hesitated. "Is everything okay?"

"No emergencies or anything like that," he said.

"What's the meeting about?" Dara asked, feeling her body freeze up.

"You'll receive the details when we get there." He began walking. She followed, her body now on autopilot, her head spinning.

He led her to a small conference room not far from her office. Two women she recognized from the Personnel Security office sat at the table.

One of the women, Teresa Ingalls, motioned for her to sit down. "Ms. Bouldin, we've called you in today because we've received derogatory information that impacts your security clearance. As a result, we are taking the action to indefinitely suspend you."

Dara could only stare.

"In this folder is a letter containing the Statement of Reasons for your suspension."

She focused on the blue folder placed in front of her for what felt like several minutes. Finally, Dara heard herself say in a small voice, "What did I do?"

"It's explained in the letter."

She opened the folder. Snippets of text sprang off the page: '...Russian national identified as an agent...' '...sexual relationship...' '...gifts...' '...close and continuing contact...' '...did not follow reporting procedures...' '...single, lonely, introverted...' '...in debt...' '...vulnerable...' Her hands clenched.

Dara cleared her throat. "I didn't do anything wrong."

"You can appeal," said the woman sitting beside Ms. Ingalls. "The procedures are specified in the letter. We will continue to pay you for thirty days."

"My boss told me that I needed to socialize with my coworkers. A couple of people even married each other."

The women exchanged glances while William Lopez stared at his hands. "You had a close and continuing relationship with a foreigner, and you didn't report him."

"I only saw him a few times. Plus, he worked with us in our office. We were told to treat the visiting scientists like everyone else because they'd been vetted, just not to let them on the LAN or share any sensitive information."

Ms. Ingalls furrowed her brows, pulled out a photograph from another folder. The photo depicted Dara, in her striped hair, transparent blouse, and silver jeans, engulfed in Dmitri's arms in front of his apartment after Jericho's show.

The other woman said, "You also accepted at least one gift from him that you didn't report." From her folder, she pulled out a copy of a receipt from a jewelry store and a grainy image of Dmitri making the purchase. Another picture in her collection showed Dara wearing the diamond necklace over her off-black Chambers U sweatshirt, taken at Alexander's party on the night of the State of the Union Address.

"We understand that you referred to the Russian who gave you the necklace as your 'boyfriend.'"

Electrical impulses fried Dara's synapses. "He isn't."

The woman bristled. "An appeals process is described in the letter. For now, Mr. Lopez will escort you off the premises."

"What about my projects? Or my personal items?"

Mr. Lopez chimed in. "We'll stop by your desk and pick up any belongings."

Her mom's tray. She looked away. "I brought some cookies for the assembly today. Can I leave a message for someone to save my tray for me?"

Ms. Ingalls' face betrayed an incredulous look. "You are not to speak to any of your coworkers." Now openly smirking, she added, "I'm sure you can live without your tray. You have more pressing issues to concern yourself with right now."

Dara went numb.

"Any further questions, Ms. Bouldin?"

She shook her head. Mr. Lopez rose, nodded at Dara to follow him. Once at her desk, Dara found an empty box on the floor.

Personal records, pictures of Albert Einstein and Marie Curie, her electric teapot, collection of teas…no access to the computer, though. Her work was no longer hers. It probably never was, at least not after she gave it away to the government.

"I'll need your badge, Ms. Bouldin." Dara handed it to him, taking one last look at her ID picture. The ghost image, now the ghost.

Mr. Lopez offered to carry the box to her car. She put on her jacket and slung her backpack over her shoulder, requiring a few tries because her entire body trembled. "If you forgot something," he said, "we can make arrangements for you to come by after hours or on the weekend to pick it up."

Dara pictured the cookie tray, bright yellow, embossed with colorful graphics of woodland creatures dancing around stylized letters spelling out "Yellowstone." She fought the quiver that came to her lips.

Escorted to the garage, Dara got into her car. Lopez eyed her every move, spoke into the walkie-talkie that spat back static. She started the engine, her hands operating on muscle memory. Her escort motioned for her to go.

As she drove around the garage levels, Dara spotted other security officers talking into radios, glaring at her car as it passed. Just drive, she told herself. The parking garage door, the road outside, red stop signs, double yellow lines, city buses, taxis — everything around her swirled.

She made it home, nearly missing the turn onto her own street. Empty apartment, empty bed. She removed her jacket and shoes, pulled the covers over her head. Waves of nausea stopped short of triggering a gag reflex, leaving her dizzy, unwell, screaming into her pillow.

***

"Dara?"

Avery returned to the apartment from his overnight shift at the Slot Lot, realizing that his daughter was still in her bedroom. He tapped on the door as quietly as he could. "Are you going to work today?"

Minutes passed. Avery was about to repeat the question when Dara finally spoke. "No," she said in a hoarse voice.

"Are you sick? Do you want me to call the doctor?"

Silence, then, "No."

Avery shook his head. He knew she'd been upset over breaking up with Dmitri, but he thought she had moved on, at least enough to get herself to the office. The reemergence of sobs through the wall told another story. "Sweetheart, I'm worried," he said. "Please tell me what's wrong."

"I don't want to talk about it," she said, louder this time.

Avery tried the knob, but the door was locked. "Dara, help me out here. You're scaring me."

No response. Avery leaned against the door. Now he heard nothing: zero movements, zero breathing. He debated kicking it in. At a loss, his voice cracked past the lump in his throat. "Please," he said. "Let me help you. I'm begging you."

Moments later, the creaking of bedsprings. She opened the door, looking even paler than usual.

"There's my girl," Avery said, softly. "Will you tell me what happened?"

Dara's face contorted, her eyes darting to the floor.

"Come with me to the kitchen, I'll make you some tea."

"I never want another cup of tea as long as I live."

"Okay, how about hot chocolate?"

"A-all right."

Aromas of cocoa and vanilla extract wafted through the apartment. Dara sat at the table, staring straight ahead.

"So," Avery said, placing their mugs onto coasters. "Why are you skipping work?"

Dara's eyes remained fixed on nothing in particular. "I'm not skipping work."

"Well, you're not sick. You didn't take leave as far as I know. Why aren't you at the office?"

Dara looked at Avery this time. "I got suspended," she said, the unsteadiness in her voice telegraphing the depth of her fear.

"Suspended?" His daughter, the perfect student, the obedient kid, the good girl? He couldn't believe it.

"Yes. Believe it."

"For how long? And why?"

"Indefinitely. For dating Dmitri."

"Dmitri?"

"Because he's Russian."

"So what? Lots of people date Russians."

Dara looked back into space. "He was working for an intelligence service. I didn't know. No one did. He was part of a formal government exchange program and was collaborating with our Reactor Safety Simulation team. How could I have known what he was up to? They investigate these people for a year before they come and told us to treat him like a regular coworker."

"Sounds like Personnel Security didn't do their due diligence, and now they're blaming you."

"I wish I knew. I never talked to Dmitri about anything that wasn't public information, but they don't believe me."

"Can you do something? Can you clear this up? It sounds like a misunderstanding."

"They gave me a letter and said I could appeal, but what can I say? It's my word against theirs. I can't deny dating him — they know I did."

"Can anyone help you?"

"It says I have a right to counsel, but all the lawyers I called charge a fortune. I don't have the money." She glared at Avery. "We don't have the money."

Avery's heart skipped. "Are you being paid?"

"For twenty-nine more days. Then I'm cut off. Pretty much every job I can get with my Ph.D. and experience requires a security clearance. You need a Safeguards Clearance just for a regular nuclear engineering job. There's no way to avoid it."

"Can you get a different type of job?"

"Not one that'll pay enough to cover our debts. And being 'indefinitely suspended' isn't going to help me impress future employers, regardless of the field."

Avery sighed. He remembered the first time the security clearance process almost sunk her chances at federal employment, all due to the debts he'd incurred on their shared accounts. The feds didn't play around. Moreover, she was right about how much she would need to earn. They were just getting by with their two incomes as it was. Maybe he could ask for extra shifts dealing blackjack? Maybe they could declare bankruptcy?

Dara took a sip of cocoa. "I'm wondering if I should call Jericho. He offered to pay off some of my debts a while back. I didn't want his charity, but I'm desperate now. At least I could hire a decent attorney and fight to get my job back."

Avery's heart sank to his stomach. Jericho. The Tyrannosaurus Regina boycott. Kids on the news, burning tee-shirts and CDs. Dara apparently hadn't checked out the music blogs or celebrity gossip web pages in a while.

"Sweetheart, I don't think things are going well for Jericho right now."

She put down her mug. "Have you talked to him?"

"No. But I saw a story on the news that some D.J. organized a boycott against him."

"Why would people want to boycott Jericho Wells?"

"Because he's not playing Detonation Day. None of the bands on the label are, so everyone's been boycotted."

Dara shook her head. "That doesn't make any sense. What's wrong with not playing?"

"They think he's in Sam Collins' pocket because she's against the CAA."

"But he was everyone's hero."

"People are fickle. They love you until they don't."

Dara got up from the table. Jericho was her last hope. Halfway between the kitchen and her bedroom, she turned to her father. "You know if you hadn't ruined my life, I wouldn't be in this mess. Right?"

Avery nodded his head slowly. "Dara, I've apologized to you every way I know how. What's done is done. I'm doing everything I can to get better."

"You spent my money. You ruined my credit. You gambled away my future. You'll be fine. My life was over before it even started."

Avery looked away. His life turned to ashes a long time ago, but there was no arguing with Dara about it now. The door slammed as she stormed out of the apartment into the brisk afternoon.

***

Dara pulled the hood of her sweatshirt over her head to ward off the unseasonable chill. *Keep moving*, she said to herself. *Walk fast. Burn off energy. Think.*

She had only a few weeks until she'd lose her income. Hardly any savings since every penny went toward rent, then food, then transportation, then debt. The monthly interest amounted to more than the previous three bills combined. Avery's income was enough to cover rent plus his own expenses — provided he worked his twelve-step Gamblers Anonymous program and didn't fall off the wagon — but it barely dented the amount owed. Not that it mattered for him. A fair amount was in Dara's name only, ostensibly for student loans earmarked for living expenses, but, in reality, covering the ever-increasing credit card debt Avery had incurred.

Student loans could not be discharged in bankruptcy, and forbearance due to unemployment wouldn't stop interest from piling up. There was no way out.

Activity buzzed around her — second-shift commuters driving to work, cops directing traffic, construction workers filling potholes, retirees on fitness walks, people working or retired from working. Except for Dara, in limbo, 'indefinitely suspended.' What kind of job could she even get, since jobs that required clearances were off limits? Her nuclear engineering degree was useless, at least in the near term. Perhaps she could teach, but an academic job search would take months.

She could go to the Black Cherry Lounge and ask if they needed someone to do live sound. Or find out if any local recording studios needed tape ops or ProTools operators. Audio engineering was unlikely to produce a living wage, though, at least at the entry level. No matter. There were twenty-four hours in a day, and she was young and energetic. Babysitting, tutoring, housecleaning, waitressing — if it took a combination of jobs to pay her bills, she was willing to do it.

Send out résumés. Make some calls. Ask for help. Ask for help? Dara drew the line at reaching out to people she knew. She didn't have many business contacts, anyway. Networking was never her forte, as Jason Houseman was quick to observe. Her acquaintances were mostly government employees, and they couldn't help. They'd probably worry that speaking to her would implicate them. Jane Canton would probably just mutter 'stupid girl' under her breath and hang up on her. If Dara wasn't in a position to help Jane, Jane wanted nothing to do with Dara.

The casino probably couldn't hire her given that she was discharged over a security violation. Dara didn't want her dad to run into any guilt by association, so it was probably best to stay away.

She couldn't call Jericho, either. The more the fact of the boycott sank in, the queasier Dara's stomach felt. He took Tyrannosaurus Regina to the top of the charts and treated his label mates like family, paying for their health insurance, fighting for high guarantees for performances, and personally calling their loved ones if anyone got ill or injured on tour. Now he was being punished for doing the right thing.

Jericho wasn't a sellout. He never was. Her stomach lurched again.

She was certain that Senator Collins hadn't told Jericho the reasons behind her and Chase Tucker's disapproval of the CAA, since Jericho had no security clearance. Still, Dara wondered if Jericho suspected anything. She should at least text him to say she heard about the boycott and was thinking about him.

Dara folded her arms to keep from shivering in the unseasonable chill, realizing that she was now a couple of miles from home. Time to turn back, buck up. This was not the time to fall apart under her blankets. She'd find a job —

something to pay the bills for the short term and didn't require a security clearance for the long term.

First she would apologize to Avery. There was no reason to argue with him. He was doing his best, seeking help for his gambling addiction, taking control of his demons. She hastened her steps, taking the shortcut behind the strip mall with renewed purpose.

Her apartment complex came into view — the makeshift soccer field the neighborhood kids set up on the lawn, the bike rack, the leasing office sign, Dara and Avery's second story unit. She spotted her father at the door, talking to a tall man in a dark suit. The man pulled a badge from his pocket and held it up. Pallor washed over Avery's face as the man continued talking. Avery shook his head, his shoulders forming a shrug.

Electrical impulses skittered down Dara's back. She pulled her hood over her face as far it would go, turned on her heel, and walked as quickly as possible in the opposite direction. Not knowing what else to do, she ducked behind a truck, pretending she'd dropped something. Her peripheral vision fixed on the parking lot's exit. Several cars, several minutes passed. Finally, a gray Ford Taurus heeded the stop sign, the man in the dark suit behind the wheel.

"Did you lose something?"

Dara gasped.

"Are you all right, hon?" An elderly woman with kind eyes looked at Dara with concern.

"Oh, I'm sorry," said Dara, jumping up, her mind racing. "I dropped some change, but I found it."

"If I find any more, I'll know it's yours," the lady replied with a smile.

Dara thanked the woman as cheerfully as she could muster and sprinted back to her apartment.

***

The principals met in one of the many Sensitive Compartmented Information Facilities (a.k.a. SCIFs) in the Capitol complex. Samantha Collins and Chase Tucker sat, flanked by representatives from the Office of Congressional Affairs, the National Security Staff, the Joint Chiefs of Staff, and the Strategic Command, waiting for Alexander Fallsworth, Jane Canton and Randall Swanson to arrive.

The Senator considered initiating a media campaign against the CAA but wanted to give the CIA reps a chance to explain themselves. There could have been a mistake on either end. Chase Tucker did his best to extrapolate the program but didn't have anywhere near the expertise of the CIA team.

If there in fact was an error on the CIA end, she'd order them to fix it. If not, she'd start the grassroots campaign to end all grassroots campaigns and bring the matter directly to the American people. Or file a lawsuit in federal court. Maybe both. Either way, she'd need evidence.

Alexander and company arrived, all smiles, pleasantries, and nice-to-see-you's. Senator Collins played along, knowing perfectly well that everyone at Alexander's agency called her Sam-I-Am behind her back.

Randall set up the secure laptop. Alexander got to the point. "Senator Collins, we appreciate the opportunity to speak with you and your colleagues today. I've brought our senior programmer, Randall Swanson, with me today, along with Dr. Jane Canton, our technical consultant."

"Thank you for coming. I understand that you've reviewed the questions Mr. Tucker sent you?" said Senator Collins.

"Yes, we have. Dr. Canton is going to go through the code with you to demonstrate that your extrapolation contains several errors."

The Senator shot a look at Jane. "Errors?"

Jane stood up and walked toward the screen, laser pointer in hand, her decades as a professor in full effect. Randall pulled up in split screen Chase Tucker's extrapolation, along with a second version of the program that he, with input from Jane, had coded.

"Yes, Senator. I'm Dr. Jane Canton, and my team at Chambers University developed the original version of this software," she said, unblinking. "I'm the leading expert, or at least the leading expert who's cleared to meet with you." She grinned, not without effort due to her Juvidermed nasolabial folds.

Senator Collins nodded. "Please proceed."

"There is no way to properly extrapolate this function. Your version makes too many assumptions of smoothness. Our version uses more advanced techniques. I'll demonstrate."

At Jane's direction, Randall imported a list of data points into each version of the program. A few clicks later, he hit the Run icon. In seconds, the results were ready to view.

"We are able to show results over time for candidate longitudes and latitudes." She asked Randall to click one of the coordinates on the map icon and input a random year. Maps of Asia appeared on each side of the screen. Neon colors denoted areas and severity of drought in the first view. Others showed temperature, monsoon activity, precipitation, and other climate conditions.

The side of the screen using Chase's program showed desert conditions. Alexander nodded in the direction of the CIA version, which showed normal conditions. Chase could only stare at the result.

Senator Collins knew better than to take them at their word. "Professor Canton," she said, "Please show your work."

Jane tittered in response, but the deadly expression on the Senator's face left no doubt that she was serious. "Sure," she said. "Randall, please pull up the code so we can do a line by line comparison."

"See, here's an example of the inadequacy of your extrapolation. You've considered only data around the x equals 0 point and estimated that the function behaves as sine of x equals approximately x. Where x equals approximately 0, this is an excellent estimate. But once you start moving away from 0, the extrapolation veers almost arbitrarily from the x-axis, and your error increases without bound."

Chase Tucker slunk low in his chair, not making eye contact with the woman brandishing the laser pointer who stood smirking at him. Senator Collins knew that Chase had dotted all his i's and crossed his t's, despite coming up short.

She didn't fault Chase. She got an answer, just not the one she was looking for. Not that the Senator believed her visitors, necessarily. Especially the director with the crewcut, his glad handing cranked up to eleven.

She watched as her colleagues from the Office of Congressional Affairs bantered back and forth with the CIA group. Those entrusted with oversight of the project seemed perfectly at ease with today's briefing. They may have professed objectivity at work, but she knew they were all planning grandiose 'Let's Get Bombed' barbeques and Detonation Day parties.

Senator Collins wanted no part of it. She would remain the lone voice in the wilderness, protecting the wilderness. Congress had sponsored decades of useless, self-serving environmental policies, and now it wanted to obliterate what little remained of America's unspoiled natural resources as a Band-Aid. Regardless of what might happen in the aftermath, the scheme was wrong on its face.

There were other, more honest ways to deal with climate change — emphasis on the word 'change.' The CAA meant no one needed to change. One or two generations from now, people would wonder why their predecessors greenlit such a pernicious idea. That is, if other countries with nuclear weapons didn't answer with similar stunts. If that happened, there might not be any generations left to speak of at all.

"Meeting adjourned," she announced, tight-lipped.

***

"**D**ad?"

"Dara!" Avery pulled his trembling daughter into his arms.

"I saw someone talking to you at the door."

Avery looked at Dara. "Sweetheart, he was from the FBI. They want to bring you in for questioning. He gave me his card. Here it is -- Kyle Anson, Special Agent, Federal Bureau of Investigation."

"Oh, my God." She felt her lungs deflate.

"Dara, you didn't do anything."

Her eyes welled with tears. "I-I don't have money for a lawyer."

"They could appoint one for you if you're being charged with a crime."

"But I didn't divulge any classified information. That would be criminal, not dating a Russian." She shook her head.

"I know you didn't break the law, sweetheart." Avery reached for a tissue to dry Dara's eyes.

"What can I do?"

Avery sighed. "All you can do is wait. Find out what the agent wants. I don't know what else you can do under the circumstances."

"Is he coming back?"

"He wouldn't say. I think that means yes."

Dara felt her head pound.

"What can I do to help you?"

Silence.

"Will you eat something? You'll need your strength."

Dara shook her head. She began pacing — living room, kitchen, hallway. Several turns around the apartment later, she went to her room and rummaged through her closet. Green fabric dye. Scissors. Clothes — her real clothes, not the costumes she'd been wearing to work in recent months. Cash. She'd empty her bank account via the ATM for the rest.

She thought of cities she'd been to with Jericho, part of his tours. So-called flyover country. She could purchase a bus ticket. She didn't need a car. She didn't need a phone. She'd buy a disposable one at Walmart and pay for minutes with a phone company gift card. Use an alias. Stay in a cheap motel or youth hostel. All those cities had nightclubs. If she could get hired at the Black Cherry Lounge, she had a decent shot at venues in other towns.

Dara also knew that clubs were happy to pay in cash, under the table. That was a plus.

She'd disappear, for now. She hadn't been charged with anything. As long as she hadn't been charged, she wasn't in trouble. If they couldn't find her, she couldn't be charged.

And if she defaulted on her debt, what would it matter? She wasn't trying to buy a house or get credit, just survive. What could they do to her if she just stopped paying, anyway? Debtors' prisons and workhouses went out with Charles Dickens.

She went into the bathroom with the dye, scissors, and rubber gloves, spread newspapers on the floor, pulled off her sweatshirt. A thousand cuts later, a pile of dark curls on the newsprint, her hair spiked around her face in a ragged pixie. Next, Dara leaned over the bathtub, gloves on, and scrubbed her hair with the fabric dye, a punk rock trick she'd picked up from the lead singer of Vitamin X.

Dara styled her now-green hair using her hair dryer, then returned to her room to change clothes. She cut up an old bandana and fashioned the strips into bracelets for her right arm in the interest of covering identifiable scars. Black jeans, black top, Chucks...nothing that would identify her as a Chambers U. alumna or former AAER employee. Sunglasses at night, anonymous, cipher girl.

The diamond on her dresser caught her eye. The last thing she wanted to see. But then she remembered its value from the receipt. In a pinch, she could try to sell it — its 18-karat gold chain alone would yield a decent sum. What she really wanted to do was throw it into the ocean, like Rose in the movie *Titanic*. But turning it in for cash could help turn the negative into a positive, and she needed all the positives she could get. She put the necklace in an envelope and tucked it into the recesses of her purse.

Minutes later, she emerged from her bedroom, green-haired, duffel bag stuffed, purse strapped across her chest.

Avery gaped. "What are you doing?"

"I'm leaving."

"Where are you going?"

"Out of town. I'm going to empty my bank account. I'll stop by Walmart and get a disposable phone. The other one's going in the trash after I run it under the faucet. I'm taking the bus. You can sell my car if you want; I'm not going to need it."

"This is a bad idea. Will you at least tell me where you're going?"

"Not if you plan to breathe a word of this to anyone."

Avery shook his head. "You're not thinking straight, Dara. You can't just run away."

"Watch me."

He moved to stand between Dara and the door, his voice rising. "I can't let you do this."

"I'm not a child, Dad. I can get a job and make my own way."

Dara wasn't going to back down. Avery's voice softened. "You'll always be my child, Dara. You'll understand that when you have kids of your own."

She looked away. "I'll send you my new phone number when I have it and let you know where I am. But I might have to lie. That way, when the FBI asks you where I'm staying, you can say you don't know and mean it."

Avery sighed, slung Dara's duffel bag over one arm while hugging her with the other. "It's been a while since you had green hair," he said. "You look like my daughter again."

Dara squeezed back tightly, blinking back tears.

"Can I at least give you a ride to the bus station?"

"Okay," she said, drying her eyes with her improvised bracelet. "First I need to go to the ATM."

Avery handed Dara the cash out of his pockets – $37.86. Progress. In the past, every cent fed the slots. "Thanks, Dad." Dara's voice caught in her throat. "Sorry I yelled at you earlier. I'm proud of how far you've come. Promise me you'll stay with your program?"

"It's okay. I promise."

"Let's go before I lose my nerve."

***

Rainy day fund – four hundred and fifty dollars, less fifteen dollars for the phone from Walmart. According to the giant screen on Greyhound station's wall, the bus to Saint Louis, Missouri, left in 30 minutes. Dara remembered Jericho talking about the city. There were bound to be cheap hotels near the bus station.

Saint Louis — as good a place as any. Maybe even better. It had great music, great food, a low cost of living, and was the setting for that fantastic movie with Judy Garland she and her dad watched every Christmas after they'd gotten their fill of *It's a Wonderful Life*. Plus, it fostered a thriving radiopharmaceutical industry. She wouldn't need a clearance to work with medical isotopes. Worth a shot.

Dara used her duffel bag as a pillow, clutched at her purse. The bus station after dark was not the most wholesome of spaces. At least the one-way ticket was cheap.

Vagrants milled around. She wondered what happened to them. Had they lost all their belongings in a fire? Been evicted? Fallen prey to their own or a loved one's addiction? Gotten fired from a job without warning? Dara looked down at her sneakers, realizing she could check off all of the above. In fact, in ducking law enforcement, her situation might have been worse.

Dara vowed not to dwell on her troubles in public. Stiff upper lip. She didn't bring any electronic devices with her, couldn't risk the location features giving her away. No tunes. Instead, she listened to the music in her head, memories of songs. One by a band called Trigger Happy, on Jericho's label, came to mind.

Someplace far where nobody knows me

I'll be as free as air is there
And water falls
Leaves its mark on me
Washes away
The way that I've been
And I'll fly, and I'll fly away

How did she end up here? She did all the right things. Studied hard, worked hard...good girlfriend, good daughter, good person.

Someplace far with horizons endless
Borders lost in time and in space
I'll erase
The demons within me
Find my new life
Make my new place
And I'll fly, and I'll fly away

The bus rolled on. Dark outside; only the occasional truck stop for miles at a time. Dara's lower back registered every bump. *Just get through it,* she thought to herself, unable to sleep. *Things will get better. They have to.*

Someplace far I'll find my courage
Test this brave new spirit inside
Become a woman
Of the world of lost borders
Forgive myself and
Get on with my life
And I'll fly, and I'll fly away

An eternity later, she looked up. The sky broke into dawn, Saint Louis' Gateway Arch stretching in the distance over the horizon.

***

"Avery?"

"Speaking."

"Jane Canton."

Given her new status as a semi-public figure, Jane must have changed her number. Her phone calls now registered as "Unknown," rendering Avery unable to screen her calls. Dara's disposable phone also flashed as "Unknown," so Avery picked up, hoping to connect with his daughter. Not this time.

"Hi, Jane," he muttered.

"It's a pleasure to speak with you, too, Avery."

"I'm busy, Jane. What can I do for you?"

"Can I speak to Dara? Her phone seems to be disconnected."

Dara had been away for a week. She called Avery once, letting him know she was in Saint Louis, at a cheap hotel near the Greyhound Station. She could check her email in the hotel's "business center" (really just a desk with a lap top chained to it), but mainly communicated on the disposable phone so as not to be traced. She told Avery she was making the rounds at nightclubs, trying to find work as a sound engineer. Avery cringed at the thought of his daughter, all five feet two of her, traipsing around at night, alone in an unfamiliar city. But what could he do? She was a grown woman.

Not to mention that she had sworn Avery to secrecy. "Dara's not here," he said, hoping to end the call.

Jane pressed on. "I understand she's on leave from her job. It's okay; I'm a consultant on her project and know all about it."

"Well, then, you should know she doesn't want to talk to anyone right now."

"Avery, I care about Dara. I'm calling because every year we mark her mother's passing by donating blood together. The date's coming up soon, and I thought if she was around, we could make plans to go."

Avery didn't know this. Dara sometimes defended her, but he just chalked it up to survivor's guilt from getting her Ph.D. with Jane's support.

"That's kind of you, Jane," Avery conceded. "But she's out of town right now."

"Oh. Where'd she go?"

"I don't know."

"Is she okay financially? The admin told me she's on non-duty status. In the government, that usually means leave without pay."

Avery hesitated. Office grapevines had a way of strangling the best-laid plans. He swore he wouldn't tell anyone his daughter's whereabouts, but what if Jane were willing to help Dara?

No. He fought the temptation. Avery promised to keep his mouth shut. Besides, the last person he could ever trust was Jane.

"She'll be fine. Thanks for calling."

"Okay, but if she needs help, you know where to find me. I'll text you my new number."

Avery added it to his contacts, felt his face flush at the realization that if Dara needed financial help, he couldn't do much. He looked up Dara's motel online and confirmed the rate of $68 a night, plus tax. Even at that price, Dara would run out of money quickly if she didn't find work soon.

***

"My fellow Americans, we are standing on the precipice of history."

President Donahue addressed the nation on television in prime time. His poll numbers were up, his posts on social media were timed to generate maximum excitement, and his surrogates — the Defense Secretary, Senator Christopher Willoughby, Dr. Jane Canton — were on a non-stop media blitz. Donahue seized the moment, his speech calling to mind a victory lap.

"We cannot say for certain what we are up against with regard to the Earth's warming," he said, a nod to his fan base of climate change deniers. Donahue had no intention of rankling them. "But we can use technology to take constructive action."

Survey after survey showed that the deniers were all too happy to "get bombed," confounding even the most jaded Sunday morning talking heads. But deep down, the pundits knew. Science and opinion had merged years ago. Correlation was causation, anecdotal evidence was conclusive evidence, and believing was seeing. The deniers chose not to believe in climate change, but they did accept that geo-engineering would improve weather patterns.

The minority party, with Samantha Collins as its most vocal member, took to the airwaves to point out these disparities. "People need to understand that nothing will change unless we make sacrifices," she'd say to whomever would listen. "The CAA is putting a Band-Aid on a gaping wound."

"Senator," asked a reporter, "regardless of what people believe, we can use technology to help ourselves. Why shouldn't we try?"

"You'll be destroying the ecosystem in Alaska, for starters," replied Senator Collins.

"The majority of Alaskans and their governor are all for the CAA. They understand that desperate times call for desperate measures. Major engineering projects throughout the centuries have changed the landscape, and by and large humanity has benefitted."

"Not every time. Humanity trying to overcome nature for its own gain hasn't always succeeded."

"With all due respect, the people have spoken, and they've chosen to think positive. Where would the world be without the Panama Canal, for instance? We dug a waterway between two continents."

"What about the Aral Sea?" the Senator countered. "The Soviets diverted the rivers feeding into it to irrigate cotton fields in Uzbekistan. How'd that work out for them? Most of the sea is literally gone, the fishing industry is dead, and what's left is polluted, causing all sorts of health problems. If we're going to discuss history's man-made environmental disasters, we'll be here all day."

"We'll just have to agree to disagree," said the reporter. No matter. The 24-hour news cycle would "cleanse the palate" soon enough. Detonation Day festivities were much easier to swallow and much better for ratings. Give the people what they want.

"Friends," said Donahue on prime time TV, looking into the camera, blue eyes reflecting the overhead spotlights, "I know you're excited for Detonation Day on August 14th. As many of you know, I'll be hosting a major celebration on the National Mall. I'll also lead the detonation countdown, which we'll broadcast live. For those of you outside the Washington area, I hope you'll tune in and mark this momentous occasion with me. A brighter future awaits. God bless you and God bless America."

***

The name of the nightclub was Club Taser. Dara remembered it from Jericho's tour schedule. The capacity, typical of venues he had played at the time, was in the four hundreds — more than the Black Cherry, but not exactly Madison Square Garden. Dara's first task upon her arrival in Saint Louis was to figure out the public transportation system and locate the club on the bus route.

Approaching the bouncer at the door, Dara realized she'd never paid a cover charge in her life. She'd always been out with Jericho, usually when he or one of the groups on his label performed. Tonight was Three Bands for Three Bucks night, so at least she wouldn't have to invest too much for the chance to ask for a job.

She'd fluffed out her green pixie, done her makeup, but kept her outfit to skinny jeans and a Lycra tee-shirt, something to show she was serious about working. Crawling around on sticky floors to mic drum sets, plug amplifiers into the public address system, and set up effects pedals required freedom of movement and a high tolerance for grime.

Whatever it takes, she told herself. Returning home and risking arrest were out of the question. She needed to put the 'oxygen mask' on herself first by finding a means of support. Then she could take the next critical step in her plan, exposing Alexander. She held that thought.

Bands never went on until after nine p.m., even on a weeknight, but Dara knew that if she was going to catch the owner, she had to arrive early. Just after eight, still light outside. The sweltering temperatures in Saint Louis, so different from Washington's unusually chilly summer, showed no mercy despite the impending sunset. She paid the admission and entered, finding the club nearly empty. Her face grew hot. She'd have welcomed the Black Cherry's wobbly ceiling fan right about now. Dara spotted a dartboard on the wall opposite the stage and decided to occupy herself, tossing darts, actually hitting the bullseye several times thanks to imagining Alexander's face in the center. As she tossed, she psyched herself up, whispering, *you can do this.*

The moment she felt herself believing the self-talk, she beelined for the bar, ordering a club soda with lime. Three dollars, plus a dollar for the bartender in hopes that she might introduce her to the owner. Not much money, but Dara didn't have much, and this was no time to get off on the wrong foot with potential new coworkers.

"Hi, I'm Dara," she said to the bartender, a black-haired woman with floral tattoos peeking out from under her low-cut tank top. Dara took a tiny sip from her glass, willing herself out of her social comfort zone. The irony of it all — Dara Bouldin, networking. If Jason Houseman could only see her now.

"Hey, I'm Jill," the woman responded, glancing politely at Dara, wiping down the counter. "You're pretty good with the darts."

"Can I ask you something?"

"Sure."

Dara took a breath, readying the thirty-second "elevator pitch" in her mind. "I'm new here, and I'm looking for a job. I do live sound, and I was wondering if I could talk to the owner about doing it here."

Jill looked at Dara. "You do sound?"

"Yeah."

"Who for?"

"I've worked with Jericho Wells, Spaceman Spiff, Vitamin X, most of the bands on the Tyrannosaurus Regina label." Dara hated to drop names, but she wasn't lying. Pulling rank was her best hope.

Jill nodded. "I don't know if we need anyone, but I'll go get Rick and you can ask him yourself." She slipped behind a door and emerged with a tall, bearded man with piercings in his neck.

He smiled. "Looks like we've got a little Martian and she wants to do sound," he said in a flat, Midwestern accent, eyeing Dara's green do.

The owner's raised eyebrows told her straight away he didn't take her seriously. "Nice to meet you," she said, shaking his hand. "I've worked sound on all kinds of systems, and I can fix anything." *Keep smiling,* she said to herself. *Make eye contact.*

"Oh really?" he replied, bemused. "I've got a board that has a short. Do you think you can fix it?"

Of course she could. But she wasn't going to fix it without getting paid, or, better yet, the promise of a gig. "If I fix it, will you hire me to do a show?"

"Do it tonight and we'll see," he said.

Not the answer Dara wanted. Still, she'd paid her admission and had nothing better to do. "Do you have a soldering iron?"

"Yep. You sure you want to do this?

"If I can convince you to hire me, I'll do it."

The owner shook his head, laughing. He led Dara back to his office where a sound board tangled in wires and cables took up most of the space. He handed her a few tools. "Enjoy," he said.

This wouldn't be enjoyable — not in the least. She didn't have access to an oscilloscope. In the past she'd borrowed one from the lab at Chambers to use for equipment repairs. Jane figured Dara was doing experiments at home and encouraged her to take whatever she wanted, as long as she brought the gear back the next day. Dara would just have to work around this obstacle tonight.

One of the bands, a local group called Asbestos Stockpile, took the stage. Dara pulled a set of earplugs from her pocket. She was going to need them.

Rick dropped in on Dara several times throughout the evening, probably to make sure she didn't steal anything. The other bands played as the night progressed, each displaying the same level of quality as Asbestos Stockpile. Dynamics were not their strong suit, nor melody, lyrics, or harmony. Nor personal hygiene, if the greasy-haired lead screamer of the second band was any indication. The third band's drummer had both meth face and meth shirt.

Finally, Rick spoke up. "I've never seen you here before. Jill said you were new in town. What brings you to Saint Louis?"

Dara removed her earplugs. "I'm from D.C., but I needed a change."

"College girl?"

Dara hesitated. "I went to Chambers," she replied, keeping the majors and advanced levels of her degrees to herself.

Rick's eyes widened. "So, you're a smart Martian. We don't get too many girls asking to mess around with wires."

"I'm good at fixing things. I'm even better at sound."

"Do you know anyone in Missouri?"

"No."

"Where are you staying?"

"At a hotel, for now."

Rick stared. "You mean you just showed up here without a job, not knowing anyone?"

Dara nodded.

"Why? I've got two daughters and I'd never let them loose by themselves where they didn't know anyone. Can't you do sound back in D.C.?"

Dara thought fast. "The cost of living's too high back home. I've got loans to pay off. Anyway, they say Midwesterners are nicer." She smiled.

"That we are," Rick said, nodding.

"Oh, and I fixed your board."

Rick examined Dara's handiwork. "Yes, you did."

"So, you think you can hire me?"

"What's your name again?"

"Dara. Dara Jones." She felt her face redden.

"You twenty-one?"

"Twenty-two, actually."

Rick smiled broadly. "Okay, Dara Jones. Even though I think you're crazy, I could probably fit you in on weeknights a few times a week. I can't pay you much. It's usually a guarantee of fifty bucks a night, cash, but if we get a decent take at the bar, I could give you a percentage of that. Drinks aren't included, by the way, only sodas or water."

Dara's heart leapt. It was a start. "I'm straightedge, so that works for me."

"Deal. Let me look at my calendar and we'll decide on a night for you to start."

"Thanks so much," Dara replied, sending Rick a text so he'd have her phone number.

"Appreciate you fixing my board. Have a safe trip back to your home planet."

Dara waited for the bus back to her hotel. Hit up for spare change only a couple times, she didn't feel any less safe than she felt back home. She could handle getting around the city at night. And she could tolerate a steady diet of microwave ramen noodles. Tomorrow she'd make flyers on the hotel business center's computer, advertising cleaning and tutoring services. She'd drop by all the cafés and coffee shops and post her flyers on every bulletin board she could find.

She'd also visit the local pawn shops and gold dealers and find out what she could get for her diamond necklace. That needed to go as soon as possible.

**

"Avery?"

"Speaking."

"It's Jericho."

Another person whose calls flashed "Unknown" — not Dara, but mercifully not Jane. "Jericho! It's great to hear your voice. Haven't talked to you in a long time."

"You, too."

"How are you?"

Hesitation from Jericho's end of the line. "Well, I've been better. You probably heard about the boycott if you haven't been in a coma."

"I did hear about it. I'm sorry things went that way. Are you all right?"

"Oh, it's only money. I'm not in the red yet, but getting there. Still have my health."

"Hang in there. It's just a matter of time before things turn around." Avery decided it was best to change the subject. "How's your mom?"

"She's great. Her new boyfriend has grandkids, so she's stopped bugging me about getting married and starting a family. For now."

Marriage and family were even touchier subjects than the boycott, so Avery opted to cut to the chase. "Jericho, what can I do for you?"

"Is Dara there? I've been trying to email and text her for couple weeks now. When I called, a recording said her phone number was out of service."

Avery hedged. "She didn't email you back?"

"No."

This caught Avery off guard. He was certain Dara and Jericho had patched up their differences a few months ago. She loved the photo he sent her for the holidays.

Only Dara hadn't responded to Avery in several days, either. The last time they spoke, she said she was doing sound engineering at a club, wiring a yoga studio's stereo system, tutoring a couple of summer school students, and reviewing a grad student's thesis. She had asked Avery to sell her car, but it was such a beater that no one wanted it, not even for spare parts. Avery did the math and knew she'd be out of cash soon, even with the odd jobs.

Could she pay her hotel bill? She had health insurance until the end of the month, but then what? Dara was stubborn about asking for help.

She'd implored Avery not to divulge her whereabouts, but Jericho was like family, and probably the most trustworthy person he'd ever known. Right now, Avery needed a friend. At one time, he and Jericho had been friends, borderline family, bonded by how much they cared for Dara.

"Jericho, I can tell you what's going on. But I need you to promise not to tell anyone. Especially not Dara."

"What are you talking about?"

"She left. She's in Saint Louis, but I can't say much more."

"Saint Louis? Did she get a new job?"

"Not exactly."

"What happened?"

Avery sighed. This was Jericho, not some stranger. "She lost her security clearance."

"How? She's the most straitlaced person around."

Avery wasn't sure if he should say more. Then again, what if Dara's silence meant she was in trouble? His ex-future son-in-law's fortunes were bound to reverse, possibly putting him in a position to help her.

"She was dating a Russian guy she met at work. Apparently, she wasn't supposed to."

"Oh."

"Right before she left, the cops started sniffing around."

"Cops?"

"Some FBI agent came by and asked about her. She's afraid they're going to accuse her of giving classified information to the Russian."

"Well, did she?"

"Of course not!"

"Are you sure?"

Avery couldn't see the lurid picture in Jericho's memory from the night Dara showed up at his concert in silver jeans, but he could hear the fury in his daughter's ex-fiance's voice. "She would never do something like that. I probably shouldn't have told you."

"You did me a favor," Jericho responded, his voice quieting down. "I don't have to miss her anymore."

"Jericho, she didn't do anything. Please, swear you won't tell anyone."

"I won't. Whatever happened is none of my business. I'm sure she'll figure it out."

After their good-byes, Avery slumped in his chair. Bad move on his part to tell Jericho about Dara's situation. But as poorly as the conversation went, it felt good to get it off his chest. It was better to be honest. Suffering alone with his secrets was not how he wanted to live. Not anymore.

***

"Dara, can you dye my hair like yours?"

Uh oh. Dara noticed that her tutoring charge, barely a month out from her *quinceanera*, had started dressing like her – Converse All-stars, shiny black leggings, striped top, black beret. Her parents, upper class and suburban, hired Dara sight unseen to usher their daughter through summer school geometry. Dara knew full well that her Ph.D. in nuclear engineering from Chambers got the job for her.

Mom and Dad's jaws hit the subflooring when Dara walked in, but fifteen-year-old Serena Ruiz took an immediate shine. The stickers on the girl's book cover gave away her musical interests, so Dara bribed the girl to study with playlists. If she got her proofs right, Dara would introduce her to a slew of new songs.

For a moment, Dara considered a grand bargain with the girl's mother to dye Serena's hair if she passed the final. But she knew this was a non-starter. The parents owned and operated a successful law firm, big fish in a larger-than-expected pond. Their baby girl would not have green hair.

"Sorry, your parents would kill me."

The teen moaned. "God, I hate geometry."

Dara stood her ground. "I hate to break it to you, but it doesn't matter. You have to pass this class."

"Why do I even need it?"

Dara sighed. The truth was that even in her graduate-level nuclear engineering classes, she never saw any Euclidean proofs. But geometry taught a thought process, one that applied to computer programming, mathematical modeling, and even everyday logical analysis.

"It trains your brain," said Dara. "Trust me."

Serena rolled her eyes. "I don't care about that stuff."

"Do you care about graduating high school?"

"Yeah."

"Then you'll have to get through it. I know you can."

"I can't. You love math, and you're good at it. You wouldn't understand."

"Oh, I do. You have to find a way to hate it less. We've got the playlists for now."

The girl pouted, folded her arms across her chest. *Cue the drama.* Dara never had the luxury of blowing off her studies at fifteen. Still, she had infinite sympathy when it came to adolescence. Teen and adult angst were similar points on the same continuum.

"Serena, I'm not coloring your hair. When you're my age, you can dye your whole body green if you want. Until then, sometimes you have to do things you don't want in order to get what you do want."

The girl eyed Dara suspiciously. "Do you do that?"

Dara smiled. "Every minute of every day."

"God, being an adult must suck."

Dara wanted to nod, particularly in light of her personal series of unfortunate events. But deep down, despite borderline homelessness and eking out a living on odd jobs, she secretly enjoyed her current life. She felt free, comfortable in her own skin. Young adulthood was a journey, all peaks and valleys, but it came with self-determination unavailable to someone Serena's age.

Of course, the tragic flaw of Dara's current position on the adulthood track was that her bank account approached zero. She'd redoubled her efforts to find work, pulling in a few extra dollars a week scrubbing the bathrooms at Club Taser and locating a co-op that gave casual workers food credit in exchange for making sandwiches behind the deli counter. Dara remained stuck in the hotel, despite all her hard work. Finding a cheap room to rent was more difficult than she'd anticipated. Even homeowners seeking boarders insisted on a credit report, and no one took cash.

"Please dye my hair," the girl pleaded. "Or just teach me how. What's the harm?"

"It's not easy being green, sweetie." *More than you'll ever know,* she thought.

Fifteen years old. Dara had barely started her period at that age. No driver's permit, no diploma, no worries. The climate modeling program was still just a game. She spiked her hair and dressed punk for fun -- not to disguise herself.

She tried not to begrudge Serena her parents' wealth. It wasn't her fault she was spoiled. Still, Dara couldn't help but wonder how differently her own life would have turned out if she'd grown up with the advantages Serena had -- if her mother hadn't died, if her father hadn't succumbed to his gambling addiction, if overcoming scarcity wasn't part of life's equation. Money wasn't everything, but it sure went a long way towards solving money problems.

One thing was certain. Dara held the solution to her financial woes in an envelope at the bottom of her purse. She needed to sell her necklace, the sooner, the better. She'd printed out a list of pawn shops and gold dealers, jotting which bus stops were closest to each.

But not before spending a couple evenings in front of the bathroom mirror, modeling the object of beauty, memorizing the way it sparkled under the lights, caressed her collarbones. She waltzed around the hotel room, her pillow serving as her dance partner, until a feeling of foolishness set in. Perish any thought of the necklace as a token of Dmitri's love for her. It wasn't.

The teenage girl across from her not only wore a diamond necklace, but matching earrings as well. Thrift store clothes were "vintage finds" to Serena, not economic necessities. From the sound of it, her *quinceanera* celebration cost more than Dara's stipend last year when she was still on fellowship.

With all that going for her, Serena could never fail. Her parents cast every possible safety net. This may have been the first time Serena flunked a class, but it probably wouldn't be the last. She'd simply repeat the subject with another down-on-her-luck math or civics or French whisperer. It didn't matter. Her future came with a guarantee.

Dara stopped herself. Who was she to judge someone else? Heartbreak was universal, and reality was bound to catch up with her pupil someday, regardless of her parents' efforts to shield her. Besides, it was no use trying to explain life to a teenager. Soon enough, Serena would figure it out for herself.

"I finished my proof," Serena said. The diamond around the teen's neck twinkled, winking like an all-seeing eye. Robert Frost's verse came to mind: "We dance round in a ring and suppose, but the secret sits in the middle and knows."

Dara wondered, uncertainty biting at her. Where would this journey lead? Why was she here? Was any of this even real?

Dara's diamond was real. She could sell the chain for now — the gold had a high yield, enough to tide her over for a while. She wasn't ready to part with the gem just yet. Her little secret.

***

Open phones typically dominated the third hour of Fat Frank's national morning show, and today was no exception. "Do I have Pittsburgh on the line?" he announced to the first of the callers.

"Yup. Morning, Frank."

"What's on your mind, Pittsburgh?"

"Detonation Day. Can't wait!"

"Me neither. Less than a month away! Got any plans?"

"I'm getting bombed, of course." The minions played explosion sound effects in the background.

"You and me both. Where at?"

"My buddies and I are driving down to D.C. for the festival on the Mall. We wanna show our support in person."

"I'm with you. We need to give James Donahue props. For once, someone in power actually gave a [cuckoo sound effect] about us."

"Damn straight. I got displaced twice, once after a flood and the second time after a hurricane. No one would rebuild because everyone knew we'd just be repeating the process in a year or two."

"How are things holding up in [fart sound effect]-burg?"

"So far, so good."

"Bless you, my friend. Thanks for tuning in. Next caller. Atlanta?"

"Morning!"

"Howdy, Hotlanta. Got any D-Day plans?"

Hesitation. "Um..."

Frank grew impatient. "Come on, Atlanta, you know how we feel about radio silence on the radio."

"Sorry. I dunno. I heard a bunch of Alaskan tribes are against the detonation. The mountain's sacred to them."

Boos from Fat Frank's peanut gallery.

"Oh, spare me," said Fat Frank. "They'll get over it."

"Not just them. Lots of people are saying we aren't thinking this through."

"Let me guess. You're on Team Jericho Wells?"

"I never said that."

Fat Frank cleared his throat. "You know, Jericho's trying to get booked on my show. Wants to explain himself, apparently. Oh, yeah, and talk about his new album. Hate to break it to him, but the boycott's working like a charm. No one's buying what he's selling."

"He's entitled to his opinion. Seems to know a lot about the CAA."

"Well, you know what they say about opinions. Everyone's got one of those, too. But whatever, I'll think about it. Might be fun to bitch slap him in person."

"If he doesn't slap you first."

The sound effects man chimed in with slapping noises, along with an effeminate voiceover that squealed, "Ouch!" Fat Frank guffawed. "As if. Give your tree a hug for me, Atlanta."

***

Unknown caller again. *Here goes nothing,* Avery said to himself. "Hello?"

"Hi, it's Jane."

Goddammit. "Jane, I don't have time right now."

"This won't take long. Is Dara around?"

"No."

"Do you know when she's going to be home?"

"No."

"Come on, Avery. I'm getting worried. Her mom's anniversary is tomorrow, and I've donated blood with Dara every year since I've known her. This isn't like her, to just disappear."

No, it wasn't. Avery hadn't heard from Dara since before Jericho called. His stomach knotted. He could barely cover his own expenses without Dara's income. Extra money wasn't going to materialize without a lottery win at this point—but Avery had promised to stay on the Gamblers Anonymous wagon, so that wasn't happening.

He considered clearing out Dara's room and finding a roommate, but that was risky. The last thing he needed was some deadbeat who'd drain him of the few assets he did have by doing drugs, punching a hole in the wall, stealing the TV, or whatever adult roommates did in nightmare scenarios. Avery had watched enough court shows to know he'd need time to screen for the right person.

The thought of Dara getting evicted from the hotel sent shudders down Avery's spine. He knew she was still staying there from the times he'd called to leave messages for her with the front desk. The staff slipped the messages under her door, but she wouldn't respond.

Avery was well acquainted with Dara's habit of withdrawing when things went badly – hiding in her room after breakups or job problems, clamming up when deal after deal for her climate modeling program fell through. He prayed her silence was simple withdrawal this time and not something else.

Revulsion welled up in Avery's throat, a bilious combination of fear over the prospect of Dara being thrown out on the street, plus his own impotence in failing to provide for her. Dara needed help, and Avery needed help to give her what she needed. His daughter's safety was at stake. Yes, Avery promised Dara he wouldn't tell anyone about her ordeal. But Jane offered assistance. Deep down, maybe Jane cared.

He couldn't stand by and let Dara wander Saint Louis alone and vulnerable, not when a solution was available. Avery made up his mind.

"Jane, I can tell you where she is. But I need to swear you to secrecy. And I need you to do us a favor."

"What can I do?"

"Dara's away. She...left Washington. She doesn't want anyone to know where she is. I can't give you her number. She isn't talking to me, and I don't think she wants to talk to anyone."

"Why is she doing this?"

"I can't say. But I'm worried about her finances. She didn't have much money to begin with, and she hasn't found a steady job yet."

"Oh. Does she need money?"

"Yes."

"And obviously you can't help her."

The statement felt like a pinprick, but Avery let it go along with the last of his pride. "Jane, I need to you pay Dara's hotel bill, and I need you to do it anonymously."

Hesitation on Jane's side. "Anonymously?"

"Yes. She'd reject the payment if she knew it was from you. She also made me swear not to tell anyone where she is, at least not until she gets on her feet. So, I need you to pay her bill using cash, or maybe a money order. Something that won't give away who paid."

"Okay. I can do that. Maybe I can talk to her when she's back on her feet."

"Maybe. But not until then. I'll tell her that I got some more hours at work and the money's from me."

"Got it. Where do I send the money?"

Avery took one last moment to convince himself that he was doing the right thing. A twinge of relief in finding help for Dara tempered his shame. He took a breath.

"Thank you, Jane," he said, his trembling voice betraying weeks of worry. "I appreciate this more than I can say. She's in Saint Louis."

T-minus Three

Sam-I-Am Collins was at it again. Media blitzes, celebrities. The other politicos were all in with their support for the CAA and couldn't renege now, even if they wanted to do so. Sam and her surrogates, on the other hand, could do as they pleased. She couldn't sue the administration because she lacked the expertise to prove Chase Tucker's hunch and disprove the CIA team. Still, the media needed a counterpoint, so the bully pulpit was her last, best hope to stop the detonation.

President Donahue's people kept tabs on Sam Collins, knowing full well that grassroots lips could sink ships. He responded in turn. Today Donahue visited a town in Louisiana that a recent spate of tornadoes had shredded. He timed his speech to make the Monday evening news in hopes of drowning out Senator Collins' sound bites from the Sunday morning talk shows.

"Friends," he said, "we must not allow opposing voices to distract us from the task at hand. There are some who'll politicize your situation, the country's situation, to fuel their own agendas, their own grabs at power. These individuals think over-regulating our industries and forcing us to live according to their rules will save us. Well, in my view, those who want to change our way of life are showing their true colors. They are trying to take away our freedom!"

The throng, hundreds deep, surrounded by rubble, roared. The president continued. "We all know fossil fuels are part of our energy mix. Louisiana depends on this industry."

Donahue looked directly into the camera. "Friends, I am not the first to say that the jury is still out on so-called 'climate change.' We can't prove that what we're dealing with is man-made. Many scientists point to volcanic eruptions and natural shifts in weather patterns as the cause of rising temperatures. They reject the notion that you and I are at fault."

The camera panned out to cheers and nods from those in attendance. Donahue continued. "Regardless, no one denies that we have problems. No one doubts that you are suffering. My heart goes out to every family who lives in the aftermath of tragedy and destruction."

The camera pulled in for a close-up, focusing in on Donahue's veneers, pores, metallic blue eyes. "I offer you and your children a promise. We have the technology to make positive changes that will preserve both our safety and our way of life. We will apply it on August 14th and solve our problems. Once again, American ingenuity will help us succeed and create a brighter tomorrow."

Delirium washed over the crowd, the President having absolved them of any guilt.

***

Dara worked nights and weekends at Club Taser, reserving afternoons for tutoring sessions or sandwich-making at the co-op. Sometimes she'd spend mornings in the library. She didn't sign up for a library card just yet given her desire for anonymity, but she could at least read the papers. The headlines were all Detonation Day, all the time.

Checking her email at the hotel's business center before she left for the library didn't offer much respite from that particular sword of Damocles, what with all the D-Day-related spam. But to her surprise, today's news wasn't all bad thanks to a message that appeared in her inbox:

Dear Dara,

I know you're not responding to e-mails, but in case you're reading them, I want you to know that I've arranged to cover your hotel bill for the rest of July. The night manager confirmed that they received the money order today. I hope this helps. Call me if I can help with anything else. Please be safe.

    Love,
    Dad

Dara re-read the message several times to convince herself she wasn't seeing things. *Way to go, Dad,* she thought, her heart racing as a smile came to her lips. She made a mental note to stop by the dollar store and buy him a thank you card. But where did he get the money? Did he sell her car? Did he find a roommate? Did he sign on for extra hours at work?

To Dara, the money was proof positive that Avery wasn't gambling away his earnings, since she (and, deep down, he) knew all too well that the house always won. Dara had worried that the stress of her situation would derail her father's recovery. Avery's ability to earn extra cash to give to her meant he was keeping his promise.

She soaked in the relief that bubbled up. Perfect timing. Dara was down to her last $70 from the sale of the chain that came with her diamond pendant. She asked the hotel manager for an extra day to pay her bill, which he granted. No need to sell the diamond just yet -- it remained in the envelope in her purse. Due to the shady characters on the bus, Dara considered getting a safety deposit box, but it cost too much. Now that she knew she wasn't getting evicted from the hotel, she could put it in the hotel safe.

A little breathing room, for now. She had a safe place to stay, could live on peanuts and orange juice from the bar at Club Taser, sandwiches from the co-op, and packages of Ramen noodles from 7-11. The extra money meant she could splurge on salad, pizza, frozen yogurt!

God, she missed real food. One night at the club, some aging hipster, probably twenty years her senior, asked her out to dinner. She almost went on the promise of a free meal but came to her senses and turned him down. The last thing she needed was to get mixed up with a new man.

With food and shelter checked off her list, Dara's mind returned to her other chief concern, the one she could focus on now that homelessness and hunger weren't immediate threats.

The pending detonation was less than a month away. What could she do to stop it? She'd lost her security clearance, and now the feds were looking for her. A textbook case of nothing left to lose, but not much time to work out a plan.

Posters festooned every floor at AAER, declaring in bold red graphics, "If you see something, say something." Dara saw something. Still, who would listen to her now that she was just some green-haired punk rocker, eking out an existence in flyover country? No longer cleared, she couldn't just ring up some hapless government employee and make allegations. They'd probably hang up on her, fearing guilt by association.

Leaking to the press, which seemed like the right option before AAER's "indefinite suspension" stunt, would likely prove futile at this point. Dismissed from her federal job ostensibly over her affair with Dmitri, she'd come across as some disgruntled ex-employee. Worse, Alexander would probably send reporters photos of Dara and Dmitri in flagrante. The story would morph into a slut-shaming exposé of the girl who – at least according to CIA claims – sold out her country.

The library was mostly empty mornings during the week – just a mom with two kids aged small and smaller, a couple of seniors browsing through the periodicals, and a disheveled man who looked even more displaced than Dara. Poster-sized photos of politicians at library events graced the building's entrance.

A thought occurred to her. Elected officials didn't undergo the same security clearance procedures as regular federal workers. She'd read that being elected and swearing an oath of office kept them from traditional background investigations. In theory, she could call someone who had been voted into power without compromising the individual's access to secure information.

There was one such person, someone who spoke in opposition to the Climate Action Act and desperately wanted to stop the detonation. Samantha Collins stood just one degree of separation away.

***

"Good morning, friends. It's your old pal, Fat Frank. We have a special guest for you today — so very, very special. Let's hear it for Jericho Wells."

The minions booed. Jericho fully expected the red meat treatment, controversy being the name of the game in radio, so he jeered along sardonically.

Fat Frank shushed his team of sycophants. "Guys, come on. Let's not be rude to our visitor. Jericho, they're just jealous because they know our female listeners are flinging their panties at their radios right now."

Laughter from the crew.

"Oh, I'm sure somebody's flinging something at me," said Jericho, playing along. "I'm not sure it's underwear, though."

"I see you brought your guitar with you."

"I did."

"So. Shall we address the elephant in the room?"

One of the minions piped up. "That would be you, boss."

Frank shook his head. "I walked right into that one, didn't I? Let's try this again. A couple of months ago, I instigated a boycott against Tyrannosaurus Regina because you guys are against the Climate Action Act. You also pal around with Sam-I-Am Collins."

Boos again from Frank's crew after he mentioned the senator.

"Am I allowed to use the word [cuckoo sound effect] on the radio?" asked Frank. "Oh, I guess not. How about 'See You Next Thursday?' Okay, we'll go with that."

It was all Jericho could do not to roll his eyes, but he remained stoic and let Frank do his shtick. Millions of people tuned in every morning and Jericho needed to get them on his side.

The host continued his rant, finally punctuating the end of his diatribe with, "Jericho Wells, are you guilty as charged? Or do you have an alibi for sitting out the Detonation Day concerts?"

As if on cue, the sound effects guy punched in Perry Mason music. Jericho cleared his throat. "Frank, I appreciate you letting me on the show today. I want to set the record straight. I respect Senator Collins and think she makes some excellent points. But make no mistake. I'm totally pro geo-engineering to reverse climate change."

"Are you? Prove it."

"It's a clever program, for starters. Do you want me to talk about Markov Chain Monte Carlo sampling? I know a little bit about it."

The sidekick army 'oohed' in unison.

"Wow," said Frank. "My listeners share a brain, so let's not do that. Assuming you know your stuff and believe in geo-engineering, why aren't you playing any of the D-Day concerts?"

Jericho had anticipated the question and tried not to sound rehearsed. "Because I was planning to drop my new album in August. I didn't want people to think I was using the detonation to promote myself or the bands on my label."

Radio silence. For once, the nonplussed contingent in the studio was Fat Frank and company.

"If I had played the D-day show, someone else might have boycotted me for being a sellout. Damned if I do, damned if I don't."

"Oh," Frank managed to say.

"I'm new at this," continued Jericho, on a roll. "I'm figuring out how to run an independent record label by running an independent record label. Just a regular guy from D.C. whose band got huge before I knew what I was doing. All I care about is artistic freedom and supporting causes I believe in and bands I like."

Another hesitation. Finally, Fat Frank spoke. "I owe you an apology. I jumped to conclusions about you, and that was wrong."

No hesitation from Jericho, only slight shock that Frank so readily bought his argument. "Apology accepted," he replied.

"Okay, I officially declare the boycott over. Friends, run out, fire up your credit cards, and buy this guy's music."

Jericho's expression betrayed his relief. "Thanks, Frank," he said, torn between hugging him and punching his bloated face.

"So, you're dropping a new album?"

"Yep, on August 20th. It's called, 'Buck the Hum.'"

One of the crew members interrupted. "Like the guitar pickups?"

Frank sighed. "You have to excuse Paulie. He's a guitar freak."

"It's okay; I am, too. 'Buck the Hum' is a play on words. I've got a Les Paul, so it refers to humbucking pickups, but also bucking the hum to shut out all the noise."

"Noise?"

"You know, the background B.S. in everybody's life. Political noise, self-doubt noise, love noise, all of it."

"Love noise?" The minions 'oohed' again.

"Talk about walking right into something," chortled Frank. "So, tell us about this 'love noise' of which you speak."

Jericho shook his head. "There's not much to tell."

Frank's eyes darted from minion to minion, then back to Jericho. "Do you want to play us a song today?"

"I do."

"No spillage of guts, no play-age of song!"

Laughter pealed.

"I've got the single from the new disc. It's called 'Medicine.' It's covered in guts."

"'Love noise' guts?"

"Yep."

"Okay, deal. Play it for us. Ladies and gentlemen, Jericho Wells."

The song, an acoustic ballad, featured a mournful cello on the recorded version. The opening arpeggio resonated from Jericho's Martin, his voice verging on a whisper.

Unexpected
Climbing up a sand dune
She is finding your gaze
She'll never be the same

Unsuspected

Now she scales the clouds
And she is closer, closer
To the sun
She'll never be the same

Oh, so much you will never know
Oh, so much you will never know
Only that she's burnt up, blackened, beaten
By the sun

The host and crew sat in silence. One of the minions closed his eyes, rocking from side to side. Jericho's voice melted, bittersweet, into the second verse.

Undetected
Feeling very much alone
Silence all around her
She suffocates in privacy

Unprotected
No defenses shield her soul
Open wounds display her ills
All revealed, none concealed

Oh, so much you will never know
Oh, so much you will never know
Only that she's burnt up, blackened, beaten
By the sun

The chorus built up to a crescendo, punctuated by a question mark.

Now then, how then, how then could it be
That the medicine
Could bring her to her knees?

Dara was the smartest person Jericho knew. Did she really sell out her country? He shuddered at the thought of her with Dmitri, smitten as she was with her Russian paramour. He saw it with his own eyes.

Was she ever that crazy about him? Maybe, but whatever she felt got tangled up in her ambition. Perhaps her feelings for Dmitri got tangled up in the same tragic flaw.

The song ended on the chorus, chanted over and over until the final chord. Sometime between the first and last verses, the studio's switchboard lit up like a holiday, sending the interns into a tizzy. The hum wasn't bucking anytime soon.

***

Dara waited a day to move forward on contacting Senator Collins, supposedly because she was helping Serena cram for her final exam, but really because she hadn't mustered up the nerve. What could she even say about her current situation? 'Senator, the FBI is after me, and the government is planning to use the Climate Action Act for nefarious purposes.' Such a spiel, however true, would relegate her to tinfoil hat territory.

The day of Serena's exam, Dara spent the entire morning at the hotel, procrastinating with a paperback she found in the giveaway bin at the library, praying for a text that the girl had passed — an iffy proposition, given her hatred for the subject. But Mrs. Ruiz called Dara after lunch with the good news, along with profuse thanks and compliments.

Dara squealed. She momentarily forgot her troubles and began daydreaming about how she might build on her success. The school year was starting in a month. Maybe she could open a tutoring company and ask the Ruizes and her other charges for references. She could hire other tutors to work for her by drawing upon the local graduate student population or finding schoolteachers hoping to moonlight for extra cash.

She went over the math in her head — how many people might use her services, what her cut would be, how much money she'd stand to earn. The thought of being able to pay off her debts in short order made her heartbeat quicken. She imagined buying her own home, or, for the first time, clothes or furniture or cars that weren't second hand. Walking through life with her head held high.

The clock radio caught Dara's eye. Two p.m. — where did the time go? She needed to get in touch with Jericho for help in reaching Senator Collins. But first things first. She'd promised herself a treat if she succeeded with Serena, drooling over the prospect since the assignment began. Her reward would be an extra-large frozen yogurt, piled with fresh fruit and anything else that would fit in the cup, from the shop she walked by every day but forced herself to resist.

She giggled like a six-year-old. Fro-yo was for special occasions, and finally she had one. Her mom started the tradition, taking her to the yogurt shop when she was a kid to celebrate her quarterly report cards. Over the years, her father, Jericho, and even Jane tagged along on her treat days, although none of them particularly cared for yogurt.

Dara brushed her hair, put on her Chucks, checked her purse to make sure she had enough cash. She spotted the envelope with the diamond. First stop, the front desk to put the diamond in the hotel safe.

"Good afternoon, Miss Jones," said the hotel manager, referring to Dara's alias. "How can I help you?"

"Hi," she said, breaking into a grin. "Call me Dara. Could you please put this in the safe?" She handed him the envelope, her room number written on the front.

"Sure, no problem," he said. "Call me Howard. How's your stay?"

"Great," she said, beaming, too excited to contain herself. "I'm going to Frogolo to eat myself silly."

"Love that place," he replied. "I'll go lock this in the vault. Have fun!"

"Thanks, Howard, I will," said Dara. Midwesterners really were nicer.

Dara barely noticed the Saint Louis heat today, didn't care that the humidity made her green pixie cut look like something on a Muppet. She laughed at her reflection in the shop windows as she walked by. Hey, who didn't love the Muppets? The past few weeks of living in her own skin, on her own terms, felt great.

Halfway down the street, a man in a dark suit approached her. "Dara Bouldin?"

Dara stopped, eyes darting, the rest of her body paralyzed in place. Finally, not knowing what else to do, she said, "Yes?"

He flashed a badge. "FBI. Come with me."

***

The next several hours played out like every bad dream Dara had attempted to squelch since she arrived in Saint Louis. The man led her into a car, drove her to a non-descript office building. A backdrop of strip malls and office parks rolled by on repeat as if she were in a grim cartoon. Dara heard herself ask, "Where are you taking me? Am I under arrest? Do I get to call a lawyer?"

"We'll answer your questions when we arrive."

After fingerprinting and directing her to a conference room table, all the man would say was that she wasn't under arrest, but rather, being detained.

Dara wouldn't let up. "Detained? Why?"

Finally, the man answered her. "Ma'am, under Section 1021 of the National Defense Authorization Act, any person who has committed what the government deems a 'belligerent' act can be detained…"

"What?" Dara stared at him.

"…without charges or trial…"

"Excuse me?"

"…indefinitely." He placed a copy of the relevant section of the NDAA in front of her.

The text, spelling out her fate in the blackest black, came into focus. Dara remembered hearing about 'detainees' from the recent past. Detention was forever, for 'any person,' even U.S. citizens. Indeed, no lawyer for her, since court-appointed attorneys were for those formally charged with crimes. Even if the FBI allowed her to retain counsel, it would cost thousands of dollars that she didn't have.

The room, heavily air conditioned, turned Dara's skin to goose flesh. How did they even find her? She felt like a microchipped animal.

The man must have read her mind. "Dara, your father is very concerned about you. You left him to fend for himself, knowing that he has a serious gambling problem. We offered a reward for information about your whereabouts, and he provided it."

Dara felt her face grow hot, despite the A/C chill. "I don't believe you," she said, shaking her head. "My father's in a twelve-step program and he's doing well. You're lying."

The man met her eyes. "Believe what you want. People relapse, especially when their loved ones disappoint them."

Dara willed herself not to tear up. Her one certainty was that people in intelligence fields were professional liars. Tears were precisely what they wanted from her, and she wasn't going to give them the satisfaction.

Several law enforcement types wandered in and out of the room. All in dark suit jackets despite the weather, even the women. One offered a bottle of water. Dara eyed it warily, saw that it was sealed, and accepted.

Finally, a stack of paperwork completed, the agent turned to Dara and said, "Okay, our plan is to transfer you to a detention center. A military flight's been arranged. We're taking you to the airport now."

Dara flinched as if she'd been slapped. "But my stuff is at the hotel. Can't I at least pack a bag?"

"No, you won't need anything. Your room will be searched as part of our investigation. I advise you to cooperate."

Dara's hands balled into fists. "I didn't do anything illegal. All you'll find is green dye and some clothes."

"Well, then, you have nothing to worry about."

She stiffened. They would plant something, or someone. Remind her in no uncertain terms of her insignificance, crush her into sand.

Dara knew that whatever did or didn't turn up didn't matter. Her life was over. Dark thoughts flooded her brain, immune to positive self-talk. Detention was purgatory on Earth, punishment for wanting too much, like the dog with the steak in its mouth from her mother's story. Love, self-expression, meaningful work, financial security…the truth was out. Wanting a better life was a cardinal sin. These people weren't going to let her get away with it.

She gulped. Their jackboot had nothing on the one crushing her from the inside out. The blood of destroying half the world with her nuclear Band-Aid would not only soak her hands but her entire essence. She'd be warehoused, ending all semblance of life, and, moreover, any ability to talk sense into anyone, anywhere, who'd listen. Yet time and consequences would trample forward. In the FBI sedan to God knows where, pent-up tears pooled in Dara's eyes, stinging like defeat.

***

As far as Alexander Fallsworth was concerned, the FBI found Dara in the nick of time. The detention process would solve two problems. First, it would keep her from leaking information. Second, in order to meet the August 14th deadline, he needed someone to repair one last but crucial bug in the software. Randall Swanson, Jane Canton, a team of TS-SCI-cleared contractors, all the king's horses and men, essentially, had failed. Since Dara developed the code from scratch and knew it inside and out, she was the one person who could solve the problem.

Of course, he already knew she would refuse. But Alexander's military training had rendered him intimately familiar with methods to make uncooperative people fall in line.

She'd been at the detention facility for a week. Small room, twin bed, desk, white walls, overhead lighting, toilet, no windows. Solitary confinement. Her room was more college dorm than cage, but the lock on the outside of the door made her predicament clear.

She may have held the cards when it came to software development, but the cameras beaming her every move to closed circuit television screens shifted the balance of power to her captors.

Mornings, Dara received a tray with a small bag of cereal, carton of milk, lukewarm coffee (not that she even drank coffee), bottle of water, scrambled eggs, orange juice. Lunch was a sandwich; supper was akin to a Hungry Man TV dinner. More bottles of water. On days one and two, she returned her food uneaten.

Alexander watched her on the monitor, lying on the sheets, staring at the ceiling, eventually climbing on the bed in a futile attempt to jump up and disable the camera. She tried to push the bed toward the wall, but it was nailed down. Then she attempted to take apart the desk, but it was bolted to the wall, and, besides, she didn't have any tools. Intermittently, she wept, splashed water on her face or hair, did jumping jacks, or used the toilet. Alexander laughed when he saw that Dara rigged her bed sheet to hide her body as she relieved herself.

Female guards milled in and out of Dara's room, usually without knocking, asking her if the temperature was okay or if she needed a blanket. The air conditioner was on blast, so Dara agreed. After the second day of returned trays, Alexander instructed one of the guards to ask Dara why she wasn't eating.

He listened in. "What's the problem? How can we help?" asked the guard, playing good cop.

Dara refused to answer or even look at her visitor.

Undeterred, she continued, "Do you have a food allergy, or a dietary requirement based on your religion? We can accommodate you. You just need to tell us."

Dara's eyes flashed this time. Her voice registered several decibels above what Alexander could ever imagine coming out of Dara's mouth. "What do you think?" she growled. "I'm in jail for no reason, probably forever. You won't even let me call my dad!"

Alexander flinched at the angry display on the monitor. The guard remained calm, shaking her head. "Dara, no. You're simply being detained. You have not been arrested. You're being treated according to our approved, standardized procedures. We don't want you to get sick, but you will if continue to refuse food."

Dara fidgeted, probably because she wasn't accustomed to prison-issue denim scraping against her skin. This time she shrieked, "I don't care!"

"Are you sure about that? You could die if you keep this up."

"Good!"

"Very well. We'll have no choice but to install a feeding tube."

Dara's face fell, along with her volume. "What?"

"A feeding tube, inserted through the nose. We've done this with other detainees, several times. Hunger strikes happen occasionally at our facility." The woman's expression and cadence remained bland. The color of Dara's face now matched her sheet.

What seemed like minutes passed. The guard sat on the edge of the desk, not budging. Finally, Dara shook her head, eyes fixed on the linoleum. "Please don't do that," she said in a half-whisper. "I'll eat."

The woman stood up. "I'm glad that's settled then."

Alexander watched the guard take her leave, nodded when Dara buried her head in the pillow. The outcome of the exchange gave him confidence that she would agree to debug the program, possibly even voluntarily. Dara was surely going stir crazy with nothing to do, read, or watch on TV.

***

"Rock star in the house!" Samantha Collins beamed as her surprise guest entered her suite in the Hart Senate Office Building.

In D.C. to visit family, Jericho Wells decided that it was time for a courtesy call on his favorite member of Congress. The senator, arms outstretched, greeted Jericho with a motherly hug and introduced him to her cadre of summer interns. Besides the post-adolescent team members, mostly middle-aged female staffers wormed their way into the vicinity of the Senator's office, armed with excuses like, 'The copy machine on my floor is broken, can I borrow yours?' and 'Oops! Must have made a wrong turn at Albuquerque — tee hee.' The congressional security guards who escorted Jericho just smiled, breaking protocol to get their own selfies with their superstar visitor.

Jericho knew what to expect from fans at this point in his career, but he was taken aback by the professionally-attired Washington types squealing his name, begging for autographs, and otherwise freaking out. One of the admins even asked him to sign her arm, asserting that she'd get a tattoo artist to make it permanent. Jericho, a native Washingtonian, knew full well that he was in that world, not of it. Still, even though he never expected Capitol Hill staffers to join his audience as fervent members, the real shocker was how much he found himself enjoying it.

A photo op with the Senator's college hires wouldn't hurt, since his 'indie cred' ship had sailed some time ago. All publicity was good publicity anyway, even if it involved hanging out with government workers. More importantly, he wanted to pick Sam Collins' brain. The Detonation Day media circus hadn't let up despite her best efforts, but she soldiered on. She clearly had more than a passing familiarity with the detonation project and its status.

With Dara no longer involved and apparently out of a job, Jericho was anxious. Did Sam Collins know what happened to her? As miffed as he was over her relationship with Dmitri, he worried. Could Dara really lose her security clearance for dating a coworker? And, more importantly, was there any proof that she tried to sell out the country?

The answer had to be no. Jericho knew Dara. She never discussed her work with anyone and forever stressed how seriously she took her clearance. Earning her own money, paying down her debts — these were points of pride for her. Jeopardizing her livelihood over a man she barely knew seemed preposterous, especially for someone whose head usually prevailed over her heart -- to a fault, as Jericho knew, all too well.

He had rehearsed what he'd say to the Senator, taking care to keep any knowledge about Dara's involvement in the project to himself. Once the fanfare ended and the Senator invited him to join her in her office, he wasted no time.

"Thanks so much for agreeing to meet with me today, Senator Collins. I wanted to talk to you because Detonation Day is still on schedule."

Sam Collins hesitated, then nodded. "I'm afraid so."

Jericho swallowed hard. "Everything's happening so fast. Do you think the plan's safe?"

The Senator shook her head. "We think it's got serious problems. Not just on an environmental level, but on a geopolitical level. I just don't have the expertise on my staff to prove it. I wish I could tell you more about it, but I can't." She trailed off.

Jericho chose his words carefully. "You know, I reach a lot of people. Maybe there's something I can do to help you."

The Senator smiled. "I know you're not blowing smoke when you say that. These kids would do anything for you. I'll definitely need your help to mobilize them down the road. Maybe if we rock the vote hard enough, we can finally reverse climate change."

Jericho nodded, wondering what she meant by 'geopolitical level.' He vowed to ask Dara—if he ever even saw her again. Just as he sensed that Senator Collins had reached the limit of what she could say, the soon-to-be-tattooed administrative assistant slipped in to let her know her next appointment had arrived.

"You know I'll always be here for you, asking what I can do for my country," said Jericho. As he exited the Capitol amid a phalanx of high-fives, he considered his next move.

***

"Ms. Bouldin, come with me."

Days into her detention, August 14th looming large on the calendar she drew on the wall, a guard Dara hadn't seen before led her through the building to a small office in a different wing. She contemplated making a run for it, but the sterile surroundings revealed cameras at every turn. Her denim coveralls would render her even more conspicuous against the white cinderblock walls.

If she screamed, would other detainees hear her? Not that she even knew if there were other detainees in the facility. She only saw her captors, thus far all female guards, probably military officers given their attire, hairstyles, and posture. She peppered them with questions which they studiously ignored. Clearly, it didn't matter if anyone heard her. Nothing that mattered to her mattered to anyone there.

Upon entering the room, it was all Dara could do not to have at the person sitting at the table: Alexander Fallsworth. Her stomach did the lurching for her, as if encountering the devil in the flesh.

Dara turned to the guard. "I have nothing to say to him. I'd like to go back to my room."

The guard smirked. "It doesn't work that way, Ms. Bouldin." She took her leave, closing the door behind her.

"So, to what do I owe this honor?" Dara glared at her adversary, refusing to join him at the table.

"Sit down, Dara. I know you're upset."

"Don't patronize me."

"You know, I can help you get out of here."

"Oh really?" Dara folded her arms, rolling her eyes. "And how do you intend to do that?"

Alexander leaned back in his chair, a bemused expression on his face. "You seem to have forgotten that you're in a hell of a lot of trouble. I'd dial back the attitude if I were you."

"Well, you're not my boss, so I don't see why I should follow your orders. Can't I at least call my dad? Or a lawyer? Or my congressman? This is B.S., and you know it."

"National security violations aren't B.S., Dara."

Her voice kicked up a decibel. "I didn't do anything."

"You did, and we have the pictures to prove it."

"I didn't commit a crime, and you know it," she said, louder this time. She turned on her heel and attempted to open the door, but it was locked.

Alexander chortled. "You'll need one of these to open the door," he said, holding up his keycard.

Dara sighed, refusing to look at his smug face. "I don't want to talk to you. I don't want to be in the same room with you."

At this, Alexander fidgeted in his chair, registering his impatience. "Calm down. Look, I didn't come all this way to argue with you. Do you want to hear what I came to say?"

It occurred to Dara that she had no idea how far 'all this way' was. She had attempted to find out, but none of the guards would reveal the detention facility's location. The windows on the plane and transport vehicles were tinted black, so no clues there. She had traveled for hours, and the air in her new whereabouts felt cool and dry, unlike the swampy midsummer conditions in Saint Louis. Other than that, she had no clue as to where she was. How far was she from her father, from her mother's grave, from anything that mattered to her?

She turned, continuing her eye contact with the floor. Alexander clearly wasn't going to leave until she heard him out. The sooner she did that, the sooner she could get back to her room. Solitary confinement beat dealing with Alexander any day.

Shuffling to the chair opposite her ex-supervisor, Dara took a seat. "Okay. Tell me."

Alexander cleared his throat. "There's a bug in the software. It's not syncing with the operational codes. You developed the system and know it better than anyone. We'd like for you to resolve the glitch so we can be ready in time for Detonation Day."

Now Dara stared at Alexander, incredulous. "You've got Swanson on your team. Get him to do it."

Alexander shook his head. "We tried. Swanson's stuck. If this isn't resolved, we'll cause a delay."

Dara's eyebrows arched. "What about Jane Canton? She's always looking for work."

"You and I both know that Jane's mainly a figurehead at Chambers nowadays. Her students carry the technical load, and she gets the credit. We don't have time to clear anyone new to join the project."

She could no longer contain her annoyance. "Why the hell should I help you? Would you agree to use the coordinates we originally planned?"

"Sure," Alexander replied. Too quickly in Dara's estimation.

"Well, you're a professional liar, so I don't believe you."

"Would you believe me if I said we'd release you back to your life? How does this sound? If you patched up the software, we'd let you go home, set you up in a job in academia or the private sector, and life would go on. You would sign a non-disclosure agreement and we'd go our separate ways."

Dara could only gape at Alexander. Was he really saying what she thought she heard?

He continued. "You could even continue your research on climate modeling if you wanted to. There's bound to be significant commercial interest after the detonation, so you'd stand to gain. The bottom line is, you would help us and we'd help you."

"You have got to be kidding me."

"Not at all. We could make it happen. Besides, I know you're going stir crazy. You love solving these types of glitches. This could even be fun for you."

Dara's eyes bored into Alexander's. "I want no part of this."

He didn't blink. "Oh, I forgot to mention. We'd clear your debt, too."

Unable to stifle a laugh, Dara could only reply, "Really, now, Alexander, bribery?"

"I'm serious, Dara. Clean slate."

She got unamused fast. Alexander meant every crazy proposition. The bead of sweat at the edge of his hairline revealed he might even be a little desperate. "Look," she replied, mustering all the authority her voice could convey, "Under no circumstances will I agree to destroy any part of the Asian continent. That's what this is about, right? If that's how you want America to get the upper hand and rise up from the ashes and droughts and floods, be my guest, but I'm not helping you."

"I'm sorry, but I don't think you have a choice in the matter, unless you want to spend the rest of your life in an eight-by-ten-foot cell. Is that what you want?"

Dara's eyes burned. No, that wasn't what she wanted. But if those were his terms, she would accept them.

"Yep," she said, affecting a breezy tone, determined to stay positive, even defiant, in the face of his attempts to destroy her. "And I'd like to go back there, right now."

"Really? You're sure about this?"

"You heard me. I'm not helping you, and I'd like to go back to my cell."

Alexander rolled his eyes, got up, and opened the door with his keycard. The guard was waiting outside. "You can escort Ms. Bouldin back to her room, now, Marta."

Dara sprang up from the chair. "Thanks *so much* for coming to visit," she said, grinning sarcastically. "My regards to Carmen and the kids."

The fake-it-till-you-make-it approach must have worked. Back in her cell, Dara felt stronger than she had in days. She'd take one for the team, humanity being the team. Her life would mean something. Maybe some future politician would take pity on her and release her, or at least let her call her father.

Dara remembered what her mother always said: "The devil knows how to make all kinds of pots, but never figured out how to make the lids." Eventually, the truth would come out. And if it didn't, at least she'd go down swinging.

She heard a knock on her door. Marta and another woman entered. "Ms. Bouldin, we understand that your discussion with Mr. Fallsworth was unproductive."

Dara shrugged. "Unproductive? I don't think I'm under any obligation to 'produce' anything. I don't work for Alexander Fallsworth anymore."

Out of nowhere, Marta slapped her hard across the face.

Dara flinched, felt a welt developing on her cheek. "What did you do that for?"

She then noticed the other woman held a straight razor. "You need to consider falling into line."

Dara stared at the razor. Steadying her breathing, she murmured, "Please put that down."

The guard grabbed Dara and pinned her into the chair. She squirmed. "Hold still," Marta said through gritted teeth.

The other woman brought the razor up to Dara's face, brushing it over her cheeks, her mouth, her neck. Dara froze, hyperaware of the cold metal against her skin.

The woman grasped a fistful of Dara's hair, shaved it off at the roots. Jagged green locks fell to the floor. Dara froze in place, her neck seizing up, eyes fixed on the hair clippings. If she moved even a millimeter, blood would drip into the pile.

After what felt like an eternity, Marta shoved Dara to the floor. She and the other woman left without a word, leaving the clippings where they had fallen. As the ache to Dara's backside from hitting the linoleum set in, she felt at her scalp, finding only stubbly skin.

She shook her head, unaccustomed to the sensation of air conditioning where her hair used to be. *Quite the craven move*, Dara thought, *even for Alexander, making the guards do his dirty work*. As if shaving her head would be enough to change her mind.

All she could do was laugh. *Imagine that,* she thought. *Me, a skinhead.* If Jericho could only see her now — he'd never again question her punk sensibilities. She scooped the remains of her doomed pixie cut from the floor with her hands and flushed them down the toilet.

***

"Professor Canton speaking."

Avery hesitated. After every conversation he'd ever had with Jane, he promised himself, never again. But she'd turn up like the proverbial bad penny, each interaction typically worse than the one that preceded it. In Avery's experience, even Jane's infrequent brushes with kindness were just a palate cleanser, designed to soften her targets so future attacks would hurt more.

Agreeing to let Jane pay for Dara's hotel bill was like making a deal with Lucifer's ex-wife. But what else could he do? Homelessness was too great a risk.

And yet, today he received a strange package. UPS left the box behind his door while he was out running errands. The return address was the hotel in Saint Louis. Contents consisted of Dara's clothes, a bottle of green dye, some magazines, and a brief message. Signed by Howard Kitson, Night Manager, the note thanked Dara for her stay and indicated that enclosed were items she "inadvertently" left behind.

Where did Dara go? Did she leave Saint Louis? Why did she leave most of her clothes at the hotel? Avery knew she had access to hotel business center computers along with a disposable phone. Still, his calls and messages went unanswered.

Not knowing what else to do, he decided to call Jane. Their last conversation featured one of her rare displays of magnanimity – perhaps she was still in a good mood? Probably not, but, regardless, she must have known what happened regarding Dara's hotel stay, since she'd been paying the bill.

"It's Avery. I hope you're well."

"Of course. What can I do for you?" No ice tinkled in the background this time since he called her at work.

"Jane, you've been paying for Dara's hotel room over the past few weeks, and I really appreciate your help with that."

"Well, I would have preferred for you to thank me by telling me she moved."

Avery went silent. So, she knew about Dara's departure?

"Are you there?" Jane tapped at the phone.

"Um, yeah. I'm here. Actually, I didn't know she moved. How did you find out?"

"The hotel returned the money order I sent. Dara left about two weeks ago."

"Do you know where she went?"

Jane laughed into the receiver. "Avery, please. I'm not your daughter's keeper. Dara's an adult, and let's face it, why would she even want to talk to you? You ruined her life, remember?"

Yes, he remembered.

Jane continued. "She probably just wants a new start without you holding her back. Let her. If she wants you in her life, she'll get in touch."

Avery tried to respond but his voice caught in his throat.

"Or not!" Jane cackled, clearly enjoying herself.

Avery's voice returned. "Okay, Jane," he said. "Sorry to bother you at work."

"No problem," she replied, still snickering.

He hung up. So much for the reasonable, kind Jane from their previous chat. Avery immediately put it out of his mind, refusing to accept that Dara would disappear without a word. Someone out there knew her whereabouts, and Avery decided it was time for a deep dive.

***

Detonation Day now two weeks away, President Donahue decided it was time for yet another pre-victory lap, this time in the form of a television interview at the White House. Most of the noise from the likes of Sam-I-Am Collins and the Native Alaskan tribes had either died down or been drowned out. Public excitement nearing a crescendo, the Commander-in-Chief sought to prolong the good will.

Majority-party friendly news network? Check. Simpering reporter in the form of morning show newsreader Champ Wilkins? Check. Softball questions provided in advance for White House approval? Check. With the Oval Office as backdrop, the stage was set. President Donahue even wore a green tie and Earth cufflinks, signaling his commitment to environmental causes in case anyone had any doubt.

Administering the customary grip and grin, he immediately turned to the camera and affected his patented Ronald Reagan twinkle. "Champ, I think your viewers will agree – you're the best young reporter in this business. It's a pleasure to see you."

"The pleasure is all mine, Mr. President," said Champ.

The men settled into high back chairs.

"Sir, Detonation Day is just around the corner. We've received thousands of messages from our viewers in support. You've given hope to so many people."

"I'm glad," he said, nodding. "This is for them."

"I hear you're going to do the countdown live on TV. Did they have to twist your arm?"

Donahue chuckled. "Not at all. I'm delighted and honored to lead the festivities."

The reporter, still grinning, then lobbed a question not on the original list. "So, in agreeing to the Climate Action Act, are you admitting that global warming is real?"

The President's head began tilting to the side, but he checked himself before it went any further. "Excuse me?" he asked, reminding himself that he was on live television.

"You campaigned on global warming being a hoax. Are you now saying that you agree with environmentalists that climate change is caused primarily by human actions, such as burning fossil fuels?"

Donahue shook his head. "Champ, you know that there are many opinions on this subject. The jury's still out on global warming. I've chosen to back the detonation in Alaska out of an abundance of caution. If we can use resources and technologies available to us to improve the environment, let's try."

Champ no longer smiled. "With all due respect, Sir, the jury isn't 'still out' on climate change. Scientists disagree with you."

"Some scientists — not all." The president felt a bead of sweat trickle down his back.

"No. Not true. The only scientists who disagree are scientists employed by polluting industries. Or by your administration."

Donahue attempted to hide his disgust, taking on an impassive expression and tone of voice. His handlers would face his wrath after the interview, but this was live, and appearances mattered. "Champ, you're an intelligent, well-spoken young man. With all due respect, I advise you to do a bit more research and stop letting your personal biases impact your work."

"Oh?" Champ responded. "Sir, I did my research. I deal in science, data, and facts. They don't come with biases."

Shaking his head, forcing a chuckle, Donahue said, "Champ, you're exactly why I love idealistic, young people."

"Well, young people would prefer that you took our concerns seriously."

From the corner of his eye Donahue noticed the producer gesticulating, her face contorted. His pleasant expression returned, eyebrows knit into an earnest furrow.

"Of course, I take your concerns and those of all Americans very seriously."

Champ nodded, but his smirk told another story. "I'm getting a signal that our time is up. Thank you for joining us today, Mr. President."

"You're most welcome, Champ." Reagan twinkle, handshake, cut.

Donahue's smile vanished the second the red light on the camera went off. The president's handlers crowded around him, attempting to shield him from view as he tore off his microphone. He walked off, unconcerned that his abrupt departure might be characterized as storming out.

Escorts whisked Champ Wilkins and crew out of the building, all but releasing a pack of hounds to chase them away. Out of earshot, Donahue smashed a vase against the wall, nicking the frame around a hapless Andrew Jackson.

Still, he knew he'd get the last laugh. Champ Wilkins would be fired. The CEO of the network was an old friend, and James Donahue was all about applying executive privilege.

***

"You have a visitor," said Marta as she entered Dara's cell without knocking.

The guard had stopped bothering with basic professionalism, let alone pleasantries, sometime after she struck Dara across the face and forced her down to get shorn. Dara, for her part, ignored her.

This was Marta's second visit of the day. Earlier that morning, she pulled the "Follow me" routine, but Dara wasn't having it. She realized that she was under no obligation to follow anyone anywhere, let alone the likes of Alexander Fallsworth or his flunkies.

Instead, she started practicing yoga on the floor, the bed sheet folded up into a makeshift yoga mat. Not that she knew anything about the practice. But she'd had a brief gig in Saint Louis installing a new sound system at a yoga studio. As she worked, she watched the exercisers stretch into different poses, fascinated at the strength and agility on display. She decided to while away her days, mimicking her mental pictures of the poses, laughing at what she must look like contorting herself in coveralls. Still, despite the DIY nature of the endeavor, she felt her muscles getting tight but loose, and liked it.

This time Alexander came to her cell, bringing along a padlocked briefcase. *Oh joy*, she thought, sitting in a lotus position on the floor.

"Like my haircut?" she said, not looking at him.

"It's an improvement. The green was a little juvenile, if you ask me."

She pretended not to hear him, closing her eyes.

Comfortable?" asked Alexander, taking a seat at the desk.

"I'm exercising. You're interrupting me."

Alexander leaned back in the chair. "Dara, I've come by today to ask you to patch up the software so we can sync up to the operations unit and –"

"You already asked me, and I already told you no," said Dara, now standing in a lunge. "Hey, this time I'm interrupting you! I guess I'm 'belligerent' after all."

Alexander glared at her. "Dara, this is not a joke. You used to believe in this project. It was your baby. You wanted to save the world, remember?"

She glared back. "Not by your terms. Fix it yourself."

Alexander turned to the briefcase he brought along and pulled out a laptop computer, placing it on the desk. "I know you must be going nuts in here. Don't you want something to do to pass the time? If you make progress on the patch, I could load some games onto the computer for you. How does that sound?"

Dara broke into peals of laughter this time. "Oh, my God, Alexander, seriously? Games?"

"Just thought you might be bored," he said, eyebrows raised.

Dara remembered the old joke about "military intelligence" being an oxymoron. It would have been funny if it weren't so true. "Look," she said, "I never get bored. I solve theorems in my head. I recite poetry I've memorized. I make up stories. I build castles in the air. I've got plenty in my imagination to keep me busy for the rest of my life, thank you very much. And I'm not patching anything for you. Ever."

"I need you to reconsider."

"No means no."

This was ridiculous. What the hell was he going to do to her, anyway? Kill her? Surely that was illegal. Not that any of this seemed legal — but Alexander had to draw the line at murder...wouldn't he? Whatever, at least she wouldn't be responsible for millions of people dying. *Go ahead*, she thought. *Take your best shot.*

"Dara, I'm warning you."

With that, Dara's patience evaporated. "Warning me? Oh, please. Come on, Alexander, you can't make me do this, and you know it. Sorry if you thought you could break me with computer games, but kudos for trying." She returned to her DIY yoga mat.

Alexander scowled, walking toward the door, opening it with his keycard. Marta had been waiting behind the door. He motioned for her to enter.

As the guard closed the door with one hand, Dara noticed she was wearing rubber gloves. A shiny object glinted in her free hand.

Alexander walked toward Dara, forcing her up from the floor by her arms.

"What are you doing? Ouch! You're hurting me!" Red marks forming where Alexander's fingers had been, he pushed her onto the bed, pinning her down from behind with his arms and legs.

"Get off!" Dara yelled, struggling with all her might to break loose. Marta walked over in silence and freed Dara's left arm, which Alexander held in place.

"If you stop squirming, this will be much easier on you," said Alexander through gritted teeth. His extremities crushed hers into submission as his hot breath wafted over the side of her face. She tried kicking, to no avail, realizing she was as good as paralyzed.

At that, Marta maneuvered the shiny object, a long-needled syringe, into a vein in Dara's arm, injecting her. Dara screamed, feeling every muscle in her body contract.

A screeching sound filled her ears. A metallic taste overtook her mouth. She felt like a cannonball on the verge of being shot. It was probably best that Alexander continued to hold her down, keeping her from flinging her body through the wall.

Dara's thoughts accelerated. *What's happening? Where am I? Why are the lines in the linoleum so sharp? How did the lights get so bright?* "Oh, God, my heart is about to explode," she heard herself say.

She felt herself wretch. Alexander dragged her to the toilet where she threw up. The woman wearing rubber gloves wiped the vomit off her face with toilet paper.

Dara stared at the Band-Aid the woman had put on her arm. "It's so hot in here," she said, unbuttoning and removing the top of her coveralls, a thin undershirt beneath. "God, I must look terrible."

"No, you're fine," said a deep male voice.

"Alexander?" said Dara, now hearing an echo.

"Yes, it's me."

"Are we at work?" asked Dara.

"Yes, we are," replied Alexander, smiling.

"Oh. Who's she?"

"It's Marta. She's here to make sure you feel okay. Let her know if you need her to crank the A/C or bring you some water. She'll give you something tonight so you'll be able to sleep."

"Okay."

"Can you do something for me?"

"What do you want me to do?"

"I need you to patch up some software."

"Mmkay." Dara was slurring at this point.

"Great. I know I can always count on you." Alexander's giddiness was palpable. Wasting no time, he led her to the desk and walked her through the problem.

***

Hotel staff members don't discuss their guests. Avery Bouldin learned this the hard way while trying to find Dara.

He called the desk at Dara's hotel in Saint Louis several times a day in hopes of catching someone off script, perhaps a new employee who didn't know the rules, or someone with children who'd empathize. But the staff wouldn't budge.

"Sir," the night manager said, "We respect a guest's right to privacy, so we can't share information about Miss Jones."

"But she disappeared and left most of her clothes behind. I'm worried about her. She's my only daughter." Avery's voice quavered.

"I understand, and I'm truly sorry, but my hands are tied. If it's an emergency, you should contact law enforcement authorities."

The card burned a hole in Avery's pocket, reminding him that Kyle Anson, Special Agent, Federal Bureau of Investigation, had asked about his daughter. If that particular law enforcement authority was still trying to find Dara, maybe he could get real answers from Anson or his staff. As opposed to the runaround into brick walls he was currently getting.

The last thing Avery wanted was for the FBI to find Dara. But at least they could assure him that she was safe so he could finally sleep again.

He dialed.

"Anson," said a deep voice.

Avery cleared his throat. "Mr. Anson, my name is Avery Bouldin. You came to my home a few weeks ago and asked about my daughter, Dara."

"Yes, I recall," said the agent.

"Um, did you happen to find her?"

"I thought she lived with you."

"Actually, she left. I haven't heard from her, and I was wondering if you had."

"Mr. Bouldin, I can't comment on an ongoing investigation."

Avery hesitated. "I understand. I'm just calling as her father. I want to make sure she's safe."

"Your daughter isn't a minor. She's free to come and go as she pleases, and she doesn't need to inform you. Do you have reason to believe she's in trouble?"

"I don't know."

"If you did, you could always file a missing person's report with the local police."

Silence on Avery's end. She wasn't exactly a 'missing person,' not in the traditional sense.

"Look, your daughter is in her twenties. Could be she just wants her independence. I'm sure she'll get back in touch with you when she's ready. It's only been a few weeks."

"What if she's in danger?"

"Mr. Bouldin, have you had any contact with your daughter since I first spoke to you? I asked you to contact me. Do you remember that?"

Avery didn't know how to respond without incriminating himself or getting Dara into more trouble. But then again, talking to Anson was voluntary. He wondered if this phone call meant he was under oath.

But Anson probably already knew the answer. "I'm not answering that," said Avery. "Talking to you was and is voluntary. Good-bye."

"I'll take that as a yes," said the agent as Avery hung up.

***

Red, orange, and yellow colors swirled. Like swimming inside an impressionist painting, breathing in color, as if through water. Or smoke.

So unbearably hot. Was she melting? Dara reached up to wipe the sweat beading on her brow, saw flames licking the bed around her. She spotted someone at the edge of her mattress.

"Mom, is that you?" Dara held out her hand.

Anne Bouldin reached for Dara through the flames. Not screaming this time but smiling. Brown hair framed her face, collarbones. She was smaller than Dara remembered. Same rosy cheeks, sparkling brown eyes.

"Don't cry, sweetheart. Come with me."

Dara held her mother's hand, walked with her through the fire.

"I miss you so much."

"I miss you, too."

"I didn't even get to know you."

"I know, sweetheart."

"Something happened to me, Mom. I'm trapped."

Dara's subconscious knew the full extent of her troubles, but the conscious version of Dara had no idea. Before the daily doses of stimulants and God knows what else wore off, Marta would inject Dara with bedtime barbiturates, literal nightmare fuel.

"You'll get through it. You've pulled through so much. I'm proud of you."

Dara shook her head. "I'm in over my head."

"Did you ask for help?"

"No," she said. Too proud, too stubborn. And when she finally decided to reach out, too late. She looked away.

"It's okay to let somebody help you."

"I can't trust anyone, Mom," Dara whispered. "I've been hurt too many times."

"It's too much for one person to be strong all the time, and it's not necessary. Pain means you're alive. But it's not all painful, I promise you." She pulled Dara close.

Dara breathed in her mom's scent. Anne worked in a department store and would sneak sprays of Chanel Number Five from the testers after her shifts. Dara hadn't smelled Chanel Number Five in years.

"Losing you was the worst thing that ever happened to me, Mom."

"Losing you was the worst thing that ever happened to me, Dara."

"But I'm the reason you died."

"Don't say that, baby. You gave me so much to live for. You made every minute of my life a treasure."

Dara dissolved into tears, reached up to touch her mom's face.

Someone grabbed at her arm. After a pinching sensation, the sound of a freight train whizzed through

Dara's head, screeching into her eardrums from the inside. She opened her eyes.

"Time to get up and back to work. Alexander told me you're nearly finished with the patch." Marta pointed to the desk. "Come on, you don't want to be late." The glare from the laptop pierced Dara's retinas. She shuffled to the workstation, her heart thumping in her chest.

T-minus Two

The Sunday morning talk show oozed from the flatscreen, complete with blow-dried, grinning host, omnipresent 'Breaking News' banner scrolling underneath. "Professor Canton," said the talking head, "Thank you for joining us this morning. According to yesterday's leaks, Detonation Day is in danger of postponement due to a software problem. Can you set the record straight?"

Jane had perfected her TV look, sitting for the interview in a bright red dress, full makeup and rhinestone American flag brooch.

Avery Bouldin watched the show in spite of himself, knowing Jane was scheduled to appear. He chuckled, noticing that she and the host had matching oversized veneers.

"Tim, this is a non-story. Detonation Day is happening on August 14th, right on schedule. And let me assure you, the president is getting to the bottom of how this falsehood got spread."

Under normal circumstances, Dara would be at the table, eating Sunday pancakes with Avery, filling the kitchen with her goofy laugh at Jane's preposterous makeover. But he still hadn't heard from Dara and had no idea of what to do about it. Bittersweet pangs pulsed in his chest.

"Can you tell us where things stand with the software?" asked Tim Dobson, the host, apparently stifling an eye-roll. "Our sources indicate that it wasn't in sync with the operational program. The last thing we want is for the detonation to miss its mark."

"That won't happen," said Jane, glowering at her inquisitor. "Are you going to believe some hacker? You're a seasoned journalist, Tim. I'm sure you're aware that people sometimes make up claims just to get a rise out of the American public."

"Yes, but intelligence sources confirmed the hacks, Dr. Canton. So as a 'seasoned journalist,' I'll need more details."

Jane stared at him, nonplussed.

He went on. "As it stands, next week, several drones will be carrying thermonuclear warheads over populated areas en route to Alaska. How can we be sure the detonation will be carried out safely?"

Jane hesitated. Finally, she said, "Our top expert, the individual who developed the code, is personally seeing to the mission's success."

Avery's heart jumped. Could it be true?

"Oh?" said the journalist, "Who?"

"Someone I know very well, personally and professionally. I trust this person's technical abilities. More than that, her work defines who she is. She'd sooner die than deliver a product that was less than perfect."

A bilious sensation crept up Avery's esophagus. Dara's work was about making sure no one else ever had to lose a loved one the way she did, not about misguided perfectionism.

"We'll be trusting this person with the lives of countless Americans. Do you understand why this question is important?"

"Of course I do. And so does the president. He calls me every day for an update on our progress. We're all on the hook. I assure you, any concerns about the software have been addressed, and we'll be ready on Detonation Day exactly as planned."

"Do you stake your reputation on it?"

Jane nodded, a little too vigorously. "Yes," she said, "And so does President Donahue."

"This program will most certainly define his legacy, regardless of how it plays out. Thank you for joining us today, Dr. Canton."

"You're very welcome," said Jane, Chiclet smile on full display. At that, the host cut to commercial.

Avery wondered. If Jane was referring to Dara, did that mean she was in Washington?

But Dara hadn't called. It wasn't like her.

Was she being held against her will?

Or perhaps she just hated him. At least that's what Jane would say. Maybe she was right.

***

Night. Not quite sleeping, not quite dreaming. From the depths of her unconscious, Dara begged all that was divine for a moment's peace. The bedtime meds were a cruel joke. Morpheus mocked her with all the rapid eye movements but zero actual rest.

Dara heard a clicking sound, caught a dark figure slipping into her cell in her peripheral vision. A midsummer night's incubus? She tried to move, but under the influence, her arms and legs became an amalgamation of lead and Jell-O.

Black ski mask, black clothes, black gloves despite it being August. Did her visitor find the air conditioning oppressive? She couldn't cool off to save her life even though she was drinking at least ten bottles of water a day.

Would he speak to her? Yesterday she chattered with the centipede she found crawling on the floor under her bed. Marta wasn't up for conversation, only administering shots and barking orders. Or taking her computer away and announcing it was bedtime. Dara finished her assignment, but her mind kept moving, desperate to talk to someone, anyone. She could have sworn she heard the insect talking back to her.

Perhaps the man in black was up for some conversation. "I miss my father. I wish I could call him. Will you help me?" The words formed in her head but emerged from her mouth as murmurs.

He approached Dara's bed, reached out to her, the leather from his gloves rough against her shoulders. He then shook her, hard.

"Mmmmph." She wanted to tell the man he was hurting her.

He slapped her face, then said in a low growl, "You have to get up."

"It's...still...dark."

"Dara, listen to me. I'm helping you escape. Get up."

"Mmmmph..."

He took something out of his pocket, a small vial, and waved it under her face. A putrid odor punched Dara in the nose.

"Oh, God," she said.

"Listen," the man said in a gruff whisper, "You have to get up and follow me as quietly as you can. Okay?"

"Follow you where?"

"Just trust me. I'm here to help you."

"Help me?"

"Yes. Now."

She looked at the dark mask through the shadows, tried to make out the eyes. His voice wafted into her consciousness as he spoke.

"Yes. I need help," she said, holding out her hand, stumbling from bed in prison issue underwear.

"Here, put these on," he said, tossing her a pair of black leggings, a black undershirt, and sneakers.

She had trouble coordinating her movements, so he dressed her. "I'm sorry," she whispered, feeling her face grow warm. "I don't know what I'm doing."

"It's okay," he said, "Follow me."

The man put on what looked like night vision goggles, led Dara by the hand through the cell door. His keycard made a soft click as he opened it. Dara's legs felt heavy, as if they'd buckle under her at any moment.

"This way," he said. Dara noticed one of the male guards, out cold on the floor.

"Aren't the cameras going to film us?" she asked.

"Don't worry about cameras."

"Aren't there motion detectors?"

"Don't worry about motion detectors. Just walk."

The only light came from the intermittent Exit signs in the corridors. Were they going outside? Dara hadn't been outdoors in weeks. The hairs on her arms pricked up at the prospect of fresh air.

They moved together, the man ensuring that Dara stayed on her feet despite her stupor. "Can we rest a little?" she asked.

"No. You need to do everything you can to stay awake."

"Mmkay." She tried pinching herself, biting the inside of her cheek, singing a song in her head. The lyrics came to her in Jericho's voice:

> *Strange days*
> *Signals crossed, time is lost*
> *Nothing falls into place*
> *You made your world*
> *Stay with it girl*
> *Or you'll fall from grace*
> *Take her away, take her away*
> *Say what you want to say*

She and the man ran toward the doorway at the end of the hall. Dara realized that the guard she saw just moments before, sprawled out on the linoleum, was now chasing after them.

"Faster," growled the man under his breath.

Strange nights, clouded skies hide the moon
Stars fade from sight
Dream away, the world is too much with you, girl
Maybe she might
Just run away, just run away
Say what you want to say

The guard caught up, grabbed the man by the back of his shirt. Dara's protector swung around, catlike, and clocked him on the temple. The guard stumbled and lunged forward, reaching for his weapon. The man kickboxed the guard's hand away from his holster, knocking him to the ground. Several blows later, he was out cold again.

She remembered her father's advice if she ever got in a fight. Block with the left, fight with the right. Hard to do when you're seeing double, tottering through what felt like a viscous substance.

The man in the mask grabbed Dara's arm. "Come on, we have to get out of here."

They made it outside. Torrential rain, damp, swampy air. The rains were always torrential nowadays, no surprise there. Half crouching, Dara followed the man toward a sign that said Employee Parking. He pushed her into the back seat of a steel gray SUV.

"Get on the floor, under the blanket."

Sounds in the background pierced through the rain. Alarms blaring through the complex penetrated the car's sealed windows and doors, the dark wool blanket, Dara's addled brain. She covered her ears, her scalp like sandpaper against her fingertips.

The SUV lurched forward, moving fast, then faster. "Brace yourself!" the man yelled as the engine revved.

She felt an impact, heard the sound of a collision. Her body hurtled off the floor, weightless for a split-second, then landed, knees first. She moaned, grabbed onto the seat, forced herself upright through the pain to look through the back window. They'd crashed through a gate, now in splinters on the ground. The SUV's front windshield, rain pouring over it in sheets, revealed several long cracks. The mirror on the passenger side sheared loose. As they sped off, she spotted another car in the distance, sirens cranked to eleven, following in pursuit.

"Down! Now!"

Dara, woozy, obeyed orders.

They'd had a head start, but the sirens grew as the other vehicle accelerated. "Hold on!" The car bounced over a hill, then swerved. If the brambles hitting the windows and tumultuous ride were any indication, they'd exited the road.

Dara sat up. Too fast — headrush. Woods, wet leaves sticking to the windows, blackness beyond them. Her guardian hadn't turned on the headlights. To her left, brakes squealed. Another steel gray SUV raced past them onto the road, emerging via the same clearing they'd used as an off ramp.

They continued forward off-road, into the forest, away from the asphalt. Dara's heart now raced, drowning out the SUV's rattle. The sirens crescendoed, then grew faint.

Her pulse ebbed with the sound, the nighttime meds resuming their consciousness-dulling mission. Dara curled up on the floor of the car. *He's going to do a number on his suspension*, she thought, as the SUV forged through the vegetation. Her clothes, skin, and shoes, drenched, she listened to the rain thump on the roof of the car. Jericho's grizzled tenor returned, singing the bridge to "Strange Days," lulling her to sleep:

> *She lost the key to her lock on life*
> *She's too lost in the dark to take flight*
> *For every venture, there's nothing gained*
> *But you made your world*
> *It's yours, girl, so stay*

***

Ringtones interrupted Avery's slumber. The graveyard shift at the Slot Lot meant he slept during the day, but Dara's silence left him no choice but to keep the phone switched on. From the bedside table, Caller ID flashed, "Unknown."

Avery's pulse registered in electrical impulses. Was it Dara? Jane? Jericho? Anson?

"Yeah?" he said into the receiver.

"Avery Bouldin?" A voice reverberated from the other end, gruff and distorted as if disguised by a computer. Avery recalled witnesses on a TV crime show.

"Who is this?" he asked, not in the mood for games.

"I'm calling to tell you your daughter is safe."

The impulses morphed into full-on shock. "Where is she?"

"In a secure location, with people concerned for her welfare."

Avery's voice rose. "Who has her? Tell me!"

"I cannot disclose this information. But I assure you, in due time, she will return home."

The voice on the other end sounded male, but the gender could have been a computer trick. The speech patterns seemed...stilted?

Avery racked his brain, attempting to place the voice, but came up null. "Why should I believe you?" he said, spittle collecting at the corners of his mouth. "Who is this?"

Silence from the other end.

"I'm calling the police!"

This time the caller responded. "I strongly advise you not to notify the authorities."

"Really? And why should I listen to you?"

"They're the ones you should be worried about."

Avery restrained himself from slamming the phone on the table. "Stop talking in riddles," he said through gritted teeth. "Can I at least talk to her?"

"No. But trust me, Dara is safe.

"I have no reason to trust you."

"I give you my word," the caller replied. "She is with people who care about her. Maybe even more than you do."

Avery erupted into a string of expletives, to no avail. The phone disconnected.

***

Dara awoke, temples pounding, pulsating in pain. She opened her eyes, regretting doing so as light singed her retinas.

Where was sunlight coming from? Her cell didn't have any windows. She blinked, eyes watering. The sheets felt softer than she remembered, much softer. She wiped her eyes on the scalloped edge of the pillowcase.

Several blinks later, Dara's eyes adjusted to a squint. Her surroundings felt new, the hints of wood and varnish calling to mind a furniture shop. This wasn't her cell at all. Exposed beams on the ceiling drew her gaze to a wall of windows. Sliding doors opened out to a deck overlooking mountains and trees that spread for miles, verdant under the cloudless sky.

She winced through her headache. Her arms and legs, covered with bruises and what looked like dirt, sank into the mattress. As far as she stretched her limbs, the bed's edges remained out of reach.

The room looked like something out of a Frank Lloyd Wright fantasy, only with higher ceilings and the world's most enormous bed. A stone fireplace and plush chairs flanked the walls, and a brightly colored area rug partially covered the wide-planked oak floor. There wasn't much else in the way of adornment, as if anything could compete with the spectacular view.

Taking in her surroundings, something felt oddly familiar. Dara tried to shrug off the feeling as a phantom memory, knowing she'd never met anyone with a home like this nor stayed in a hotel remotely this nice. Maybe she'd seen something similar in a magazine?

Dara spotted the door to the bathroom, hoping it came with extra-strength ibuprofen in the medicine cabinet. She maneuvered her aching body through the piles of Egyptian cotton, careful to avoid sullying the sheets with dirt.

The en-suite bathroom housed a massive shower and Jacuzzi tub. Should she take a bath? She certainly needed one. Alas, no meds, just piles of towels. And mirrors. Catching her reflection for the first time in weeks, Dara's heart dropped. The woman staring back at her in a ripped undershirt and black leggings was bald, scarred, ghastly. She looked away, deciding that she'd better wash up lest the proprietor throw her out on sight.

Tears welled, mingling with water from the shower. *Where am I? How did I get here?* The last she could remember, she was in the detention center. This wasn't prison at all. The view from the bathroom window suggested heaven. *Am I dead?*

The deceased don't get splitting headaches. Perhaps she was Schrödinger's fugitive, alive and dead at the same time. Dara laughed sardonically through her tears.

She scrubbed at the dirt, inhaling the soap's minty fragrance and growing steadier with each breath. Her mouth parched, she gulped water from the shower head as she washed. Find the owners, she told herself. They could tell her how she got here, or at least let her call her father.

She located a tube of toothpaste but no toothbrush, so she improvised with her finger. At least she didn't need to worry about drying her hair. Toweling off, she was loath to wear her filthy leggings-undershirt combo again, but the bedroom-sized closet was empty. She hoped a clean body would count for something.

Deep breath. She walked toward the door, reached for the knob. But just as her fingers touched brass, the lock clicked, opened, sent shockwaves down her spine.

"Dara." A man's voice quavered.

Unable to move, she managed a whisper: "Jericho."

He pulled her into his arms. A year's worth of tears poured between them.

She found her voice. "Where am I?"

Jericho smiled through his tears, led her by the hand through the corridor to a cavernous living room. "My cabin. Welcome to Boonieville."

She eyed the room, its oversized sofa, puffy chairs, cream-colored shag rug. Reclaimed wood and stonework, hearth, home. Dara's headache throbbed harder as confusion took over. "How did I get here?"

"Do you remember anything?"

"I was in a detention center. They wouldn't let me call my father or get a lawyer."

"What else?"

Dara wondered what Jericho knew, but surmised that her presence here meant he probably knew something, if not everything. "They wanted me to patch the detonation software, the operational version that's supposed to sync up to the modeling program I developed. I've been working on Donahue's climate project these past few months."

Jericho nodded. "Yeah, I know. Did anything else happen to you?"

"They slapped me around, shaved my head. Alexander made his underlings do it for him."

"Such a goddamn coward."

Dara's lip resumed trembling.

"Hey, don't cry," Jericho said softly. "Your hair's really cute like that."

Dara shook her head. "I couldn't care less about my hair. They weren't going to change the coordinates back to the ones I proposed, so I refused to patch the software. And then I woke up in your house. I can't remember anything else. How did I even get here?"

Jericho furrowed his brow. "You must be hungry. Come on, I'll make you some lunch."

"Got any aspirin? I've got the worst headache."

"I'll get you some. By the way, the doctor I keep on retainer for our tour insurance is coming tomorrow to check you out."

"Doctor?"

She followed Jericho to the kitchen, all stainless-steel appliances, marble countertops, and white cabinets. It finally hit her. This was the house she and Jericho imagined they'd build together.

"Yeah, just to be on the safe side. I'm sorry to tell you this, but Alexander and his goons had you drugged."

Dara heard nothing. For a moment, all she could process in her mind was déjà vu, all over again. Her memory sharpened into focus, its point all too fine. This was the house Dara dreamed of building with Jericho, before they broke up, before her life went off the rails. She stared at the floor.

"Hey, are you okay?" Jericho reached over to stroke Dara's forehead.

"I probably just need some food," she said in a quiet voice.

"Well, they injected you with something. The drugs might be the reason for your headache."

She looked up. "What did they make me take?"

"We're not sure. Probably some sort of amphetamine cocktail during the day and sleep medication at night."

"Why did they do that?" asked Dara, praying the answer wasn't what she suspected.

"To force you to patch the software. Alexander's dead set on making the detonation happen, and medicating you was the means to the end."

Dara's face grew hot.

"It's not your fault," said Jericho, catching the tear that streamed down her cheek with his finger. "It's going to be all right."

She shook her head. "The detonation can't happen. You don't understand."

"No, I do understand."

"What do you know?"

"I know about Alexander changing the coordinates. I know that he wants to advance America by turning parts of Russia, China, and other countries in Asia into wastelands. He wants to crush the competition, play dirty and settle scores."

Dara could only stare at Jericho, unblinking, unsure of what to ask next.

"Here's a couple aspirin and some water," said Jericho. Assembling a sandwich on a plate, he continued, "But eat some of this first. You don't need an ulcer on top of everything else."

The smell of roast beef and tomato reminded Dara that she hadn't eaten in what felt like days. "Thanks," she said, sitting on a stool at the edge of the kitchen island. "What time is it anyway?"

"Two p.m., August ninth."

Dara sighed. In her mind-altered state, the hours seeped in and out of the detention facility without her realization. How could anything be "all right" with so little time left?

She started on her lunch, hoping it would settle her stomach. "Jericho, how do you know all this? Is this public knowledge?"

He looked at her, choosing his words carefully. "The person who rescued you told me."

Dara dropped her sandwich back onto the plate. "Rescued me? Are you serious? I'm not some damsel in distress!"

"Hey, I know you don't like it when people help you, but it was either get rescued or stay in the detention center for the rest of your life."

Dara felt her shoulders tense at the edge in Jericho's response. "Why did they tell you?"

"Your rescuer knows I'll do whatever it takes to help. And that no one would ever find you here."

"Was it my father?"

Jericho hesitated. "Avery knows you're safe, but we can't tell him the whole story just yet."

"Who's this 'we' you keep talking about? Who rescued me? I don't understand."

What seemed like minutes passed before Jericho mustered the courage to answer Dara's question. "Reg," he said, his voice halting, "It was Dmitri."

***

Rescuing Dara meant Dmitri – who skipped his flight back to Russia and remained in D.C. under deep cover -- needed to find Jericho, who 1) resided in a luxury hermitage in Middle of Nowhere, West Virginia, and 2) had strong ties to Senator Samantha Collins, the lone voice of reason when it came to the Climate Action Act. It also meant keeping tabs on Dara, which got tricky when Alexander Fallsworth forced her into the detention center. Hacking the security cameras and closed-circuit TVs took time, a resource in short supply.

Procuring twin sport utility vehicles from Center, including one that could operate without a driver, came next, along with forged credentials, fake license plates, night vision goggles, and a uniform. Mapping the escape route in consultation with Jericho followed. The plan involved waiting for the night that called for downpours, all the better to wash away any tire tracks.

Dmitri, in hiding at his Russian Embassy office, watched Dara defy Alexander in real time, cheering her on, dreading what could happen. When the henchwoman began drugging her, he felt every needle that plunged into her arm. Worse, he realized the meds turned Dara into a zombie, Alexander's drone. He needed to get her out of there, as quickly as possible—but also as safely as possible. Detonation be damned.

He entered the facility in his usual guise as a night watchman. Once on the premises, he switched to black clothes in order to blend into the shadows. He located Dara's cell, incapacitating a guard in the process, gently awakened her and helped her into civilian clothes. They made it back to the parking lot, giving the guards and police the slip by tearing through the rain and into the woods in the SUV outfitted with signal jammers. Then Dmitri activated the driverless decoy for the cops to follow. Center in Moscow had programmed the vehicle to crash into a tree some distance away.

Dmitri drove to Jericho's cabin, mostly via back roads, arriving as planned before sunup. Once they'd gotten away from the police sirens, Dara passed out, sleeping through the thunder and lightning.

Jericho's cabin. The air smelled of ozone from all the lightning, of pine and greenery. Dmitri scooped Dara's limp body from the floor of the vehicle, carrying her into the house. A broken bird, heart thumping, limbs scarred from past injuries, bruised from recent assaults.

The life she'd led pained him. Surviving a wildfire only to lose her mother. Bouncing around the country, always the misfit. Working for Jason Houseman, a pompous ass who refused to acknowledge her prodigious talents. Alexander Fallsworth, chewing her up and spitting her out after he'd gained her trust.

Dara's thesis advisor Jane Canton used her for her own money-grubbing purposes. Even her own father had used her. Avery Bouldin gambled away her future, refusing to seek help for his own demons until it was too late.

In the darkened room, Dara's face pale against the white sheets, Dmitri remembered better times, how he'd run his hands through her glossy dark hair, spread out below him on his pillow. Such sweet moments they'd had. He longed for them, kissed her on the forehead. *"May God grant you to be so beloved by another,"* he thought, recalling the lines from Pushkin's poem, *Ya vas Lyubil.* Such was his life: fall in love, fall away.

Jericho would take care of her, and Dmitri knew Dara would do the right thing. She would access the right people, develop a plan. Russia, the fatherland, along with all of the other countries in the detonation's crosshairs, would be in her debt, never even knowing it. But he would.

***

Dara paced the kitchen, the gravity of the situation sinking in as the aspirin took the edge off her headache. "We're running out of time."

"Any ideas?" asked Jericho, setting out a bowl of grapes.

"Jericho, I had every intention of contacting you when I was in Saint Louis, but I got detained. I need you to put me in touch with Chase Tucker. He's Samantha Collins' Science Advisor. They'll take your calls."

"Does he know you?"

"Yes. He called me at AAER with questions about the software months ago. He knows I developed it, and he figured out that something was up with the coordinates. I confronted Alexander about it, and the next thing I knew, I was out of a job. Alexander and his yes men probably made up a bunch of data to try to throw him off."

"I'll call right now," he said, placing a handful of grapes in Dara's palm. "In the meantime, you eat. They obviously starved you in there."

Dara sighed, but knew he was right. After lunch, Jericho handed her a clean Vitamin X tee-shirt from his Tyrannosaurus Regina merchandise cache to wear in lieu of her torn undershirt. Size extra small hung off her body. She vowed that after all this was over, she was going to take better care of herself, eat right, get strong.

She needed decent clothes, maybe even a wig if she was going to meet with the senator and Chase Tucker. Were there even any stores in the area? Dara noticed the solar panels on the roof when she stepped onto the deck with her grapes. Jericho had mentioned a solar water heater, and most of the rooms had fireplaces. He'd made good on his vow to go off the grid. She made a mental note to tell him how proud she was of what he had accomplished -- although as wondrous as she found the Middle of Nowhere, she still needed proper business attire.

Through the sliding glass doors, Jericho handed Dara the phone, which he'd placed on mute. "It's Sam Collins along with Chase Tucker, on speaker. I told her what happened, and they want to speak to you."

"Do they believe you?"

"Not sure. But I helped Senator Collins get elected, so she owes me," said Jericho as he returned to the kitchen.

She unmuted the phone. "Dara Bouldin speaking."

"Good afternoon, Dara, this is Samantha Collins. Jericho tells us you've been through quite an ordeal."

"Yes, ma'am, I have. I'm the Dara Bouldin who developed the detonation software. After I started working at AAER, Alexander Fallsworth from CIA approached me about adapting it for implementation. I talked to Chase months ago about the coordinates being off."

"Chase, is this the person you told me about?" asked Senator Collins.

"Yes," he said.

Dara continued. "I confronted Alexander, and he had my clearance revoked on trumped-up espionage allegations. I wanted to get back in touch with Chase, but I got thrown into a detention center before I could track him down."

"Chase believes the coordinates Mr. Fallsworth proposed would result in adverse changes to climate conditions overseas. Is this true?"

"Yes, parts of Russia, China, and other parts of Asia would become uninhabitable. Millions of innocent civilians would suffer."

Chase piped up. "A while back, Fallsworth, Jane Canton, and a few others met with us and claimed those assertions were incorrect."

"I'm convinced they made up data after I got forced out. That's Alexander's style."

Hesitation from the other end, then Senator Collins spoke. "Dara, we had no idea until after the fact that you were arrested and sent to a detention center. We knew you developed the software, and we should have pressed Fallsworth to explain why you weren't in that meeting."

"I wasn't even arrested, just detained and pretty much tortured. I did nothing illegal, and they knew it. They never read me my rights, never let me call an attorney, never even let me call…my father." Dara gulped, hoping the Senator and Chase hadn't noticed the catch in her throat.

"I understand they drugged you."

"That's how they forced me to debug the software. Alexander said he'd let me go if I coded a patch, but I refused. I knew what he was planning to do. He wants to build up America by crushing our economic and military competition from Asia. He thinks we need to retaliate for the wars we've lost, including the political and economic ones."

Dara felt her stomach clench. "Senator, I know this must sound crazy," she added, "but I swear on my life, it happened."

The senator cleared her throat. "Dara, your line isn't secure, and there's much that I can't say. But rest assured, I believe you."

Dara exhaled. "I appreciate that."

"Do you know what drugs they gave you?"

"No, but Jericho arranged for a doctor to come tomorrow to examine me and give me a drug test."

"Sounds like you're in good hands."

"Definitely," replied Dara.

"How do you know Jericho?"

Dara searched for words. "He's...my oldest friend. Probably my best friend. We grew up together." She hoped Jericho couldn't see her through the glass, on the verge of tears.

"He obviously cares about you very much."

"Yes," said Dara, "he does."

The Senator's tone shifted. "Dara, we haven't a moment to spare. After your medical appointment, can you come meet us in Washington? I'd like you to go through the software with Chase and explain what's in store if we go through with Alexander's version of the detonation."

"I can do that."

"I'm going to call an emergency session of the Intelligence Committee to convene immediately. Are you willing to testify?"

"Absolutely." She spotted Jericho watching her through the glass doors, gave him the thumbs up.

T-minus One

"Rex, I'm going to need to buy some clothes. Does Boonieville have any stores?"

"There's a big box place about 50 miles from here. It's on the way to D.C."

"We could buy me a new outfit and replace your tires at the same time."

"Hey, let's not dis West Virginia. Did you not see the view?"

"Yeah, I saw it," she replied, a smile coming to her lips. But it vanished when she realized she didn't have any cash or credit cards. "You know, if we left super early and stopped at my apartment, I could just wear my own clothes. We wouldn't have to buy anything. I could even get my car back if my dad didn't sell it."

"You realize your place is being surveilled, right? And we can't drag your dad into this yet, for his own safety. Dmitri was clear about that."

Dmitri. Dara hadn't fully processed his role in her escape. Feeling herself stiffen, she opted to change the subject. "I'm going to need some hair, too."

Jericho gave her the once over. "I'm sorry, Reg, but I don't think we'll be able to find you a wig in time. You've got a nice buzz growing, though. The weather got hot again and it's going to be 100 degrees by the time we get to D.C. You might even prefer it."

Oh well – vanity, meet bonfire. So tomorrow morning the doctor would swing by at six, then the drive to D.C. would take around three hours. Fifty miles in, she'd procure what would pass for business clothes in grab-and-go fashion at Boonie-Mart, changing in the car. Maybe pick up a McBreakfast/lunch combo somewhere. The cherry atop the slop sundae was to finish the day getting grilled by members of Congress. *Lovely.*

But Dara brightened. At first, she wasn't sure why. Then it hit her – three hours alone on the road with Jericho. When was the last time that happened? She stifled a laugh, picturing him hiding in the vehicle while she shopped, the tinted windows rolled up so as not to incite a teen girl riot. When they were a couple, he'd play the role of sounding board for her Avery Bouldin/Jane Canton-engendered anxieties, knowing exactly how to build her confidence, buck the hum in her head. Something she desperately needed right now.

***

A voice boomed through the car speakers. "Good morning! Friends, I'm not gonna lie. I'm excited today. So much that I'm about to jump out of my skin."

A second voice piped up. "That's a lot of skin to jump out of, boss!"

Dara rolled her eyes. "Jericho, do we have to listen to Fat Frank?"

"Just for a while — he promised to play one of my new songs. I need to make sure he does it."

Another voice ribbed, "Did it ever occur to you to order the salad?"

"Hey, I get Caesar salads all the time."

"Not quite," countered Frank's lackey. "You get a giant bowl of dressing, croutons, and cheese, with a dollop of lettuce."

Frank sighed. "Guilty as charged. Actually, I call it the Brutus. It's the salad that stabs you in the back."

Unwarranted cackles flew from the speakers, filling the car.

Dara shook her head, catching a glimpse of her arms in the process. Besides the scarring from her childhood, she now had bonus track marks from Alexander's goons' injections, plus fresh scabs from vials of blood drawn this morning. A long-sleeved blouse was in order, despite the heat.

Sun-lit clouds shaped like valentines, seashells and horses rolled by as the Appalachians stretched before them like open arms. Curious vegetation grew lush in spots. On closer inspection, it was mostly felled or stunted trees, choked by new growth.

Jericho swerved. Screeching tires drowned out the radio.

"What was that?" Dara yelled, gripping the armrest.

"The storms have been pretty terrible. They haven't had time to move the rocks off the road."

Dara stared at the netting on the sides of the mountains, holding the boulders in place. "Watch for Falling Rocks" signs seemed like a threat. West Virginia already struggled with economic and other malaise; climate problems added insult to injury. She thought back to the days when her modeling program was still a game, how she'd pinpoint coordinates to help places that needed it most.

"Listeners, it's seventy-two hours until Detonation Day. I for one can't wait. I'm gonna host the concert on the Mall in Washington with our pals from Total Static Head."

Jericho grimaced. "Those guys hate me."

"Yeah, I heard," said Dara.

Frank continued. "Today on the show we've got actress Sailor Angelo and Emerson Smith from Planet Plan It, plus new music from another friend of the show, Jericho Wells."

"Oooooh, Jericho!" squealed the sycophants in falsetto.

Dara guffawed.

"Yes, he's dreamy," said Frank, "and his new song isn't half bad. We're giving him the benefit of the doubt even though he isn't playing at any of the Detonation celebrations. I think his record deserves to be heard. Besides, you know what they say about a tree falling in the forest and no one hearing it."

"It's the same as the sound of one hand clapping," mused a morning zoo denizen.

"Are you talking about masturbation again, Paulie?" asked Frank.

"Just play the damn song," said Jericho.

"Before we slide completely into the gutter, let's welcome our guests, Sailor and Emerson!"

Cheers from the yes-men.

Dara recalled the viral Planet Plan It video and its role in convincing the public to accept the proposal to drop the bomb. Her stomach clenched.

Sailor spoke in talking points, smattered with "likes" and "y'knows." Emerson dove in when the conversation needed stats and gravitas. Midway through the discussion, the tweener said, "Artists need to band together and stand up for what they believe in. We can get ideas into people's heads. When you change people's minds, you change their actions!"

Dara smiled. "She's a mini-Jericho Wells!"

Jericho smirked. "She's a corporate product, not an artist." But the smirk gave way when he added, "Okay, I agree with what she's saying and appreciate her handlers for making her say it. So sue me."

Dara remembered castigating Jericho as a sellout, seemingly eons ago. Making a living, a life, an impact -- who was she to judge how someone else navigated the world? Besides, she was starting to see the wisdom in Jericho's approach.

Dara looked at him. "Rex?"

"Yeah?"

"I'm starting to see the wisdom in your approach."

Jericho stared at her for a second, reverted his eyes back to the road. "What do you mean?"

"There was a lot of time to think in solitary confinement. Before they drugged me, that is."

He reached over and touched her hand. "I can't fathom what you went through, but I get that too much time alone is dangerous. I've been completely by myself since Jennie left, and I worry all the time. Way too many death threats against me since I bowed out of the D-Day events."

"Fame can't possibly be worth it if it's like that," she replied, hoping he didn't notice her wincing when he said Jennie's name.

Jericho hesitated, his hand still on Dara's. "When we were together, all I wanted was what I have now. I'd see you working so hard and doing so well. You created something unique."

"Well, it backfired."

"No, Reg. That's not on you. You believed in what you were doing, and you inspired me to want to do something just as important."

Dara stared at Jericho's hand on hers. "Rex, we didn't get along. You were always upset with me. If I got too busy, you'd yell that all I cared about was success."

Jericho's voice barely registered over the radio din. "We were living on your fellowship, and it looked like you were on your way. I was nowhere. So, yeah, I was jealous." He was quiet for a moment, then continued. "Now I know what it takes to get an idea off the ground, how much work. It's not easy."

Dara squeezed his hand. "All that matters is what's ahead. And we'll always have each other. We know better now."

Jericho smiled, brushing her cheek before he returned his hand to the steering wheel. "Hey, there's the exit for the store."

The road led to a big box El Dorado. Dara couldn't contain her glee: "Civilization!"

He pulled into a parking space and handed Dara a pile of bills. "Pick up some snacks and a few bottles of water while you're at it. We're going to need our strength."

***

"Private Lies," the song Fat Frank played, burrowed into the consciousness like an earworm. The verse swung into a go-go funk chorus, with the intro solo and fills seething angry blues.

> *Dreaming I am falling*
> *Headlights trip my eyes*
> *Almost dawn and you've been gone*
> *And you're all alibis*

> *I am not clairvoyant*
> *I can't read your mind*
> *But I've watched you tell every color of lie*
> *Got you memorized*

"Eyes on the road!" chided Dara as she changed clothes in the back seat, catching Jericho watching her in the rear-view mirror. She laughed, remembering the quick-change routine en route to his gigs back in the day. Old habits died hard.

Dara had rushed through the purchase, with buyer's remorse setting in immediately after the fact. She'd roast in the black knee-length skirt, white long-sleeved blouse, and tan closed-toe pumps. The lipstick, blush, and foundation she'd picked up in hopes of hiding her ravaged complexion would probably melt. At least she got new underwear, saving her from one more second in prison-issue bra and panties.

"Well, at least not a single living thing was sacrificed for this outfit. Polyester, polyurethane, and plastic – better living through chemistry."

"Just don't stand near an open flame," laughed Jericho in response.

The song continued. Jericho's tenor melted like caramel over the bridge and verses, transmuting into Skip James crossed with Johnny Rotten on the hook.

> *Don't say it*
> *Don't say it*
> *Private lies are what you're made of*
> *Don't say it*
> *Don't say it*
> *Private lies are what you're made of*

The lyrics were like an incantation, ringing in Dara's ears even after the chorus ended. She bristled. They made her think of Alexander Fallsworth.

"I think I've had enough radio."

"You don't like 'Private Lies?'"

"It's a great song, but it's making me think of you-know-who. I can't deal with the thought of him right now."

"No worries. I'll shut it off. We're almost there, anyway."

"Thanks."

"If it makes you feel any better, the chorus is about Donahue."

Dara grew quiet. Was President Donahue really that bad? Even though his reasons were self-serving, he did sign on to her ideas. She wanted to believe the president's heart was in the right place and Alexander had lied to him, too.

But then again, she'd trusted Alexander and he took advantage of her. So much for her instincts.

***

The U.S. Capitol loomed as the shrill of a traffic cop's whistle jarred Dara awake. She dug into her black pleather clutch for a mint.

"Hey, Sleepyhead," said Jericho.

She rubbed her eyes. "I almost forgot how huge this building is."

Jericho handed Dara a tissue from the packet on the dashboard. "I'm going to drop you off and spend the rest of the day at my mom's. Text me when you're done, and I'll come pick you up."

Dara had procured a new disposable phone at the megamart. The person she really wanted to text was Avery.

"What about tonight? Are we driving back to West Virginia?"

"DC's lousy with hotels," Jericho replied, smiling. "We could be Mr. and Mrs. Smith."

Dara felt herself redden.

"I'm kidding. Ask Sam Collins if the FBI still thinks you're a fugitive and we'll decide from there."

"If I'm in the clear, I'm going to stay with my dad," replied Dara, jaw set.

Jericho found a shady spot near the Capitol building. As he switched on the hazard lights, Dara felt her body tense up.

"Are you okay?"

"N-no," she said. She fumbled through her bag, her brain no longer registering what she saw.

Jericho zipped Dara's clutch. "Hey, look at me," he said, touching her cheek, kissing her on the forehead, pulling her close. "If you were anybody else, I'd worry. But you're the strongest person I know."

Dara willed back tears. "No. I'm not."

"You are."

She shook her head. "All the work I've done to try to make everything better is coming apart. When I fall, all I want to do is hide."

"You never stay down for long."

The space between them, sunshine streaming through the window, the scent of mint soap on Jericho's skin, the sound of their hearts beating — Dara would have traded facing the members of Congress to live inside that space forever.

"I wish you could come with me."

"I wish I could, too." Alas, it was a closed hearing. Jericho pressed his forehead against Dara's. "You know, when I have a show, I look for someone in the audience who looks like you, at least from far away. It's as if you're there."

Dara smiled. "Really?"

"Yeah. I know it's not you, but a guy can pretend, right?"

"I won't find anyone in that chamber who looks like you."

Jericho regarded the clock on the dashboard. "It's time." He checked Dara's bag, made sure she had what she needed, unhooked her seatbelt. Sunglasses on and hat pulled low, he slid out of the car and opened the passenger-side door.

Dara rubbed her back, sore from sitting for so long. Standing on the scorching pavement, her new shoes already pinched her toes.

"Deep breath, Reg. You can do this."

She squeezed Jericho's arm and turned toward the building.

***

Dara knew the drill when entering federal buildings, only this time she was doing so as escapee from Alexander Fallsworth and company. She kept her head down, named her contact in Senator Collins' office and laid her purse on the metal detector's conveyor belt. Harsh air conditioning replaced the warmth of Jericho's skin against hers.

The Senator had explained Dara's situation to the guards. They ran a name check in advance so she didn't need to present ID — not that she had one, since it remained under lock and key at the detention center.

She exhaled a bit when Samantha Collins herself, along with a young man she introduced as Chase Tucker, arrived to greet her. They escorted her back to the Senator's office.

Dara had toured the U.S. Capitol years ago on a high school field trip, but had only vague recollections of the beaux-arts splendor, the resolve in the eyes of the founding fathers staring back at her from frescoes and statues that lined the halls.

A smiling intern welcomed Dara into the mahogany-paneled receiving area of Samantha Collins' office, asked if she wanted water or coffee.

"Some water, please," said Dara, dehydration from the stifling walk to the building causing her voice to crack. The synthetic material of her outfit only made matters worse, trapping sweat. She tried not to fidget. As self-conscious as she was about her buzz cut, at least she didn't have to worry about her hair going limp with perspiration.

Senator Collins wore a royal blue shift and heels that added to her already imposing height. She extended her hand to Dara. "You've certainly been through the wringer."

"But I survived it," said Dara. "Thanks for all your work, Senator."

The two women sat across from each other at a small conference table. Dara noticed photos on the wall — Sam Collins in a mortar board giving a commencement address, wearing an evening gown while chatting with First Lady Camille Donahue, eating apples with school children, hugging a dread-locked teenager Dara remembered as the senator's son, fist bumping at a rally with the one and only Jericho Wells. Dara smiled.

Chase joined them at the table, flipping to a clean page on his yellow legal pad. Dara gulped her water, wondering if she also should take notes, but Sam Collins began speaking before she could grab her notebook. Too late.

"Dara, we're glad you're here today. I first want to clarify that we know you escaped from the CIA facility, but we also know how you got there and what happened to you while you were in custody. You needn't worry about any repercussions associated with your departure from the facility, and rest assured, we're working to get all that expunged from your personnel and FBI records."

Dara looked into the woman's deep-set eyes, sensing her kindness and wanting with all her heart to believe her. But as Dmitri, her father, and Ronald Reagan always said, "Trust but verify."

"Ma'am," she said in a small voice, "the past several weeks have been...difficult. Devastating, actually. I'm living in fear of my own government. I want to get on with my life, but I'm afraid the FBI will come after me again. They'll say I escaped from detention and they'll arrest me. It would be their word against mine."

The senator shook her head. "I understand your concerns, and we're absolutely horrified about what you went through. But you have nothing to fear. We have evidence."

The intern slipped in to refill Dara's water glass.

"Evidence?" asked Dara, eyebrows raised.

Collins exchanged looks with Chase, then watched as the intern left the room. After the door shut behind him, she continued, "Yes. We received videos of your detention from a foreign intelligence agency."

Chase piped up as if on cue. "The source who got the tape did so at great risk to himself and his government."

Dara mustered a nod, her heart pounding against her scratchy new blouse.

"We have every intention of opening an investigation into Fallsworth and his cohorts," added Senator Collins. "But for now, our priority is to stop the detonation. Chase wrote the testimony we're going to present to the Joint Subcommittee later today. I'd like you to flesh out the technical section, and also prepare a statement to introduce yourself and describe how you got involved with the program. We'll do a mock Q&A before we go in. We have a strong sense of what the subcommittee members will ask you."

Dara caught Jericho's eye in the campaign photo on the wall. She nodded back to Senator Collins, this time with more strength.

***

Dour faces in the gallery. Opening remarks from Samantha Collins, grim testimony from Chase. The roulette wheel of words spun for more than an hour, then landed on Dara. She stood, knees trembling on the long walk to the front of the room, silently praying for luck.

Reading from her script, she introduced herself. "Chairman Willoughby, distinguished members of the Joint Subcommittee, thank you for hearing our testimony today. My name is Dara Bouldin. I completed my Ph.D. in nuclear engineering at Chambers University last year. For my dissertation, I developed software to model climate responses to geological engineering applications using nuclear weapons."

She cleared her throat. "I have devoted my life to climate modelling since I was a teenager. My life changed after my family fell victim to a major wildfire in Colorado ten years ago, one that was exacerbated by severe drought conditions. I lost my mother in the blaze and nearly my own life."

Dara hesitated for a moment, then rolled up her sleeve, held up her scarred right arm for the committee members to see. "These scars remind me every day what climate change has done to me personally and to the planet we all call home."

After a murmur spread through the chamber, Dara rolled down her sleeve. She continued. "Alexander Fallsworth of CIA contacted me a few months into my tenure at the Agency for Advanced Energy Research to participate in a black project and implement my ideas."

Dara's pulse raced as she explained the basics of her project to the audience, but, to her surprise, her voice remained steady. "I can tell you, unequivocally, that Alexander Fallsworth intends to use my innovation for nefarious ends. Allow me to outline how his team's coordinates for detonation would result in consequences that do not align with the original planned outcomes."

Dara proceeded to refute Alexander's thesis, point-by-point. But she wasn't finished.

"Distinguished members of the subcommittee, I'd like to conclude by reading something to you that I hope you'll find relevant. It's from the Franck Report, which was sent to Interim Committee members of Congress and the Secretary of War on June 11, 1945, not long before the end of World War II. The preamble to the report states, 'We felt it our duty to urge that the political problems arising from the mastering of atomic power be recognized in all their gravity, and that appropriate steps be taken for their study and the preparation of necessary decisions.'"

She felt every eye in the chamber drill through her. *You can do this.*

"At the time, the Interim Committee in Congress advised President Truman to use nuclear weapons against Japan. The Franck Report stated that the 'use of nuclear bombs for an early, unannounced attack against Japan' was 'inadvisable,' and went on to say, 'If the United States would be the first to release this new means of indiscriminate destruction upon mankind, she would sacrifice public support throughout the world, precipitate the race of armaments and prejudice the possibility of reaching an international agreement on the future control of such weapons.'"

Dara took a sip of water. *You're the strongest person I know.* "Members of the subcommittee, I urge you to learn from this, from our history. Geo-engineering as prescribed by Alexander Fallsworth, against all advisement, amounts to a new means of indiscriminate destruction. All signs point to an environmental arms race. That would ruin us even faster than climate change. We need to join together with our fellow nations, particularly with other nuclear weapons states, to determine how we can use these ideas to solve climate problems but do no harm. The decision must not be unilateral."

She stared back at the audience members, memorizing every face, knowing they held the Earth's fate in their hands. "In closing, the Franck Report said what we're here to say: '...the scientific elements of the situation and prolonged preoccupation with its world-wide implications imposes on us the obligation to offer...suggestions as to the possible solution of these grave problems.' Members of the subcommittee, I urge you to vote against the detonation. Thank you."

Cheering and applause from both sides of the aisle. Dara exhaled.

***

"Unknown Caller" flashed. "Hello?"

"Jericho?"

"Reg, how did it go?"

"We got through the testimony. Now all we can do is wait for the emergency vote later tonight. Senator Collins is setting up a press conference."

"I knew you could do it."

"Thanks. She told me they're planning to investigate Alexander."

"His ass belongs in jail. Just for what he did to you, let alone for what he's trying to do to the planet."

Dara was quiet for a moment. "Something else happened," she said into the burner phone.

"What?"

"Sam Collins offered me a job. Chase Tucker's going to graduate school, so she'll need a new Science Advisor starting in September."

"Wow. Are you going to take it?"

"I need a job and I have to pay off my debts. I can't say no."

"You don't sound so sure."

Dara sighed. "I want to get past this like it never happened. I'll get dragged into the investigation either way. It'll be worse if I'm working for her, in the eye of the storm. Still, I don't have the luxury of saying no."

"You know I'll help you."

Dara knew. She also knew how good it felt to make her own way.

"Are you going to pick me up?" she asked.

"Yeah. Where are you?"

Dara nursed a cup of chamomile in a patisserie on 7th Street, realizing halfway into her cup how long it had been since she'd had tea. "I'm right by Archives Metro. You know, I still have the rest of the cash you gave me. I could just take the Green Line back to my apartment. I need to see my father. Thanks to some calls Senator Collins made on my behalf, the FBI isn't after me anymore."

Jericho hesitated. "Okay. You could do that. Do you want to come back to West Virginia with me after you see Avery?"

Dara searched her mind for words, came up empty.

"You still there?"

"I'm here." Her voice was quiet.

"So, what do you want to do?"

"I love you, Rex. But I need time." She hoped the other patrons wouldn't notice her eyes welling up.

"Hey, it's okay. You've been to hell and back. Just know I'm here for you."

Dara dabbed her eyes with her napkin. "I'll take the Metro," she said, finally. "I'd better call home."

"Okay. Be careful."

"I will."

**

The front door clicked, breaking through the din of the Washington Commanders preseason game streaming from the TV upstairs. Alexander Fallsworth set down his beer, glanced at his phone. Four thirty p.m.? His wife and kids had left for their movie only twenty minutes earlier.

"Carmen?" he called out from the second-floor man cave. No response, only footsteps.

"Babe?" he asked, louder this time. The footsteps morphed into stomps. Alexander got up, reached for the door. "Did you forget some –"

The sight of a tall man in black clothing rather than his small blonde wife froze him in place. The intruder said nothing, only glared.

Finally, Alexander recovered his voice, albeit through gritted teeth. "What the hell are you doing in my house?"

"You know exactly why I'm here."

"No, I don't," he lied, eyes darting past his adversary toward the corridor.

"I know where you keep your guns. Don't even bother."

Alexander stared. "You need to get out of my house. Now."

"Not until you do what I say." The man was taller than him, with a lean build and taut muscles that strained against his shirt. Traces of an accent colored his voice.

"Not going to happen."

The dark-eyed figure inched closer. "I know all about you."

"You know nothing about me."

"You're wrong. I know everything."

Alexander's eyes shifted to his phone on the coffee table. He thought of calling the cops, but the possibility of ending up on the Fairfax County police blotter for all to see made him reconsider. He opted to call the intruder's bluff instead.

"Really?" he asked, eyebrows arched. "What could you possibly know?"

The man glanced at the TV past Alexander's shoulder. "You think the world is some game that your country is losing, and you're willing to punish innocent people to win. Yes?"

Alexander steeled himself at the insinuation. "Look, I don't know what you're talking about. My family will be home soon, and you need to leave."

The man was now close enough for him to hear his breath quicken. "You know, I could easily do to your wife and children what you intend to do to every man, woman, and child in my homeland."

Alexander laughed sardonically. "Oh, please. You're not going to do that. Get the hell out of my house." On the verge of punctuating his statement with knuckles to the bridge of the intruder's nose, visions of polonium-based poisonings and broad daylight assassinations came to mind, tempering his outburst.

Smiling as if reading his mind, the man replied, "You underestimate me. Of course, I'd make it look like you were responsible. Murder-suicides are very easy to stage."

Alexander swallowed hard. "Sure, good luck with that," he said, attempting an impassive expression. "Now go."

"Not until you call the National Security Staff and tell your President to call off the detonation."

Alexander smirked, maintaining the mask. "Absolutely not."

"Maybe I should let you live –"

"Get out!"

"— because when your Congress is through investigating you for what you did to that girl, you'll wish you were dead."

Alexander felt sweat bead on his forehead. Dara had escaped from the detention facility, but it wasn't clear to him precisely how because the cameras had been disabled. Now he knew.

"Dara Bouldin is nobody. She should be happy we didn't throw her in prison for espionage."

"She never divulged classified information. You would have no case."

Alexander was out of patience. "Look, you said you know all about me, right? So, you know I was in the Army. You broke into my home and threatened to kill my family, so I have every motivation to rip your spine out of your mouth."

At that, the intruder grabbed Alexander's throat with gloved hands and a force that knocked the wind out of him. He dragged him further into the den, the stylized NFL violence onscreen like a play-within-a-play. Grabbing the phone from the table with his free hand, he began inputting numbers.

His adversary on the verge of hitting send, Alexander's hand-to-hand combat training came to him like a reflex. Mustering the strength to break from the chokehold, he swatted the phone to the carpet.

But the man's reflexes were swift. He delivered a star-conjuring blow to Alexander's temple, flattening him to a sprawl.

Alexander sprang to his feet, adrenaline masking the pain. He lunged, pushing the man into the wall, but his response came fast. As if having an out-of-body experience, Alexander realized that he'd been thrown against the bookcase, its contents raining down on the floor.

"Third and long," said the announcer in reverberating stereo.

The room spun. Alexander shook his head, found his bearings, delivered a punch that missed, but followed up with one that connected with the side of the man's face.

Blood spurted from his nose causing him to stagger a bit, but his wits were about him. The man dove for the phone, grasping. Alexander tackled him, struggling to reach it first. He came close, but then felt his body flip over onto the thick pile carpet, followed by a firm grip around his throat.

Alexander caught sight of the phone next to his head, flailed his right arm in a doomed attempt to grab it. His other arm, pinned under the man's knee, was of zero use to save him from death by strangulation. Alexander heard himself gurgle and felt his face grow hot, the vein in his temple close to bursting.

Echoes, ticking. "Two-minute warning." The only part of the room that wasn't circling the drain of Alexander's consciousness was the photo of Carmen, Molly, and Jackson smiling back at him through a frame decorated with glitter and macaroni seashells.

Unable to move or breathe, he could only watch as the photo dimmed. A deep snarl bulldozed through the sound of blood pounding in his head. "You have a choice. Make the call or die."

No time to think. Not that his oxygen-deprived brain was in any condition to do so. Still pinned, sweating profusely, he moved his mouth, futilely trying to speak.

His adversary used one of his hands to grab the phone, unleashing animalistic sounds, Alexander's gasps for air. A wave of relief poured through his now-limp body, half-crushed under the man's weight.

On speakerphone he heard ringing, followed by the gruff voice of Victor Rawls of the National Security Staff. The man, breathing heavily, retained a partial grasp on Alexander's throat with his other arm, allowing just enough give for him to speak. "Fallsworth," barked Rawls, "Why the hell are you bothering me at home?"

Alexander hesitated as strength slowly returned to his body. "I have something important to tell you," he croaked.

"I can barely hear you. This had better be important."

Alexander cleared his throat. "There's…been a mistake."

"Oh?"

"Yes. A mistake."

"What kind of mistake?"

He hesitated, feeling the chokehold on his neck tighten. "The coordinates for the detonation are incorrect."

The official on the other end began shouting. "And you're just figuring this out now?"

"Yes sir. But we can correct them. It's a relatively easy fix…"

"Easy how? We've spent ages preparing for this. We evacuated thousands of people and spent millions settling lawsuits with the native tribes, not to mention the Canadians. The Army Corps of Engineers spent months digging the tunnels. What in God's name are you saying?"

Alexander steadied his voice, now conscious of pain inflicted by the intruder's knee. "The fix would cause a delay, but we could move forward. NASA delays launches all the time for safety reasons. That's what this is. There could be unintended environmental damage."

"Oh really? Sounds to me like you've been drinking Sam Collins' Kool-Aid."

Alexander locked eyes with the picture of Carmen and his children, quiet for a moment. The hold around his neck tightened again, just enough to snap him back to reality. "Look, Rawls, I need to talk to the president. This is an emergency. I'm begging you to put me through."

***

Light filtered through the blinds, drawing stripes on Dara's arm, obscuring her scars. She didn't recognize herself for a moment, not just for the play of sunshine on her damaged skin, but for the fact that her head and body weren't aching. The doctor warned her of withdrawal pains and accompanying depression, noting that it could take at least a couple of weeks to feel normal again. Thankfully, it hadn't taken anywhere near that long. She leapt out of bed at the thought of her body being freed of toxins.

Hungry, sweaty — Avery must have turned off the air conditioner before he left for his shift at the Slot Lot. She thought about her homecoming last night, seeing her dad tear up.

Avery told her everything. How he hadn't sold her car. How he'd taken on extra shifts to cover the minimum payments on the debts. How he hadn't relapsed thanks to Gamblers Anonymous meetings, working out in the gym, prayer.

He also told her how he'd made the mistake of trusting Jane Canton.

Dara hadn't the heart to yell at him. The hotel payments made terrifying sense now: Jane was cooperating with the FBI. Jane was working with Alexander. Jane was the puppet master, Dara the puppet. History repeated itself.

Instead, she told her father that Senator Collins offered her a job. She also told him that she decided to decline.

Based on his silence, she surmised that Avery hadn't the heart to yell at her, either. Dara recalled the first time the government offered her a job when all she wanted was to find investors and start her own business. Avery raised his voice to the rafters, calling her every synonym of foolish, scaring the neighbors.

He had no right to yell at her, then or now. She loved him, but he had no say in her future.

In a quiet voice, Avery finally broke the silence, asking her why she didn't want the job. She'd be perfect for it. She'd make a difference, plus make a great living. Unspoken was the need to pay off the debt -- his debt, in her name.

"Dad," she replied, "All I ever wanted to do was start my own business, and I think I can do it. I just want to be independent. I had a taste of freedom when I was in Saint Louis, and I've figured out what I need to do."

After she'd spoken her piece to Avery, she reviewed the script in her head, prepared to counter his anticipated response: What kind of business would you start, especially in light of what just happened to you? What about the debt? Where will you find investors? How will you make a living until the business takes off?

Bullet pointed answers were at the ready:

• Tutoring and consulting -- possibly even consulting part-time to Sam Collins. (After all, where else would the senator find someone at a moment's notice with expertise in geo-engineering using nuclear weapons? Not too many people panhandled out on South Capitol Street holding signs saying, "Will Geo-Engineer for Food");

• It's YOUR debt, not mine, so YOU should pay it;

• The same way everyone else raises money to start a business – applying to banks, appealing to friends, pitching to venture capitalists;

• Teaching engineering classes as an adjunct at any college that would have me during the day, doing live sound at night and on weekends, and living on ramen noodles and vitamin pills for as long as it took.

But Avery didn't ask any questions. Instead, he said, "Okay, sweetheart. I'll do everything I can to help you. Plus, the debt is mine. I've been working my 12-step program, and I'm getting promoted at the casino. There's a lot more I can do now."

Dara's eyes moistened as she mentally replayed her father's response, especially at the thought of him overcoming his gambling addiction after so many attempts. Happy tears.

The doorbell rang. Dara stiffened, unsure of what to do, wondering if on top of everything else, she'd contracted post-traumatic stress disorder. It rang again.

She pulled on her robe, padded to the door. A man in uniform stood behind the peephole. On closer inspection, it was UPS.

She opened the door a crack, realizing the extent of her morning look in the mirror by the entrance. A hydrating facial was in order. "Hi. I slept in this morning. Sorry it took me so long to get the door."

"Sign here," said the man in brown, mercifully all business. He handed her a tiny package. "Have a nice day."

Dara closed the door, stared at the box. Had she left something at Jericho's house? Then she spotted the return address: Howard Kitson, St. Louis, MO.

Her heart pulsed. She tore off the wrapping. A slip of paper inside read, "Hi, Miss Jones, you left this in the safe and I figured you'd want it back. Hope you're in a good place with lots of fro-yo. Take care, HK."

The object of beauty captured every ray of sunlight that streamed into the apartment, reflecting it back in prisms. Dara cradled the diamond in her fist, clutched it to her heart.

T-minus Zero

*B*oom.

In the end, it didn't matter that both houses of Congress voted against the detonation with convincing 'Nays,' nor that Senator Collins' office leaked the consequences of the project to the media. A team of well-coifed scientists in American flag lapel pins led by Dr. Jane Canton flooded the airwaves once again, proclaiming the minority party both wrong and foolish. Before anyone could counter them, the 24-hour news cycle segued to the next topic: the celebrity-studded 'Let's Get Bombed' parties, set for cities throughout the nation.

Alexander Fallsworth got through to President Donahue just in time to avoid death at Dmitri Ivanov's gloved hands, sparing no details to his Commander-in-Chief on every possible outcome and worst-case scenario of the detonation, including consequences both now and generations from now.

But Alexander's pleas fell on deaf ears. Or perhaps partially deaf ears, since the president willfully took the decision to drop the bomb, knowing full well it would result, however indirectly, in death and destruction to America's competitors. After all, other countries would do the same to the United States if they could. In some ways, they already had.

Donahue's next official act was the veto heard 'round the globe, without the votes to override. Detonation Day went on as planned.

The president himself emceed the countdown from Washington on live TV, all smiles. Millions of Americans watched from their living rooms as swaths of Alaska, precisely at Alexander's coordinates, imploded into dust. Sailor Angelo, Total Static Head, Fat Frank, and countless other notables tweeted cheers of approval, got the parties started.

Dara knew what was coming, beyond the festivities. Fire, ice, rinse, repeat. She couldn't watch. Just the thought of it bubbled up in her throat, burnt through every synapse. A new countdown had started, the silent count to the future that would arrive soon enough.

About E. A. Smiroldo

E. A. Smiroldo is a nuclear engineer specializing in weapons nonproliferation. She's also a Washington Area Music Association Award-nominated singer-songwriter and has won prizes in writing competitions sponsored by the Bethesda Literary Festival and the International Screenwriters' Dig. After placing in the latter, she optioned the treatment for her screenplay, *Blood Like Water*, with X-ray Media. Premised on real science, *The Silent Count* is her debut novel.

Social Media

Author website: www.easmiroldo.com

Facebook: https://www.facebook.com/EASmiroldo

Twitter: https://twitter.com/EASmiroldo @EASmiroldo

Acknowledgements

I'm fortunate to come from a family of storytellers. My sister Maria made up bedtime stories for me every night, usually starring one or more of our dolls, and our parents kept us spellbound with tales of their lives in Italy rivalling any adventure novel.

I ended up becoming an engineer, but the storytelling drive never left. Great writing teachers, editors, and kindred spirits have crossed my path. James Oppenheim, my creative writing professor at University of Maryland, told me I had talent. Two outstanding instructors at the Writer's

Center in Bethesda, Maryland, John DeDakis and Kathryn Johnson, served as early editors of my manuscript. My novel writers' group – Jennifer Hale, Julie Corrigan, Maria Karametou, Rose Ann Cleveland, and Sally DiPaula – provided invaluable advice as we went through the revision process (every other Sunday for two years!).

I'm ever grateful to friends who've been there for me as well. Susan Long, BFF-in-chief, knows *The Silent Count's* origin story and treats me like a normal person when I talk about my characters as if they were real people. Herbert Massie, dear friend and engineering mentor, was one of my first beta readers. Carlotta Coates was a font of kindness and encouragement when I doubted myself, which was often. Huge thanks also go to those who supported my songwriting life, which wormed its way into the novel, especially Brad Lehman (is there a bigger-hearted guy anywhere? I think not), and Jerry Del Rosso and Jed Prentice who played bass and drums in my band.

Finally, my heartfelt appreciation goes to Solstice Publishing for this marvelous opportunity!

Printed in Great Britain
by Amazon

84424928R00169